Neurotic November

A MARY MAGRUDER KATZ MYSTERY

Barbara Levenson

This book is dedicated to Mac, my constant companion, who sat patiently by my computer desk waiting for his daily walk.

ADDITIONAL BOOKS BY BARBARA LEVENSON

FATAL FEBRUARY

JUSTICE IN JUNE

OUTRAGEOUS OCTOBER

CAST OF CHARACTERS

Mary Magruder Katz	Defense Attorney and star of the show
Carlos Martin	Mary's Hot Latin Lover
Sam, the German Shepherd	Mary's constant companion
Hope Magruder Katz and Abe Katz	Mary's Parents
Angelina and J.C. Martin	Carlos's Parents
Celia Martin (Chicky)	Carlos's sister
Catherine Aynsworth	Mary's indomitable paralegal
Brady Aynsworth	Catherine's deadbeat ex-husband
Patty and Doug Larsen	Catherine's parents
Mrs. Morehouse	Catherine's landlady
Marco Perez	Cousin of Carlos, boyfriend of Catherine and head of Pit Bull Investigations
Franco Perez	Marco's brother. Car repair expert
Lucinda Perez	Franco's wife and sparring partner
Franklin Fieldstone (Frank)	Mary's old boss and former boyfriend
Jay Lincoln	University of Miami Quarterback
Lorena and Horace Lincoln	Jay Lincoln's Parents
Jennifer de Leon	Hotty High School Girl and Jay's Accuser
Tim de Leon	Jennifer's Father
Candy Gomez	Jennifer's best friend
Jonelle Geiger	Housekeeper in the de Leon House
Fred Mercer	Vindictive Prosecutor in Jay's case
Dr. Andreas	The Martin family's trusted physician
Louise Margolis	Prosecutor in Marco's case
Judge Sylvia Cohen-Cueto	Judge in Marco's case

Judge Luongo	Judge in Jay's case
Reuben Porter	Investigator from the Pit Bull Agency
Renee Francis	Drug dealer ex-girlfriend of Brady Aynsworth
Sheila Bird	Native American ex-girlfriend of Brady Aynsworth
Oscar Songbird	Sheila's Uncle and head of a casino
Detective Ruiz	Arresting officer of Marco
Detective Vivian Suarez	Investigating officer in the shooting at the Homecoming game
Aunt Myrna and Uncle Max	Mary's Aunt and Uncle; Abe Katz's brother
Grandma Katz and her new husband	Ronald Morgan
DEA agent Roberto Padron	Assists in Marco's case
Witnesses in Marco's Case	Marty and Drucilla Lantz, Mr. Habib, Manny

Chapter One

Jay Lincoln thought he was the greatest. In fact, he knew he was the greatest. He recounted all the reasons he knew this: first Black quarterback on the University of Miami football team, already being stroked by fat cat agents who promised super-sized NFL contracts in the next draft, litters of groupies waiting outside the locker room after every game, and now this hot white chick, Jennifer, on her way over to his dorm. If she really looked like the photo she sexted him, well, he was totally hard just looking at that photo.

She knocked on his unlocked door and opened it. "Hi, it's me," she said as she slid into the half darkened room.

He was lying on the bed wearing only his gym shorts that he knew showed off his wad. Jennifer moved toward him. He saw her in the half light. Her long blond hair was loose and half covered what looked like a sports bra. Her denim skirt was so short that her legs looked like they stretched for a mile with nothing to break that silky look until his eyes hit her jeweled flip-flops that she was removing and kicking under the bed.

"Hey, babe, what's up?" Jay used his sleepy voice that usually turned the chicks on.

"I can see what's up." Jennifer giggled.

"Well, come on up here," he said

In a minute she was next to him. He pulled the long straight hair. It felt so soft, so different than Melanie, his usual girlfriend with her puffy Afro and muscled body. Jennifer felt soft everywhere.

He pulled at her bra and she completed the job removing it and tossing it to the floor. He kissed her and pulled her lips open. In an instant, they were both out of what little was left to restrict their bodies already moving in rhythm like the beat of the music blasting from a room down the hall.

He tried to hold back but he came rapidly. Jennifer was still moving against him.

She moaned and he thought she was expecting more. He looked at her and knew she looked as good as the sext she had sent him.

A noise startled both of them. It sounded like a key in the door.

"I thought you said your roommate was away," Jennifer said, sitting up.

A female voice called out. "Hey, Jay, I just got back, and---," the voice trailed off.

"Melanie," Jay said. "I, uh, you didn't call, and"

"You big shit. Couldn't keep it in your pants for one night? I am through with you, you arrogant no good Liberty City ghetto asshole." Melanie moved towards Jennifer. Her hands were balled into fists.

"Wait, Melanie, it was just a mistake." Jay was trying to put on his shorts as he rushed to separate the two women.

Jennifer took a step back. Her face was crimson. "Don't blame me if Jay likes some white meat on his plate," she hissed.

Melanie tried to punch Jennifer, but Jennifer ducked leaving Melanie to grasp a blond handful of hair and pull hard. Jennifer screamed almost drowning out Melanie's words. "Why don't you run back to your sorority whorehouse, you bitch."

"Stop it, both of you, before we all get in trouble and I get suspended from the team," Jay said. He pushed the two out of control girls away from each other.

Melanie gave one more furious look at Jay and strode out of the still open door slamming it so hard that the lamp fell off the desk and crashed against the wall.

"Hey, shut up in there," a voice from the room next door bellowed.

"So that's the roommate who was away for the night," Jennifer said. She was picking up clothes and throwing them on. "You didn't mention that the roommate was your girlfriend. So I'm just a mistake? Well, thanks for nothing."

"I'm sorry, Jennifer, I didn't mean you were a mistake. Please, let me at least walk you back to your dorm."

"I don't need anyone to walk me anywhere," she said.

"Can I call you? Where do you live?"

"You've got my e-mail. But I probably won't answer. How could you want that Black humongous bitch when you could have me?" Jennifer opened the door and looked up and down the hall. Then she was gone. Gone out of Jay Lincoln's life. At least that's what he thought.

Chapter Two

Miami Herald, October 31

Herald Sports

WILL JAY LINCOLN START AT QUARTERBACK??
University ponders ethics questions

Jay Lincoln, star junior quarterback for the Miami Hurricane football team, is scheduled for trial on pending charges of sexual battery on a minor female. The alleged victim is fifteen and a high school sophomore.

Lincoln was arrested and charged on August first, at the start of the fall practice season. Bail was set at $100,000. A group of faculty and concerned citizens raised the money for Lincoln's release.

To date, the university has allowed Mr. Lincoln to attend classes. Coach Wizotski has started Lincoln in every game. However, in the past week a group of parents, students, and Miami citizens are calling for the university to take action to suspend the quarterback from further team participation. Caring Representatives Upholding Morals in Sports (CRUMS) claim that the continued participation of the current quarterback is sending the wrong message to young athletes and to the general public.

Coach Wizotski has repeatedly stated that the charges against Jay Lincoln are only unproven allegations. "Until a jury finds someone guilty they are just accusations. Jay shouldn't be deprived of continuing his football career," Wizotski stated.

University President, Landry Phillips, was unavailable for comment and has not returned messages left by The Herald.

The next home game is homecoming on November 16, against rival Florida State. CRUMS has threatened to protest at the game if Lincoln is not replaced.

Luis Marina, chairperson of CRUMS states that at least 500 concerned citizens plan to attend the demonstration. "Maybe the university is more interested in winning games than in the plight of an under-age victim," he said. Perhaps the NCAA will be interested in monitoring this situation."

Miami Herald, November 1st Business Section
Seaside Bank Investigation Continues
Seaside Bank, chartered only three years ago, continues to be investigated for alleged irregularities. Both the Securities and Exchange Commission and the Justice Department have subpoenaed records from the bank.
The Herald has learned that a special grand jury is being empaneled to question officers and clients of the bank. Bank President, Alejandro Nardo, Vice-President and board member Juan Carlos Martin, and Treasurer Javier Montenegro were unavailable for comment. Bank spokesperson, Rhonda Feliciano, stated that no one at the bank has been subpoenaed to testify before a grand jury.
United States Attorney for the Southern District of Florida, Jose Upshaw, said that he was unable to comment on ongoing investigations. "In general, this office is dedicated to seeing that banking laws are adhered to in this district including the Bank Secrecy Act," he said.
Nardo was formerly connected to Bank Oficina, a Spanish bank that attempted to buy the defunct First Bank of Doral. That bank was forced to close after numerous irregularities were found.

Chapter Three

I had only been back in my familiar law office in Miami for two weeks when one client visit, one phone call, and one unforeseen event changed my life.

My getaway to Vermont seemed far behind me. My breakup and subsequent re-coupling with Carlos, my hot Latin boyfriend, colored all my thoughts. How could I not love a guy who paid blackmail to an ex-spouse just to protect his father? Carlos did that, as I found out when he came to High Pines, Vermont, and I finally listened to his explanation of why I caught him having dinner with his ex. How could I not love a guy who drove 1700 miles to bring me home when my father suffered a life-threatening heart attack? Carlos did that too and now we are closer than ever.

I was dividing my time during these first weeks back in Miami between the hospital vigil after Dad's heart surgery, my distraught mother, and my almost non-existent law practice. Clients deserted in droves while I hung out in New England. In spite of my paralegal, Catherine Aynsworth's heroic efforts to keep them happy and in the fold, clients expect to have their attorney available on a regular basis.

So several nerve wracking days later I sat in my office examining my disappearing bank account. My best friend, Sam, my German shepherd, was pacing the length of the office. He was suffering from climate adjustment syndrome. When we left Vermont, the temperature was consistently in the mid-forties. Here in Miami the thermometer registered eighty-five as we drove from my house in Coral Gables to my Coconut Grove office. Sam was shedding his beautiful coat that he grew in High Pines. Clumps of silky hair fell from him as he paced.

I was also shedding, having stored away my Ugg boots and heavy leather jacket to return to sleeveless shirts and flip-flops.

I heard Catherine clear her throat. I looked away from my lean bank statement and saw her standing in front of my desk.

"There's a woman in the waiting room. She doesn't have an appointment but says it's urgent that she see you," Catherine said.

"What's her name? Did you get some information about her problem, her contact numbers and address?" I asked.

"No, I'm sorry. I guess I forgot to screen her and fill out an intake form." Catherine looked at me absent-mindedly.

Catherine is an A-1 assistant. She rarely forgets anything and keeps me focused so I was surprised and puzzled.

"Catherine, is everything okay? Are you angry at me for taking off so much time? I promise you, I will get this practice up and running again. You'll never miss a paycheck, ever."

"No, Mary, I'm not angry. I just have stuff on my mind."

"Well, sit down here and let's talk about whatever is bothering you. Is it your boys?"

"No, they're fine. We'll talk when things quiet down for you. This woman is waiting. Shall I go out and get her information?"

"No, just show her in, but get her name at least," I said.

Catherine is a divorced single mother with two great sons. She manages to keep work and kids going and has a great boyfriend, Marco, who runs Pit Bull Investigations and is one of Carlos's many cousins. Her normally calm demeanor was totally missing. Just one more worry to add to my growing list.

Catherine returned accompanying a heavyset light skinned African American of indeterminate age. She was dressed in a going-to-church outfit; a navy dress with long sleeves, a small hat with a flower, and high heeled bright red shoes.

"Mary, this is Lorena Lincoln. She says she has an urgent problem."

Chapter Four

"Please, have a seat, Mrs. Lincoln," I said as I nodded toward the chair on the other side of the desk. "Is it Mrs. or Ms. Lincoln?"

"Oh, it's Mrs. I'm sorry to bother you without calling first, but I'm just so worried and I wanted Jay to get you for his lawyer but you were out of town and now maybe it's too late." Mrs. Lincoln wiped away the beginning of tears with a flowered handkerchief she pulled from her pocket.

"Okay, let's start from the beginning," I said. "I'm going to take some notes if you don't mind. Let's move over to the sofa." I stood up and took the woman by the arm and led her over to the sofa. Would you like some coffee?" Without waiting for an answer, I called Catherine on the intercom and asked her to bring coffee and mugs.

"Now, are you the one with the problem?" I asked after pouring coffee and watching Mrs. Lincoln get herself under control.

"No, it's my son, Jay Lincoln. Maybe you know who he is. He's the quarterback on the Hurricane team. I know you are an alumna of the university, and that's one of the reasons I want you for Jay's lawyer. You probably read about Jay's problem."

"No, I've been out of Miami for several weeks. Is Jay accused of something criminal?"

"Jay got arrested in August and they said he raped some high school girl. He was in that Dade County Jail for four days while we got people to help with his bail. I was so upset and his daddy nearly had a stroke. My husband is a counselor at Central High School. Jay is our only son and Horace, that's my husband, has spent his life lecturing Jay about all the way kids get in trouble. Jay has never done anything but make us proud."

"Okay, now Mrs. Lincoln. Give me some facts about this. Who is this girl, this alleged victim? When was this sexual contact supposed to have happened?"

"Please, call me Lorena. The girl's name is Jennifer de Leon. The so-called rape was supposed to have happened last May. The girl is fifteen or sixteen, I'm not sure. She goes to Coral Gables High School. The first thing Jay said to me when I went to the jail was 'Mama, I didn't rape no one. That girl came on to me, big time.'

"Now, they've set a trial date for November twenty-third, and the university sent us to some lawyer who never does criminal work. He's some business lawyer, Fieldstone's his name, who does work for the university and he's not even nice to Jay. He won't even meet with us, says he's too busy and that he's just doing this as a favor to the university. We tried to contact you over a month ago when we saw what a mess this was. One of Jay's professors told Jay to call you."

"That's a pretty quick trial date. I don't know if I can be of help so close to the trial, and there's another thing. I know Franklin Fieldstone quite well. I used to work for him. We've had some unpleasantness since – well, since I opened my own office. He might refuse to get off Jay's case."

Mrs. Lincoln reached over and gripped my arm. I looked into her terrified eyes. "I'll see what I can do," I said. "But the first thing is for me to meet Jay and interview him. When can he be here?"

"I'll get him here tomorrow morning. How early can you see him?"

As I contemplated my current morning schedule now that my mother was staying at my house, Catherine stuck her head in the door.

"Excuse me for interrupting." She handed me a phone message. "He says it can't wait."

I glanced down at the message: "J.C. Martin, Carlos's dad is on line one, says he must speak to you at once regarding a subpoena."

"Thanks, Catherine. Tell him to wait. Mrs. Lincoln, have Jay here at eight o'clock. Follow Catherine out to the front desk. She needs to get all of your contact information; address, phone numbers."

"One more important thing. Our church is raising a defense fund for Jay. We will have money for your fee. I'm not asking you to give us charity," Mrs. Lincoln said. She stood and looked me in the eye, the flower on her hat bobbing as she turned and sailed out of my office.

Chapter Five

I picked up the phone as soon as Catherine closed the door. "J.C. how good to hear from you."

"This isn't a family call, Mary. I need your legal help right away. I know you were so kind to tell me that you would help me the day you got back to Miami. I was hoping I wouldn't have to take up your offer."

"Just tell me what's wrong," I said. "Catherine said something about a subpoena."

"I've been summoned to the grand jury as a witness. The subpoena says Investigation Re: Seaside Bank. It says bring all relevant records and papers. What should I do?"

"When are you to appear?"

"Let me look. Oh, it's for November thirtieth at ten o'clock at the federal courthouse."

"Okay, that gives us time to prepare. Can you come to my office in the morning around ten? And bring the subpoena and anything else you think I should look at, like notes, e-mails or letters. Maybe records you've made about your work at the bank, and J.C., don't panic. It's just an investigation."

"Mary, Angie doesn't know much about this. Please, don't tell her anything. You know how emotional she gets. Carlos gets his Latin temper from her. We are all so glad you're back in Miami and I've never seen Carlos so happy. I'm still sick when I think how Carlos was being blackmailed by his ex, all because of my mistakes at the bank, and how I almost caused you two to break up."

"Please stop blaming yourself. Carlos is a big boy. Just because you're his father doesn't mean you're responsible for his decisions. Let's not discuss this further on the phone. We'll talk tomorrow."

"You mean you think my line is tapped?"

"Bye, J.C."

Chapter Six

It wasn't even noon yet, but I felt like I'd been at work for hours, and I still hadn't gotten back to my house to pick up my mother and get over to the hospital to check on Dad. I threw my notes about Jay and J.C. in my brief-case and stopped at Catherine's desk to let her know about the appointments for tomorrow morning. She was speaking in almost a whisper into the phone. As soon as she saw me she hung up.

"Sorry, Mary, did you need something?" she asked. She looked pale and I noticed the lines around her mouth and circles under her eyes.

"No, just to give you some info about new appointments and to remind you that I'll be at the hospital if you need me. You didn't need to hang up on my account. Are you okay?"

"Sure, I'm fine. I wanted to get off of that call anyway. Give your parents my best."

I thought about what could be wrong with Catherine while I drove back home. I hoped she would share what was going on, but I knew better than to push her. Catherine is a very private person.

Mother was watching out the front window as I drove up. She was halfway out the door before I could even get out of my car. Her hands were full carrying a bag filled with books and newspapers for Dad. I tried to remind her that Sam was in the back of the SUV. She opened the back door and Sam flew out almost knocking her over. He headed for the Martinez yard next door looking for their tiger striped cat. He ran in circles, barking. This brought Mrs. Martinez into her yard where she began another ten minute tirade about how annoying Sam is and how she enjoyed the quiet while I was away.

Mother apologized while I captured Sam and dragged him by his collar into the house and into his crate. I locked up the house, got Mother into the car and began the trip through Dixie Highway traffic to the University

Hospital. Traffic used to quiet down after rush hour, but since my return to Miami, I was struck by the fact that every hour is now rush hour.

"We must be part of a population explosion. Just look at the backup waiting to get on the freeway. Dad will be out of sorts waiting for your visit."

"Well, he's a captive audience, so he'll just have to be patient waiting for his morning sports section," Mother said. "Mary, I need to talk with you. I can't keep staying at your house or moving from one place to another. Since Dad's heart attack, I've stayed with Jonathan and his family, with two old friends on the beach and now with you. It's like camping out. I think the doctor is going to release Dad soon."

"So then you'll go back to Boynton Beach and be in your own house again."

"That's just my point. I can't go back up there. It's too far from the doctors here. Dad will need follow up appointments and tests, and if he has another attack, we need to be here in Miami."

"You don't need to move around. You and Dad can stay with me for as long as you like, or you can stay in Pinecrest in Carlos's mega mansion."

"That's very generous, but I don't want to be in the way especially now that you and Carlos are getting your relationship back on track. Here's what I'm really trying to say. I've never liked being in Boynton Beach. I miss family and friends and places to go. Up there it's the same couples all the time and frankly, they're boring. All I hear is golf or mahjong. No one is interested in discussing religion or art or music." Mother's eyes clouded with the beginning of tears.

"Hey, you're just stressed out with Dad being sick. Once he's well everything will fall into place. You loved your Sunday School class and your Tuesday ecumenical group."

"The Sunday School is very small. There aren't families with children, just retirees, and the Tuesday class is down to six women. I think they're just hanging on to be polite. No, what I want is to move back to Miami. I thought about it before Dad's attack. He loves the golf course, but while he's convalescing, he may not be playing anyway, so this is my chance to sort of ease us back here. Maybe rent a condo for a few months, and maybe Abe will see how nice it would be to be close to Jonathan and William and the kids and you and Carlos."

I stared ahead at the traffic while I collected what to say.

"Well, say something, Mary. You think I'm selfish, don't you?"

"No, I'm just surprised. I didn't know you were unhappy. Why did you agree to the move in the first place?"

"I knew how much your dad wanted to do it. He was so tired when he sold the store. I wanted to be a good sport."

"Why didn't you speak up and tell him how you felt? Why don't you ever assert yourself? You always just go along," I blurted this out. Then I saw the look of pain on Mother's face and wished I had just shut up.

"I'm not independent like you, Mary. I asserted myself once when I said I wouldn't convert to Judaism. You and William weren't born yet, just Jonathan. Grandma and Grandpa Katz wanted a big *briss.* I put my foot down and had Jonathan circumcised at the hospital. That's when everyone on the Katz side realized that they were stuck with a *goy* for life daughter-in-law. It took some time before the hurt feelings subsided. After that, I tried to compromise most of the time."

"I never sensed any strain with Grandma or Grandpa Katz."

"By the time you came along, everyone was so excited to have a little girl to dress up, and I guess they were all used to me. I'll tell you a secret, just between us. I made such a stand about not converting. Maybe, if I had kept quiet and considered it over time, I might have converted."

I almost crashed into the slow moving truck in front of me. "I'm surprised to hear you say that," I said when I got the SUV under control again. "Are you saying that now, because you think it would have made our family life easier?"

"Partly, but now that I'm older, I can see many parts of Judaism that I feel right about."

"Well, look it's never too late. You can still join up, but as far as I'm concerned, I have no need in my life for organized religion. I didn't feel good about yours or Dad's. All the politics in the church and the temple, and a lot of people who do mean things trying to make themselves feel morally right. They're places for people to bask in some false happiness, sort of like masturbation."

"Mary, that's ugly. You don't mean that."

"Sure, I do. Now let's talk about how we can ease you and Dad back into life in the Magic City." I pulled into the hospital parking garage. As I collected the reading materials to take into Dad, I glanced at my mother who I realized I barely knew.

Chapter Seven

Dad was sitting in the armchair in the corner of his hospital room reading a newspaper. Seated in the straight back chair across from him was a surprise visitor. Carlos was flipping the remote control on the TV. He was not wearing his usual jeans and boots signifying that he was coming or going from a construction site. Instead he was clad in neat dark slacks and a polo shirt with the alligator insignia, a highly preppy un-Carlos look.

"Well, this is a pleasant surprise," Mother said. She gave Carlos a kiss on the cheek.

"What are you doing here?" I asked.

"Carlos brought me the sports pages from the Herald and the Sun-Sentinel, and the media guide for the Miami Hurricanes football team, that's what. It's a good thing too. I'm tired of waiting for you girls to get here." Dad's voice of impatience had returned, a sign he was almost healthy again.

"I knew you had to be in the office this morning, and I really didn't need to be on the apartment construction site, so I came here to check up on Abe myself." Carlos put the remote down and in one stride was next to me, looking down at me and smiling. He planted a light kiss on my forehead, and started my almost forgotten heart flips.

"Hope, call that damn doctor and find out when I'm getting sprung from this jail," Dad snarled. "And where's the corn beef sandwich I asked you to bring?"

"You've got to be kidding," I said. "If you don't like the last weeks you've spent in this hospital, you're going to stay with the diet the doctor gives you," I said. "While you and Mother talk, Carlos and I are going to get a cup of coffee."

I took Carlos by the arm and escorted him out to the hallway. There weren't going to be anymore secrets between us, so now was the time to tell him that I had to contact Franklin Fieldstone about Jay Lincoln's case. Not only was Frank my old boss, he was also my old fiancé who Carlos detested.

We were seated in the hospital cafeteria, surrounded by Carlos's favorite *Café Cubano*, and my iced coffee and donuts. The lunch crowd of doctors, nurses, and families hadn't yet arrived giving us a quiet place to talk.

"It's really nice of you to visit Dad, and I see you dressed for your role as appropriate boyfriend."

"I came to the hospital several times when I learned your dad had the attack. I think he's getting used to me."

"I'm glad you're here for many reasons, but one reason is I wanted to talk to you about something that might upset you a little, and I didn't want a misunderstanding." I leaned over and covered his hand with mine. "A new case walked in the door this morning. The client is already represented by another attorney who he wants to fire. I have to contact the attorney and try to make him understand that the client is firing him and hiring me. I may have to meet with him to get the case file."

"Why are you telling me this? Is this illegal or something?"

"No, people change their minds about attorneys frequently. It's just that the attorney who's getting fired is Frank Fieldstone. I wanted you to know that I have to call him and possibly see him to obtain the case file."

Carlos immediately balled his hands into fists at the mention of Frank. His face took on a red glow that wasn't from the Florida sun.

"Can't you just have Catherine call him and I can have Marco pick up the file for you," Carlos said.

"I have to do it and I have to go over the work that's been done so far. I'm telling you this so we won't have any secrets. Like how I got the wrong idea about your having dinner with Margarita. If you had told me that she was blackmailing you, we wouldn't have almost broken up forever. Do you understand?"

"Yeah, I understand, but I don't like you having anything to do with that guy. He made so much trouble for you."

"He's not going to make any more trouble. Now here's something else that I just learned. I may need your help. Mother doesn't want to go back to Boynton Beach, at least not right now and maybe never, if she can convince Dad to move back here. She's right about not going back there for a while. Dad will need to be near the doctor here for checkups or any problems."

"Will they stay with you or Jonathan or William?"

"Mother says she doesn't want to stay with anyone. I think she wants to rent a condo or something. Then maybe Dad will enjoy being here. That's how she wants to ease him into the move."

"This is no problem. I can find them a condo in one of my buildings. Don't worry. Everything will be fine. Just get rid of Fieldstone fast."

Chapter Eight

At seven forty-five the next morning, I opened the office to prepare to meet Jay Lincoln. Another semi-sleepless night made my eyes feel like they were filled with prickly sand.

Mother paced around the house on and off during the night which kept Sam on guard emitting low growls from the foot of my bed. Carlos and I were caught in a cycle of privacy prevention. Sounds traveled from one room to another so any attempt at enjoying our sex life was inhibited. I couldn't leave Mother alone in the house while I stayed with Carlos in his humongous house, and I couldn't ask Mother to move again. After the weeks of separation, I felt annoyed and antsy waiting for Carlos to make my life exciting again. Yes, I was selfish in whining about my needs when my parents were undergoing the pangs of aging. Selfish or not, my libido was eating away at my solicitude for others.

By eight o'clock, Jay Lincoln did not appear, nor did Catherine. This was so unlike her when she knew I had an early client appointment. It was not unlike many clients to either show up late or not at all. I passed the time by glancing through the mail piled on a corner of my desk. Among the bills was a letter with the return address of Dash Mellman's law office in High Pines, Vermont. Dash and I had shared some legal work and, on one occasion a bed, while I hid out in Vermont. I set the letter aside when I heard the front door open.

"Catherine, is that you?" I called.

"No, ma'am, it's Jay Lincoln, I have an appointment," a deep voice answered me.

I glanced at my watch as I moved to the waiting room. Eight-twenty, only twenty minutes late, but a harbinger of carelessness. I made a mental note as I began my impression of this potential client.

Jay was the picture of a football player, tall, well over six feet, and a square shape. He appeared heavily muscled and more heavily tattooed. He was glancing through a magazine from my waiting room assortment. Sports Illustrated looked like a slip of paper in his huge hands. His hair was done in "dreads" and I tried to picture how they would look hanging from his helmet. He was dressed in baggy shorts, a tee-shirt which read "U. of Miami-Show the Swagger". His feet were packaged in the largest Nike's I had ever seen. He also was incredibly handsome.

"Hello, Jay, I'm Mary Katz. Come on back to my office," I said as I led the way. "You're a bit late."

"Yes. Ma'am, sorry, I had to do my morning routine; running and weights, and then I had to shower, you know."

"Well, have a seat and let's talk about your case and why you're here. Your mother told me you are already represented by an attorney."

"That's true, but, you know, it's like he's supposed to be my lawyer, but all he ever talks about, when I can get ahold of him is take a plea. I'm not going to say I'm guilty when I'm not. I need someone to fight for me and my future, you know."

"Jay, have you told Mr. Fieldstone that you want to replace him?"

"No, Mom tried to call him yesterday but he never returned her call."

"If I decide to take your case, and you decide you want to retain me, you will have to fire your old attorney before we can have an agreement. Do you understand what I'm saying?" I could see that Jay's attention was on the parking lot outside the window and not on our conversation.

"Yeah, I guess so. Why can't you fire him for me?"

"There are rules that say I can't do that. It would be an ethics violation. What are you looking at out there?"

"Somebody just got out of a super Corvette. Man, what a set of wheels."

I looked up and saw Carlos's Corvette in the parking lot. "Excuse me for a minute, Jay. I'll be right back."

I walked into the waiting room just as Carlos came in. There still was no Catherine at her desk. Carlos was wearing a navy sport coat and grey slacks and looked like he was dressed for a business meeting. He smiled as I walked in and I kissed him without even thinking about my waiting client.

"What are you doing here?" I asked when I finally let him breath.

"I'm on my way to pick up your mother and take her to look at some condos. Then I'll take her to the hospital."

"So that's why you're dressed like a page from *GQ*. Does she know you're taking her on this real estate safari?"

"I called her first thing and she's excited."

"This is so great of you."

"I have to admit, my motivation is selfish. If we get her situated, we get our privacy back and from that kiss, you must want that, too."

"I have a client waiting in my office and Catherine is a no-show so far this morning, so I better get back to work."

"Marco mentioned that he's worried about Catherine. She's been acting strange and distant lately. I'll call you later with a report on the condo caper." Carlos gave me a quick kiss and a pat on my behind as I hurried back to my interview with Jay.

Jay was playing with his cell phone, sending a text, and laughing at an answer as I seated myself at my desk and pulled my yellow pad out of a drawer.

"Okay, Jay, let's talk about your case," I said.

"Oh, sure, are you going to write stuff down?"

"Yes. I need to see if I can help you. Let's start with how you met this girl who is accusing you."

"Her name is Jennifer. The first time I saw her was at the end of the spring scrimmage. It was the first game since the last season when we beat North Carolina. I threw three passes for touchdowns. The tackle for their team"---

"Jay, whoa, I need to hear about Jennifer, not the game."

"Oh, yeah, well she was waiting outside the locker room with some other girls. She came up and started talking about congrats on a good game. She said she didn't know how good looking I was without my helmet, or something like that, I noticed her more than the other girls because she was wearing, or I guess I should say what she wasn't wearing, so she stood out. I asked her did she go to the U. and she said yes, she was a freshman. That was about it because my girlfriend was waiting for me back at the dorm, so I left."

"When did you see her again?"

"I think it was in February or probably March. There was a big party at one of the fraternity houses and one of my friends invited me and some of the other football players. Melanie, that's my girlfriend, couldn't go. She was away with the women's basketball team. I spotted Jennifer as soon as I walked in. She was dressed in a short skirt and a kinda' sports bra thing or something. She came over to me and asked did I remember her from outside the locker room. When she said that, I did remember. She asked if I was with anyone. I said no, and asked if she was. She said she wasn't, so we started talking, and then we went outside and sat down by the lake. She just leaned over and kissed me and leaned against me, so we started, you know, making out. Things were getting real hot, and then she just stood up and said she had to go. So I said I'd take her back to her dorm. She said no, she had to go get her girlfriend that she came with. It was like she was supposed to get her friend home or something. So I said I'd call her, but she ran back to the party and didn't give me her cell or anything."

"Did she ever mention where she lived or anything about classes?"

"No, but I didn't think anything about that."

"So what happened next with Jennifer?"

"A few days later, she sent me something on my Facebook page about how she liked being with me at the Sigma Alpha party and she still felt crazy when she thought about me."

"Did you answer her?"

"Of course. I thought she was one bad chick. She was so into me at that party, I thought we were going to hook up that night or soon. So I sent her my cell number and asked her to send hers. The next thing I know, she sexted me. She had great tits, and looked awesome."

"Wait a minute, Jay, what did you do with the photo in your phone? You didn't show it around did you?"

"Sure I did. Here was this really hot white bitch, ah sorry ma'am, hot white girl looking for action with me. I sent it to most of the football team."

"Jay, do you have a copy of the charges against you? You know, the information that the state attorney filed against you?"

"I guess I do at home. I didn't know I was supposed to bring it."

"Were there other charges besides the sexual battery?"

"There was lewd and some other word with a minor. Am I in some other trouble?"

"You may be. When you sent the photo to others you were distributing what is called child pornography. She was only fourteen or fifteen. That's what your mother told me when she came to see me."

"She isn't any child. Not looking like that."

"We'll worry about that later. Tell me when you saw her again."

"Melanie's team finished their season and she and I went to stay at Ft. Lauderdale Beach for part of spring break, so I wasn't looking for Jennifer. We got back and spring practice started. I guess it was maybe April when I got a text from Jennifer. She said why didn't I let her know if I liked the picture she sent. So I texted back, yeah I liked it. Send me some more. She answered how about let's get together. It'd be better than a picture. We went back and forth about when we could meet. I had practice and she said she was getting ready for finals. I said I'd come to her room, but she said her roommate was always around, so I told her to come over to my room. We made a date for the weekend in May before the semester was over. It was a Friday night. She came over around nine. She was all over me the minute she got there. Listen, I'm human and she wanted it so I gave her what she wanted. She was something else. She wanted more. I was finally getting exhausted, and then the shit really hit. Melanie walked in on us. It was a bad scene. She ended up slapping Jennifer. Jennifer was screaming at me. It turned really ugly. I told Jennifer she better leave. She was pissed, said how could I like a big black woman like Melanie when I could have her any time.

"I offered to take Jennifer back to her dorm, but she grabbed her clothes and split. Melanie and I had it out and she said she never wanted to see me again."

"When was the next time you saw Jennifer?"

"I didn't hear from her anymore. I sent her a few texts. Told her I was sorry, and couldn't we get together again. I guess I said some stuff about what a good time we had. She didn't answer."

"Didn't you ever suspect that she wasn't a student at the university?"

"No, never. The next thing I knew was when we started fall practice. The first day, I was out running shifts when Coach called me to come to his office. I walked in and there was the campus police and the Coral Gables cops and they arrested me. I kept asking what did I do? They read me some stuff, and finally Coach told me that I was accused of raping some high school kid. I didn't know what they were talking about. When I got to the station, they showed me a paper with Jennifer's name on it. I still can't believe this is happening."

"If you want me to represent you, you'll need to let Mr. Fieldstone know right away."

"I want you to help me. That Fieldstone, he keeps saying there's no way to beat this. That it doesn't matter what Jennifer said or did. She was too young, so it's no defense. Is that true, or maybe he doesn't like Black people."

"It's true that because of her age it's as if she didn't consent to the sex. That's what he was trying to tell you. We will have to go to a jury trial. That's your best shot, but let me get the file and see what work has been done and see what else I can do. Keep a pen and paper around, and write down anything else you think of that you may have forgotten to tell me. And let me know after you speak to Frank Fieldstone."

"I like you, and I want you to be my lawyer. You really listened to me. No one else has heard everything about this."

"Didn't Frank sit down with you and ask you questions?"

"No, he just said I was in big trouble."

"It figures."

Chapter Nine

I walked Jay out to the reception room. Catherine was standing by her desk putting away her backpack. All signs pointed to the fact that she had just arrived. I glanced at my watch and saw it was 9:30. I instructed Jay again about communicating with Frank. Then I turned my attention to Catherine.

She was seating herself at her desk with her head bent over her computer. "J.C. left a message that he was running a bit late," she said.

"Catherine, look at me, please. What's wrong?"

As she slowly looked up I saw a huge purple bruise around her eye. It looked like she tried to cover it with makeup, to no avail. I moved closer and saw another dark bruise on her arm.

"Catherine, come into my office," I said. I guided her from the chair and led her into the office. She winced when I touched her arm. "What has happened? Please, talk to me."

She collapsed onto the sofa and I sat next to her. She tried to stifle a sob.

"I really don't want to bother you with my problems. You have enough on your plate with your dad and all."

"Catherine, we're friends, not just office colleagues. Whatever it is, I want to help."

"Brady surfaced a few days ago, my-ex. I was late getting home that day. Cory is really old enough for him to watch out for his little brother for an hour after school so I wasn't worried about the boys. When I walked in, there was Brady in the kitchen with Cory and Phillip. Both the boys looked scared. That's when all this started."

Chapter Ten

Catherine's Story

"What the hell are you doing in my apartment?" Catherine moved quickly to place herself between the boys and Brady.

Brady looked disheveled. His face was flushed and his eyes looked like those of a trapped animal.

"I came to see my sons," he slurred.

"Mommy, he said he was our dad. He pushed me when I opened the door." Phillip's lip was trembling and his hands were locked in fists.

"How many times have I told you not to open the door if I'm not home," Catherine raised her voice and was immediately sorry. Phillip began to cry.

"And where were you, Cory?" Catherine asked.

"I was in the bathroom. I kind of remember him, but I wasn't sure." Cory eyed Brady. "Is he our dad?"

"Boys, go to your room now and close the door. I'll be in to talk to you in a minute." Catherine waited while they grabbed their backpacks. She was quiet until she heard the click of their door closing.

"Brady, what are you doing here? Did you deliberately come here when I was at work? And what are you on?"

"I saw the kids coming from school. I have a right to see them."

"As a matter of fact, you don't. I have full custody and you know it. You gave up you visitation rights years ago when you failed to appear for visitation eleven times and the one time you did show up, you showed up drunk. Now tell me what you are doing here?"

"I missed you. I thought we could talk about getting back together." Brady took a step towards her, staggered and steadied himself on the edge of the kitchen table.

"This is laughable. Where's your Ft. Lauderdale bimbo?"

"We decided to break up."

"Break up? You mean she finally got smart and threw you out?"

"Cathy, I need a place to stay for just a couple of days. I want to stay here with you and the kids."

"You've got to be out of your mind. I want you out of here now. I never want you around here again. I've worked so hard to build my life and raise my sons. You left me penniless with two babies to feed and clothe. We've been divorced for years and you have failed to even make token child support payments or even ask about Cory and Phillip."

Brady took a step closer. He grabbed Catherine's arm. "I am not leaving," he shouted.

As Catherine pulled away from him, the doorbell rang followed by pounding on the front door.

Cory ran out of the bedroom and opened the door. Marco raced in almost knocking Cory over.

"Catherine, it's Marco. Where are you?"

"Marco, in here," Catherine called as she continued to pull from Brady's grasp.

"Who is this?" Brady whirled around. "So this is why you don't want me here."

"Marco, how did you--?" Catherine said.

"Cory called me from his cell phone. He asked me to come. He said you were in trouble. I was in Coconut Grove on a case so I came right over."

"Okay, Buddy, step outside with me now." Marco grabbed Brady by the collar and propelled him out of the apartment.

"You bitch, Cathy. We're not through with this, you whore," Brady screamed.

Phillip ran to his mother and threw himself against her.

Catherine and the boys huddled together on Cory's bed. In a few minutes, Marco let himself back into the apartment. He sat down on the bed with them and tried to hug all three at once.

"Is he gone?" Catherine asked,

"He's clearly on some drug. I gave him a few bucks and told him not to come near you again. It appears that he's homeless so that's how he turned up here. I gave him enough to get a motel room. Tomorrow you need to get a restraining order. Talk to Mary. She can help or I'll go with you to the courthouse."

Chapter Eleven

The next day Marco volunteered to pick the boys up at school and Catherine at work and take them to his house for dinner. All was quiet when they finally came back to the apartment in the later evening. Catherine was being lulled into believing that Brady had once again disappeared into whatever weird world he inhabited.

Two mornings later Catherine delivered the boys to early morning soccer practice and returned home to dress for work. Mrs. Morehouse, her landlady, stopped her on the steps.

"Catherine, I thought I should let you know that some guy was trying to get into your apartment. Connie Barrow, across the hall from you, called me and I came upstairs and saw him. He claimed that he was your ex-husband and that you were getting back together but he lost the key you gave him. I told him to leave or I'd call the police."

"My former husband has been hanging around. He's been out of my life for years. You did the right thing."

"He's a little scary, honey. You be careful. I don't want no rough stuff in the building."

"Thanks Mrs. Morehouse. Don't worry. He's not going to cause any trouble."

Catherine opened the door cautiously. Everything looked quiet. Then she spotted a dirty plate on the kitchen counter. She turned quickly, but not quickly enough. Brady stepped in front of her and grabbed her arm. He twisted it behind her and she screamed.

"Don't think you can get rid of me so fast. Not your shitty boyfriend neither. You've got my kids and that bastard isn't going to be their father. I'm coming back, you hear, you bitch?"

Catherine tried to get out of his grip. As she struggled, he punched her in the eye. She felt dizzy and tried to scream again. He threw her to the floor and she did scream as loud as she could. As he tried to hold her down on the floor, she kicked him as hard as she could in the groin.

Now Brady was the one screaming as he rolled on the floor in pain. Catherine rushed out of the apartment and pounded on Connie Barrow's door. Connie opened it immediately.

"Catherine, what's happened. I heard you scream. I just called the police. Was it that guy who tried to get in your place?"

"Yes, thanks. Can I make a call from here?"

Connie handed Catherine her cell phone. Catherine dialed Marco's beeper and put in her number and 911. Then they waited.

Marco arrived before the police with one of his Pit Bull investigators. That wasn't a surprise. The Miami Police were understaffed and over-whelmed with calls. Budget cuts had reduced what was already a lean number of cops and cars.

Catherine was dazed and sitting with ice on her eye. Connie informed Marco that there was a man in the apartment. The Pit Bull and Marco raced across the hall just as a bent-over Brady came out the door.

"Okay, that's it, Brady. I warned you to leave Catherine alone. Maybe we can make this completely clear to you," Marco said.

Marco had his gun out of his waistband. The Pit Bull had Brady by the shoulders and was escorting him down the stairs. That's when two Miami officers appeared in the hallway.

Brady began screaming. "Officer, help me. These guys attacked me."

"Marco, what's going on here?" Officer Dominquez asked. "We got a call about a break-in. Is this some case of yours?"

Marco quickly explained that this was his girlfriend's ex-husband who had been warned to stay away.

"Listen, Marco, your agency does good work but we gotta interview the alleged victim, and I think you need to put away your gun. Tempers are running a little too high here," Officer Dominquez said.

In the end, the officers told Catherine to get a restraining order and gave her a copy of their report. They took Brady to the Dade County Jail charged with simple battery and trespass, two misdemeanors that insured that he would be back out on the street as soon as he went to his first appearance hearing. They also warned Marco not to get in the middle of a domestic .

"Someone is sure to get hurt, especially when guns are being displayed," Dominquez said.

Chapter Twelve

"Catherine, you should have come to me right away. As soon as I finish with J.C.'s appointment, we're going to the courthouse to get a restraining order," I said.

"I didn't want to bother you with my problems, and anyway, what good will a restraining order do? It's just a piece of paper. Do you think that will stop Brady?"

"If he tries to hurt you again, the police will have grounds to arrest him. That will entitle you to a full hearing before a domestic violence judge. The judge can make the restraining order permanent and put some teeth into it. Where has Brady been and why is he suddenly trying to get back in your life?"

"Marco did some checking on him. He's been living with some woman up in Broward County. It's not even the same woman he moved in with when we split. This one has a record for drug possession and sales of small amounts of cocaine. Brady has one charge of cocaine possession, but he got off with a pre-trial diversion program. Marco was going to send someone to talk to the woman, Renee Francis. I told him not to bother. She probably threw him out and that's why he came here. He could never make a living. He just sponges off of whoever is dumb enough to let him move in. I can't believe I was so stupid to have married that creep."

"You and the boys need to stay out of your apartment for a while. Why don't you move in with me?"

"You've already got your mom there. You're not running a hotel. Marco has been insisting that we stay with him, and I think that's what I'll do. I've got to protect Cory and Phillip and they are crazy about Marco."

We both heard the front door open and a male voice called "hello." I jumped up, and pushed Catherine back on the sofa. I rushed to the door of my office only to bump into J.C. coming around the corner.

"Am I glad it's you," I said giving him a hug.

Chapter Thirteen

"Who were you expecting?" J.C. patted my shoulder.

"It's a long story," I said. "Catherine, I'm going to help you. Just hang in there."

I motioned J.C. to the chair across from my desk. Catherine closed the door on her way out to her desk.

"J.C., I know we have a personal relationship, and you may not feel comfortable with me as your attorney. I want you to be able to speak freely to the lawyer who is to represent you. If you would feel more at ease with someone else, I can help you obtain excellent counsel. At this point, we don't know that you will need an attorney, but it's important that you be able to explain everything that has led to this grand jury subpoena."

"Mary, I trust you and I like you. I've seen you in action in court more than once. I have no reservations about your being my attorney. Carlos always says you are the best."

"Thanks, but if you change your mind there won't be any hard feelings," I said.

I was wondering what Carlos was referring to when he said I was the best. Part of me hoped he meant as an attorney. The other part hoped he meant in bed.

"Okay, the first thing you need to know about appearing before a grand jury is that your lawyer cannot be with you in the grand jury room. You are not accused of any crime. The grand jury is investigating allegations against Seaside Bank. Here's how it works."

"Wait, stop, you can't be sitting with me while they ask me questions?"

"That's correct. I will be right outside the room. At any time, you can ask to go outside and confer with your attorney and you'll be permitted to do this. The prosecutor who is an assistant U.S. attorney will be asking the questions. The grand jurors will take notes. Grand jurors aren't going to find someone guilty or not guilty. Their job, after they hear all the witnesses and evidence presented by the government, is to decide whether to bring an indictment against anyone. I won't lie to you. The government leads the jurors in their decision."

"So it's all rigged against me."

"Not necessarily. As I understand it, you are a vice president and board member of the bank. I need to hear what part you play in the policies and day to day operation of the bank. You aren't the president or CEO, so let's talk about everything you have done for the bank, and what you think the government might be looking for. Start at the beginning. How did you become involved with the bank? Don't leave out anything. Even a small detail may be important."

"This all seems surreal. I've known Alex Nardo for years. He belongs to the Yacht Club and his kids went to Country Day with my kids. He called me and said he was starting a new bank and he wanted my help."

"Alejandro Nardo? Wasn't he mixed up in the closing of Bank Oficina or that Doral bank a few years ago?"

"I guess so. He's been with a few banks. He and I met for dinner and he outlined what he was offering me. He wanted me to be vice president with marketing duties for the bank. He knew that I had a lot of connections to South Americans who spend time in Miami. He offered me a salary of $200,000 a year with bonuses for bringing in clients who opened accounts of $100,000 or more. I would also be a voting member of the board of directors, so I would be in on the ground floor of what he said would be a very profitable bank."

"I know you and Angelina have served as directors in other companies. I remember Angelina is on the board of the Yarmouths' wine company."

"That's right. I used to be on the board of Eastern Seaboard Bank until they were bought out by Bank of America, and I was on the board of Jarett Investments for many years. Those positions were largely ceremonial."

"What do you mean?"

"I just went to the board meetings and voted like the president suggested."

"Well, you were paid a salary. Weren't you supposed to review their financial statements and other papers?"

"I always looked at everything, but I'm not an accountant. I'm an entrepreneur. I invest in businesses here and there. That's why I thought a new bank would be something good. I was getting stock and paying a minimum for it."

"Okay, did you refer clients to the bank?"

"I did a very good job. I brought in numerous accounts."

"Who were these accounts? Were they people you knew?"

"Yes, at first they were friends from Argentina, and other South Americans that I met socially. Then those clients referred other clients to me."

"The ones that were referred to you, did you check on their backgrounds, their business connections?"

"That wasn't my job. There were staff members to do that."

"J.C. have you heard of the Bank Secrecy Act?"

"Well, sure I've heard of it. Why?"

"The Bank Secrecy Act was passed to inhibit banks from accepting large cash deposits. Banks have been utilized by drug cartels to launder dirty money, proceeds of criminal enterprises. Every bank must have a policy in place to red flag suspicious accounts. Does Seaside Bank have a procedure for this?"

"I'm sure they do, but this wasn't my job."

"Was it discussed at board meetings?"

"I'm not sure."

"You need to go through all your papers from the bank and see what you can find about any procedures used to investigate large clients. Look through any e-mails on your computer at the bank, and one more thing, J.C. You do not have to answer any question if the answer may tend to incriminate you, and I will write that statement our for you so you can read it as your answer to any question that you feel is trying to lead to charges being filed against you. You do not have to incriminate yourself. Do you understand?"

"Mary, you're scaring me."

"Don't be scared; just be aware that you may have brought in clients that are not coming by their money from legitimate sources. We'll sit down again as soon as you go through your documents."

Mary, could I go to jail?"

Chapter Fourteen

I sat looking at the scant notes from my interview with J.C. I heard J.C.'s booming baritone saying goodbye to Catherine, and wondered if he understood how much trouble he could be facing.

Catherine came through the door so quietly that I didn't know she was there until she cleared her throat. "J.C. looked happy as he left, but you look worried. Is he in real hot water?" she asked.

"It doesn't look good. Either J.C. is naïve or he's a great actor. Let's hope he's a great actor and can convince a jury that he's just naïve. Right now we need to take care of your problem. Do you have the report the police officer gave you? We need to close up here and get over to the courthouse for that restraining order."

"I have the report in my backpack. I'll get it." Catherine hurried back to her desk.

I began to read as soon as she handed it to me. As usual, the writing looked like bird scratches. Why aren't cops given a course in sensible, legible writing? I thought. I finished the brief one page mish-mash and stared at Catherine.

"Did you read this?" I asked.

"Not really. I was so upset and I was late for work. I just threw it in my bag. What's wrong?"

"This report makes it look like the cop wasn't sure who was at fault. It says 'both parties were injured, but female party showed bruises on her eye and arms. Male party is ex-spouse of female. New boyfriend on scene and displayed a firearm which he has a license for. Cleared scene after charging male with misdemeanors. All parties warned to stay away from each other.'

"This report makes it look like the officer wasn't sure who the perpetrator was and it puts Marco in a bad light also. Didn't the police interview your neighbor?"

"She was trying to get to work, so he said she could contact him if she wanted. I don't think she wanted to get involved. She did tell him that she saw Brady trying to get into my apartment."

"Get your backpack and let's get over to the courthouse," I said.

"What about getting your mother to the hospital to see your dad?"

"Carlos has her with him. No excuses. Let's go."

Chapter Fifteen

It was almost noon. People were streaming out of the courthouse in long lines. As we approached, it looked like the starting line for a marathon. They couldn't get away from court fast enough. In the interim hour before the afternoon session, parking places opened up. I eased the Explorer into a legal place for a change.

"Do I have to tell a judge about all of this?" Catherine asked.

"Not today. We need to speak to a domestic violence intake officer. They will interview you and issue a temporary stay-away order. The next time we come over here, there will be a hearing to see if we can obtain a permanent order. Don't worry, I'll be right there with you through all of this." I tried to reassure Catherine.

I checked in at the front desk. Most of the seats in the waiting area were filled. The receptionist said we would have at least a thirty minute wait. "There must be a full moon. Everyone wants to batter someone," the receptionist giggled. When she saw I wasn't joining her try at humor, she turned away and put the initial information in her computer; name of complaining party, request for order of restraint. Addresses and phone numbers are kept out of computers to protect the victims.

I sat down next to Catherine and put my hand on her arm to steady her. I could feel her trembling.

"I really don't want to sit here for a half hour. Please, Mary, let's leave."

As Catherine stood up, I heard a familiar voice. "Mary, how great to run into you." I turned and saw Judge Liz Maxwell striding across the room in our direction. She had her robe slung over her arm.

"Liz, how great to run into you! You remember Catherine," I said.

Liz was a former client who I helped quash an investigation and save her judicial reputation last June. Now she was a close friend. I pulled her over to the elevator area and told her why we were here.

"I came over to help with the backlog of domestic cases and I was just about to go to lunch. Can I be of some help?" Liz said.

"Can you do the intake interview and issue a temporary order for Catherine's ex to stay away from her?"

"I don't see why not. Let me get the forms and I'll take you back to the judges' chambers."

"What a break for us, Catherine. You won't feel embarrassed talking to Liz and she'll understand the cop's inability to write a readable report."

Catherine nodded and actually half smiled. I smiled, too. I was afraid one of the counselors would have been reluctant to issue the order after reading the police report.

Chapter Sixteen

The phone light was blinking as we walked into the office. Catherine deposited her backpack and her new restraining order on the desk and began retrieving messages.

I picked up the order and glanced through it again. The only problem we encountered was where to serve Brady with the order. He had no known address. A phone call to Marco gave us the address he had uncovered for the Ft. Lauderdale babe Brady was last living with. We also ventured the name of a few cheap motels in the area of the Grove, thinking maybe Brady used the money Marco gave him for a place to stay. I was of the opinion that he either snorted it or smoked it depending on his current inclination.

The order must be served on him to put him on notice and to inform him of the date next week for a hearing before a domestic violence judge. My hope was that he had disappeared down some sewer and Catherine could return to her happy life.

"Mary, listen up. Guess who called; Frank Fieldstone ranting and raving about your theft of his client, Jay Lincoln. Want to hear the message?" Catherine asked.

"No thanks. I'll call him back. Jay must have given him the news that he was fired. Any other calls?"

"A bunch, but the other important one was from Carlos. He said your cell didn't answer. He was taking your mother to the hospital and he wants you to meet him there later. Oh, and Mrs. Lincoln called and said she went to Frank's office and fired him in person. She said she tried to get the file from him but he wouldn't turn it over to her."

I went into my office and picked up the phone to call Frank when Catherine buzzed me.

"Fieldstone's on the line again. I told him I wasn't sure if you were in a client conference. Do you want me to get rid of him?"

"No, I have to talk to him and get Jay's file quickly." I took a few deep breaths and pushed the button for line one.

"Hello, Frank. I was just about to call you," I said in as friendly a voice as I could muster.

"So you're at it again; stealing my clients. Times must be hard." Frank's voice dripped sarcasm, as annoying as a dripping water faucet.

"I understood you were representing Jay *pro bono*, so it's not much of a theft. Jay and his mother contacted me. They felt it was necessary to be represented by a criminal defense attorney. I'd like to have the file as soon as possible. The trial date is approaching."

"Trial? You're going to try this case? It's a slam dunk for the state. I told the mother and that kid that all we could do is get the best plea bargain possible."

"Well, he doesn't want to plead guilty, and I have a different strategy. Can I come by and get the file this afternoon?"

"The kid is nuts. He'll be lucky if he doesn't rot in prison. I'm just trying to keep the university from getting sued."

"The kid has a name, Jay Lincoln, and I can see you really never were representing Jay. Your client was the university Thank God Jay fired you. You never change, Frank."

"Too bad we can't even have a civil conversation. You can pick up the file tomorrow morning. I'll leave it with Esther, my paralegal. You remember Esther, don't you?"

"Sure, she was the one staff person in the office who hated me. Why can't I get the file today?"

"Because I'm busy. Take it or leave it. It'll be here from 9:30 tomorrow."

"Oh, I get it, you have to create a file. You haven't done any work on the case, have you?"

"Think anything you want." Frank clicked off.

Chapter Seventeen

"Your mother's on the phone. She sounds happy or excited or something," Catherine said.

I had been researching case law in Jay's case for over two hours. For once Frank was right. This case was a slam dunk for the state. Even a minor who consents to sex with someone older is thought to be incapable of consent. In cruder terms, if you bang a fifteen year old it's a sexual battery. I put aside my yellow pad which consisted of more doodles than ideas.

"Hi, Mother, what's up?"

"Carlos is a genius, that's what. He found six furnished condos right on the beach. Some were willing to take a short term lease. I think this is all going to work out, but I wanted you and William and Jonathon to be here when I talk to Dad."

"Of course, I'll be there before dinner. Is Carlos there now?"

"No, he went to his office, but he'll be back around five and the boys will be here as soon as they leave their offices. I'm really excited about this. This could be a first step in getting moved back here."

I answered a few phone messages including one from West Publishing telling me my bill for their research materials was overdue. Then I went out to tell Catherine to call it a day.

"Thanks, Mary. Marco is getting the boys from school and then he'll pick me up here, so I won't be alone. Give your parents my love."

In a few minutes, I was easing into Dixie Highway and the traffic that formed an endless flow like a river whose banks can't contain it. The flood of cars, trucks, and vans crawled along. I turned up the radio and listened to a country music singer lamenting the heartbreak of cheating. That made me hope Carlos wouldn't go into a Latin tizzy over my visit to my ex fiancé, Franklin Fieldstone.

Chapter Eighteen

The hospital smelled of antiseptic and dinner trays, a strange mixture, but one that reminded me that I hadn't stopped for lunch. I was famished. I made a stop at the vending machine and inserted two dollar bills which netted me a Baby Ruth Candy Bar and no change. I devoured the gooey candy, satisfying even though slightly stale.

As I headed down the hall to Dad's room, I saw my two brothers and Carlos engrossed in what looked like a heated discussion or an argument. Carlos was moving his hands in arcs, a dead give-away for annoyance.

"Hi, guys," I said.

They all stopped talking and stared at me. Jonathan's face was red.

"Why didn't you talk to me before you let Mother go running around looking at condos, and deciding to move her and Dad back here?" Jonathan spit his words out.

"Maybe we should step into the waiting room and out of the hallway," I said leading the way.

I closed the door and motioned everyone into a corner of sofas and chairs.

"What's the problem here? Mother wants to stay down here close to Dad's doctors until he recuperates. I thought that was sensible and Carlos was nice enough to arrange for her to look at some apartments." I said.

"It's more than that, isn't it, Mary? Be honest with us. She's going to force Dad to move back here," William was on the attack now.

Both of my brothers are successful attorneys and they know how to argue effectively. I can hold my own, but I sensed they were ganging up on me.

"Yes, Mother confided in me that she's not happy up there in retirement land. She thought giving this a try might be a way for Dad to see that he'd enjoy being closer to all of us. Why is this a problem, or should I ask, why is this a problem for the two of you?"

"Look, Mary, Randy has finally been able to have a little space from having Mother and Dad offering advice about our parenting and about our kids. If they are around the corner from us and Dad has nothing to do all day, where do you think they'll be; either dropping in at the house or at my office every other minute." Jonathan said.

"I'm a little further away in Ft. Lauderdale, but my office is opening a branch in downtown Miami. I've been asked to manage it so Joanie and I have been looking at houses on the beach and in the Grove. I have to agree with Jon. They'll be expecting us for Sunday dinners and wanting to have the kids available at their condo all the time." William got up and began to pace.

"I never thought you two were so mean-spirited," Carlos said. You're lucky to have parents who care about you. In my world, families like to be living close by."

"This isn't your world and this isn't your business. You've butted in enough," Jonathan shouted.

"No, you butt out, and listen up," I said. Our mother has a right to live where she wants. And this is Carlos's business. He's part of our family now. When Dad had his heart attack, did you call me, Jonathan? Did you, William? No, you sent Carlos to get me. Who sat at the hospital every day with Mother while you were busy at work? Carlos did. How dare you tell him to butt out.

"Does this mean you and Carlos are getting married?" Jonathan asked. "We didn't call you because you didn't tell us you were taking off for Vermont. We weren't sure where to reach you, so now that you're together again are you getting married?"

"Don't change the subject. All four of us are going in to see Dad and support Mother when she brings up the subject of a temporary stay in Miami. If they decide to stay in Miami or go back to Boynton Beach, that's their business. If our parents interfere with your lives, deal with it like an adult and talk it out with them. I never thought I'd have to lecture my two older brothers to quit acting like children."

"Let's go see Abe and Hope before they get suspicious about where we are and remember that your dad can't get upset. He's still not well." Carlos said. "I think a few months in a condo right on the beach would be great therapy. By the way, Hope told me about all the friends they still have in the area. I wouldn't worry so much about their being bored. Hope's got some great ideas to keep your dad busy including some travel when Abe gets clearance from the doctors. So Mary, what about the question Jonathan asked. Are we getting married?"

Chapter Nineteen

Carlos and Mother and I were sitting on the patio of the hospital cafeteria having dinner. Jonathan and William were gone to their respective wives and kids. They kept their mouths shut most of the time while Mother explained to Dad her plan to stay in the area for a while. She sugar coated this pill by telling him that the doctors were ready to release him as long as he would be nearby.

That did it for Dad. He would have moved into a yurt in order to leave the hospital. Mother described beautiful views of the beach and the board-walk, and Carlos chimed in with locations and real estate brochures.

Mother and Carlos were zeroing in on a lease offer for three months on a two bedroom seventeenth floor apartment on Collins Avenue near the Fontainebleau Hotel, a place Dad always loved. He was a teenager when it was built, and it reminded him of when he and Mother met on the public beach nearby.

I was listening with half a brain while I thought about Jay Lincoln's case and my dreaded visit to Frank's office. It was my old office that I hadn't entered since the day I quit Frank and his firm. I was jarred back to reality when my cell phone rang. Before I could answer, Carlos's phone also sounded.

I answered and heard a jumble of voices. Then I heard Catherine who was sobbing.

"Mary, I need you. Can you come here right now, please?"

"Just a minute Catherine, I can hardly hear you. I need to step away where it's quieter," I said, excusing myself from the table. As I walked to the edge of the patio, I saw Carlos frowning as he spoke into his phone.

"Okay, Catherine, what's wrong? Where are you?"

"I'm in front of my apartment. The police are here."

"Is Brady bothering you again? Show the police the restraining order."

"Mary, Brady is dead. Please come." Catherine ended the call.

Chapter Twenty

Carlos was standing next to me. "Marco just called. We have to get over to Catherine's right away."

"My call was from Catherine. She said Brady is dead. What did Marco say?"

"He and Catherine and her kids went over to the apartment after dinner to pick up some things to take to his house. When they got there, police cars were all over the place. Brady was found on the sidewalk outside the apartment building. He was shot. I guess it was a gruesome scene. The boys saw it all too. I told your mother we would have to leave right away."

I left my car in the hospital garage and we climbed into Carlos's Corvette. Carlos drove through the back streets of Little Havana trying to avoid dinner hour traffic. Carlos knows every lane and alley in Miami and he used a lot of them to get to Catherine's building in just under fifteen minutes, a new record even for Carlos.

We pulled on to Bird Road in Coconut Grove, but we were unable to turn the corner onto Catherine's street. Police had cordoned it off. We left the car in a convenience store parking lot and walked to the yellow taped area. I could see an ambulance and the covered body on a gurney. Crowds of on-lookers stood behind the yellow tape.

"Sorry folks, nobody can go beyond this tape," a young patrolman stopped us.

"I need to see my cousin. He called me to come right over," Carlos said.

"I said no one. I don't know anything about anyone's cousin. This is a crime scene," the patrolman took a step toward Carlos.

Just then I spotted Jim Avery. He's the detective who was assigned to my case when I was hit on the head in my parking lot last June. "Jim, remember me, Mary Katz? Can I talk to you for a minute?"

Jim looked in my directions. He was talking with another detective. He smiled and walked over. I had forgotten how good looking he is.

"Mary, sure I remember you. What are you doing here?"

I quickly told him that the ex-wife of the dead guy is my assistant, and her boyfriend is Marco from Pit Bull Investigators. They called and asked me to come here and I need to speak to them.

"They're being questioned right now," Jim said.

"Are they being questioned as suspects?" I asked.

"Right now, everyone is a suspect," he answered.

"Well, I'm their lawyer and no one is to question them without me being present."

"Okay, Mary, only because it's you that's asking." He lifted the tape and led me over to the side of the building.

Catherine was seated in a city police car. A detective was standing in front of the open door with his notepad open. Catherine was sobbing. In the months I worked with her, I never saw her cry or lose her cool until the last few days.

Jim told the detective that I was Catherine's lawyer and employer and had exercised the right to remain with Catherine throughout any questioning. "Mary, this is Detective Jaime Ruiz."

"Detective, I also represent Marco Perez. Is he being questioned at this time?"

"You're a busy girl. Do you also chase ambulances?" the detective asked.

"No need for sarcasm. Mary was a victim in a case I handled. I told her she could have access to her clients," Jim said.

"Okay. Everyone cool it. When I finish talking to Ms. Aynsworth, we'll move on to Marco." Detective Ruiz unbuttoned the top button of his blue striped "plain clothes" shirt that strained over his ample belly. Sweat ran down his face even though the evening breeze had picked up a hint of the changing season. Yes, Miami does have a change of season from the rainy to the dry season, but I digress.

Catherine was trying to regain her control. She swallowed a sob and blew her nose.

"Ms. Aynsworth, what time did you arrive at the apartment building this afternoon?"

"It was this evening, maybe an hour ago."

"Well, didn't you come home after work?"

"No, Marco picked me up and we all went out to dinner. Then we came here and that's when we saw the police and--." Catherine went into full sobbing mode again.

I handed her a wad of tissues from my purse. "Detective Ruiz, could you finish talking to Catherine tomorrow? She's in no condition to answer questions now."

"Just tell me one more thing, Catherine. Where were you from noon on today until Marco picked you up?" Detective Ruiz stared at Catherine.

"I was at work in Mary's office all day except when we went to the courthouse to get my restraining order.

Did you see Brady today?"

"He broke into my apartment early this morning. The police arrested him and took him away." Catherine put her head in her hands. Her body shook violently.

"We'll finish this in the morning, but don't leave Dade County and tell your lawyer your whereabouts until I see you early tomorrow. Better make arrangements for her, counselor."

Detective Ruiz checked his note pad. "I'm going to talk to Marco in a minute. He's in my car right over there." He pointed to the apartment parking lot. "If you want to be present, meet me over there."

I put my arm around Catherine and pulled her out of the squad car. "I know this is an awful mess, but you need to pull yourself together. Catherine, where are the boys?" I asked.

"I took them upstairs to my apartment and told them to wait there and not to answer the door or the phone. They're really scared," she said.

I instructed Carlos to take the three of them to my house. Playing with Sam might calm them and it would give Catherine time to pull herself together.

"What about your mother. We left her at the hospital," Carlos reminded me.

"Please, call her cell phone and explain what happened. But we can't just leave her there."

Carlos thought for a second. "I'll call my mother. She can pick her up and bring her to your house."

"This should be some scene. Our two mothers, Catherine and her kids, Marco, and the details of a murder. Just another day in the Magic City."

Chapter Twenty-One

Marco looked calm as I approached. He and Detective Ruiz were leaning against the Ford sedan that served as an undercover police car that everyone in Miami recognized as a police vehicle in spite of its lack of marking. Marco was smoking a cigarette so I knew he really wasn't calm. He gave up smoking shortly after he and Catherine began dating.

"I've already mirandized him. Do you want me to go through it again, Ms. Katz?" Ruiz gave me an annoyed glance. "And I've swabbed his hands for gun powder residue. Do you want me to repeat that test?"

"No, please go ahead with your interview. Marco, if you need to consult me before answering any question, please tell the detective. If I object to your answering any question, please don't answer." I instructed him.

"Okay, Marco, tell me what you were doing at this building this evening."

"I brought my fiancé, Catherine Aynsworth, and her two sons here to pick up some clothes. They were going to be staying at my house for a while, because her ex had been stalking her and abusing her. He broke into her apartment."

"I know all that. I've read the report. Tell me where you were this afternoon."

"I picked up the boys at school at 3:30 at the middle school on Ponce Boulevard. I took them to get some ice cream at the little stand down the street. We stopped at my office on Dixie Highway."

"What's that address?"

"It's 2255 South Dixie. They worked on their homework while I checked on a few matters. Then we went to pick up Catherine at Mary's office. It's just a few blocks south on Dixie."

"What time was that?"

"Around 5:00, I think, or a little before. Then we all stopped for dinner at Casey's, the sports bar over on Grand Avenue. Then we came over here to pack whatever they needed to take to my house. That's when we found out about Brady."

"Okay. Now before you went to the school, where were you for the early afternoon, say from noon on?"

"Noon, let's see, I had a client come in to go over a report we just finished. You know, I run a private investigation firm."

"How long were you in the office? What's the name of the client?"

"I can't tell you the name of the client. It's a delicate matter, but my secretary was there.

She can tell you how long we were there."

"After that, where were you?"

"Oh, boy, let me think. This whole thing has been upsetting. Mind if I bum another cigarette?"

"No problem. Here you go." The detective handed Marco a Marlborough and his lighter.

"Oh, yeah, now I remember. One of my guys, Francisco, was supposed to be doing surveillance in a case, but he was stuck watching a guy for an attorney we work for. Anyway, we got a tip that the man in Francisco's other case was headed to the Ritz Carlton in the Grove. No one else was available so I went over there to set up surveillance."

"What time was that?"

"Maybe one-thirty or so. Again, my secretary probably can tell you. She handled the phone calls about it."

"So how long were you there?"

"I concluded that surveillance right before I picked up the kids at school."

"Did anyone see you there?"

"I hope not. I wouldn't be very good at my job if everyone saw me there."

"So you really can't prove that you spent the afternoon outside the Ritz Carlton."

"I have my notes for my log."

"There's nothing to show that you actually made those notes this afternoon, is there?"

"Just a minute, detective, don't be calling my client a liar. He's doing his best to give you answers," I said.

"Nobody used the word liar accept you, counselor," Ruiz said. "Now Marco, you displayed your firearm to Brady Aynsworth this morning. It says so right in this police report. What kind of gun do you carry and may I see it?"

"Sure, it's in my glove compartment locked in my car. I have a license to carry it in my business."

"Do you have any other firearms?'

"There are others in the safe in my office."

"For now, I'll take a look at the one in your car, with your permission, of course."

"You're welcome to see it. Anything else?"

"Not right now but write down your home and office addresses for me, and don't leave the county until I contact you again. I want to have a look at the other weapons in your office after I search your car, and I'll need the clothes you're wearing."

"What?" I asked. "is he supposed to go home in the nude?"

"It's okay, Mary. I have nothing to hide and I do have a change of clothes at the office," Marco said.

Chapter Twenty-Two

An exhausting evening at my overcrowded house left me confused. Marco brought me home after I accompanied him and the detective on his fishing trip through Marco's car. He stayed long enough to down a beer and the snacks put together by Angie and my mother. He kept assuring me that he was not the shooter of Brady, although he admitted that he wouldn't have minded permanently disposing of him.

The last of the "guests" left around ten. I told Catherine not to worry about working the next day. She agreed that her boys would need her attention and assurances for a while.

Angie offered to have Mother stay at her condo, but the offer was politely refused. Carlos stayed the night in order to deliver me to the hospital parking garage where I had left my car, and finally everyone turned in including Sam who wormed his way between Carlos and me, making sleep a feat of moving parts.

Sometime during the evening, I remembered that I was due at Frank's office in the morning to pick up Jay Lincoln's file. I decided we had all had our fill of drama for the night, so I didn't discuss this with Carlos.

As I tried to sleep, I counted the problems in my life: Jay Lincoln's impending trial, J.C.'s trip to the grand jury, the suspicion surrounding Marco in Brady's murder, and mother's move to Miami with Dad still in precarious health. I pushed Sam out of the way and snuggled against Carlos. Problems could wait. Carlos and I were together again, no matter what else was on the horizon.

Chapter Twenty-Three

Mother accompanied Carlos and me to the hospital and went directly to Dad's room. Carlos went with her to finalize the lease offer on the condo she and Dad decided was the best of the bunch she visited.

I retrieved my faithful Ford Explorer from the garage and set out for the Fieldstone Law Firm. I pulled into the garage of the expensive office complex and was greeted by Charlie, the guard who had been with the building since it opened.

"Mary Katz, what a great surprise. Are you coming back to work here?" Charlie limped over to my car window smiling and pushing his meaty fist through the opening to shake my hand.

"No, Charlie, just here to pick up some papers, but thanks for the great greeting."

He handed me a guest pass. "Park anywhere on the second floor. I wish you were coming back. Frank has been a sorry sight since you left, always frowning and angry."

"Frank was always like that, before I left." I waved as I drove up the ramp. I passed Frank's black Mercedes. I was hoping he wasn't in his office, but now I knew I would have to confront him.

A quick trip up the smooth quiet elevator with the mural of Biscayne Bay, deposited me on the twenty-third floor. Thick carpet muted the noise of voices or footsteps. I approached Francine, the French receptionist, dressed in a black wool suit whose jacket's plunging neckline displayed the best cleavage surgery can buy.

"Hello, Mary, may I help you?"

"I'm here to pick up a file from Esther. Is she in the paralegal area?"

"We're expecting you. Mr. Fieldstone is waiting for you in his office. You're to see him, not Esther," she said in her semi-French accent. No one was ever sure if she really was French, because when she was excited she sounded like she was from New York.

"Please let him know I'm here and he can bring me the file," I said.

"He told me to send you back to his office. I'll let him know you're on your way. You do remember where it is, don't you? You spent enough time there." Sarcasm dripped from Francine, like a perfumed bubble bath.

"I'll find my way," I said as I went through the glass double doors into the inner sanctum of big law.

The long hallway passed by a myriad of office doors made of dark oak. As the hallway turned to the left, the doors were further apart denoting larger and larger offices until the dead end of the hallway led to ornate double doors and the gold lettering Franklin Fieldstone, Managing Partner.

I was about to knock when the door opened. Frank stood directly in front of me dressed in a Bruno Magli navy suit, white shirt, and red patterned tie.

"Hello, Frank, were you just leaving for court?" I asked.

"No, I was expecting you. Francine called from reception."

"You look like you're in your usual courtroom power attire. I thought I was supposed to see Esther about Jay's file."

"I thought it best to go over the file with you myself. Please come in and sit down." He gestured to the conference table positioned for the view of the bay and the sailboats dancing on the water.

I moved to the far end of the table. Frank picked up a file and sat in the chair closest to mine.

He pulled a folder of case law from the file and handed it to me. "One of the associates did this research that will show you there is no defense to sexual battery on a minor. Whether the minor gave consent or not is unimportant."

Frank pulled another folder with his handwritten notes. "These notes embody the conversations I had with Jay and his mother. I explained that we should attempt to work out the best plea agreement possible and keep publicity to a minimum. This third folder contains background material on Jay and his family. So you can see that I've done your work for you."

I returned the folders to the brown file. "What depositions have you taken? Are they in the file? And how about background on the alleged victim and her family?"

"No sense running up a bunch of bills for depositions and I just told you, it doesn't matter about the girl's background. She was only fifteen years old at the time of the rape and he's nineteen or twenty."

I stood up and picked up the file. "Thanks, Frank. I can see that I have a lot of work to do before I go to trial."

"Wait, Mary. You just got here. I'll call for some coffee and some of those chocolate croissants you always liked." Frank picked up the phone.

"Please don't order anything. I'm really in a hurry."

"Well, at least tell me how your dad is doing. I ran into Jonathan at the courthouse and he told me about the heart attack."

"He's doing better. Thanks for asking.

"I always liked your dad. He was a great businessman and he and I always had such good rapport, talking golf. Does your new friend, Carlos play golf?"

"No, he doesn't."

"I didn't think so."

"Look Frank, we're not going to be buddies. After everything you did to me when I left this firm, stalking me, breaking into my house, suing me. I'm not going to sit here like none of that happened."

"I only did those things because I loved you. I still do, and I'm sorry to have behaved like that. You look beautiful even though I can see you're tired. Please, let me do something for you. I can't see how you're going to go to trial in this case, but you seem determined. Let me be your second chair." Frank looked pitiful standing there in his expensive suit and begging to be part of a criminal case.

"You don't know anything about criminal law and you don't believe in the case at all. What help can you be?"

"I can lend my reputation for handling million dollar corporations and clients. You know judges love that stuff, and this case is assigned to Judge Luongo. He just moved to criminal from the civil courthouse. I've won two trials in front of him. Whatever theory you're going to present, maybe he'll be more apt to listen."

"I'll think about it, Frank. I'll let you know." I picked up the file and headed for the double doors. If I could keep Frank from saying anything and just sitting and looking pretty, maybe it could work. Of course, Carlos would have a fit. I wished that Frank hadn't brought up the 'L' word. How uncomfortable would it be to have him sitting at the defense table knowing I was continuing to hurt him.

Chapter Twenty-Four

The office was locked and dark. It was almost eleven when I arrived. I forgot that there would be no Catherine to open the office and keep things humming.

The telephone was blinking with ten voicemails. I beamed up the computer and found forty new e-mails. I started with the voicemails. Five were ads for a variety of office products and insurance; one was from my dentist telling me I was overdue for a checkup. The last three caught my attention.

J.C. was calling to tell me he had collected all the documents and e-mails from his files and needed to go over them with me before his grand jury date. Mother was calling to say that the doctor would release Dad the day after tomorrow. She was renting a car to go to the condo and ascertain what she would need and would I please go with her to Boynton Beach tomorrow to help her pack. Marco was the last call. He sounded strange and asked me to call him at once.

I reached Marco on his cell phone. At least I reached someone on his cell. A strange voice answered. "Who's calling?" the voice grumbled.

"It's Mary Katz returning Marco's call. Who is this?"

"Just a minute." the voice snarled.

"Mary, thank God." Marco's voice finally spoke.

"Marco, what's wrong and where are you? What's that noise in the background? Who answered your phone?"

"Mary, the police have a warrant for my arrest. They came to the office and my secretary called to warn me they were coming to the house. I left right away. I'm at Franco's body shop."

"You left Catherine and the boys alone to deal with the police at your house? What were you thinking? Haven't they been through enough?"

"I'm sorry, Mary. I'm so scared. I guess I'm not thinking."

"No, Marco, you're not thinking. Trying to elude arrest just adds to the picture of guilt that the police will use against you."

"What should I do? Don't desert me, Mary."

"Of course, I won't. Stay put. I'll call Jim Avery and tell him that I will accompany you to surrender at the police station. Don't leave. I'm on my way. Marco, be prepared for the media to be there. This won't be pleasant."

I locked the office after forwarding the phone to my cell. Back on the road I drove through a series of side streets headed to Franco's Auto Advisory, the fancy name for Marco's brother's auto repair. Franco spent a lot of his time tending to the cars and trucks belonging to Carlos's extended family. Rumors abounded that Franco ran a "chop shop" in the back bay of his establishment, but I had never been allowed back there to see for myself His only arrests were for domestic violence. He and his wife routinely resorted to physical violence to express their love. And, of course there was his last arrest for alleged bribery. I got that case dismissed that stemmed from his freeing my SUV from a police impound lot.

As I drove, I returned J.C's call, leaving him a message that I might have to meet with him over the weekend due to several other urgent matters. I reached Mother on the first ring. Before she could begin her litany of all she had to do to get ready for the move to the beach, I interrupted. I told her about Marco, and heard her gasp.

"Catherine has the worst luck with men, poor girl," she said. "I guess this means you're too busy with strangers' problems to help your family."

"Marco is a wonderful guy. I know he's not guilty of anything," I said. I was sure Mother heard my annoyance with the guilt trip she was creating. "I'll work out something to get you up to Boynton Beach tomorrow, but it may be late in the day." I clicked off before she could answer.

I pulled into the gravel lot in front of Franco's shop and prepared for the ominous event of turning Marco over to the Miami cops. Guilt was washing over me for cutting my mother off.

Chapter Twenty-Five

Marco met me at the door. He looked like a guilty man, pale and sweating with dark bags under his eyes. Franco appeared from under a disassembled car wiping his hands on a rag.

"How bad is this?" Franco asked, raising his voice to be heard over the din of repair equipment that interfered with meaningful conversation.

"Please, Franco, can we go in your office?"

Franco motioned Marco and me into the glassed in area next to the shop. When he closed the door the noise subsided enough for me to explain what was about to happen to his brother,

"Let's just take this one step at a time, I said. "Marco, leave your car here. I will drive you downtown and stay with you through the booking process. I won't lie to you. You will be booked into the Dade County Jail, and you'll have to stay there until your first appearance hearing. It will be too late for the afternoon bond hearings, so you'll be on the docket first thing tomorrow morning.

"Florida law mandates that everyone charged with a crime must have a first appearance within twenty-four hours of arrest. In order to obey this law, the Dade County Courts hold bond hearings seven days a week. Monday through Friday there are hearings in the morning and afternoon. On the weekends, hearings are held Saturday and Sunday morning from nine a.m. until the previous night's arrestees have all been heard. Judges take turns manning the weekend hearings. The judges are generally disgruntled having to give up their weekend, so I'm relieved that your hearing is during the regular work week."

"Why can't I just post a bond right away at the police station?" Marco asked.

"If this was a simple case without violence, you might be able to do that, but we know they are going to charge you with Brady's murder.

I need to prepare you that if the charge is first degree murder, that means premeditated murder, there is no bond."

"What's that mean, premeditated?" Franco asked.

"It means I thought about it and planned it," Marco said.

"We don't know that's what the charge is. It could be second degree or even manslaughter," I said. "Let's get this over with, before they put out a real search for you."

"Don't worry about anything, Bro'. I'm here for you, and I'll service your car while it's here," Franco said.

Chapter Twenty-Six

As I drove, I telephoned Catherine on her cell. She answered on the first ring.

"Mary, where are you? The Miami police just left here. I don't know where Marco is and they said they had a warrant for his arrest. Is that true? This just can't be happening. What should I do? This is all my fault."

"First of all, Marco is with me, here in my car. It's true about the warrant. I called Detective Avery and told him I was bringing Marco in to surrender. We don't want the cops putting out a BOLO for him. Second, this is not your fault. You and Marco tried to get Brady to leave you alone, and you did everything you could do legally. There isn't a lot for you to do right now except to stay with Cory and Phillip and keep them calm. I think you should go back to your apartment. Chances are the media will start hanging around Marco's house."

"When can I see Marco? Where will he be?"

"At the Dade County Jail. I'll stay with him while he's booked in. Let's wait and see what the charges are. Try to keep as calm as you can for the sake of the kids. I'll keep you informed of everything. And maybe it's best if the boys go back to school tomorrow"

I pulled into the visitor's lot at the Miami Police Station and dragged Marco out of the passenger door. He leaned heavily on my arm as we walked through the front door.

Jim Avery and another officer met us at the front desk. Mercifully, no media were present. Jim introduced the uniformed officer as Sergeant Forrester from the warrants division.

"Thanks for voluntarily surrendering, Marco. Josh Forrester will be transporting you to the Dade County Jail for booking." Jim removed handcuffs from his back pocket.

"Wait, do you have to use those? Why can't my lawyer drive me to the jail?" Marco reached for a fresh cigarette.

"Sorry, I can't do that. Mary can follow us to the jail and I'll ask the corrections guys to let her stay with you while they print you and photograph you."

"Will you please let Marco know what he's being charged with?" I said.

"I'm about to do that." Jim said. "Marco Perez, you are charged with the first degree murder of Brady Aynsworth. You have a right to remain silent. Should you choose to talk to me or any other officer, anything you say"

I tuned out the rest of Jim's spiel. I couldn't believe that this was actually happening. Now there would be no bond and Marco would be stuck in the miserable hellhole known as the Dade County Jail. It was my job to get him out. My head was spinning as I realized that Marco was the second member of Carlos's family to be in big trouble. J.C. would undoubtedly be in the news media as the investigation of Seaside Bank unfolded. The Herald front page would have pictures of Marco. If I failed in their defense, the intertwined family structure would pressure Carlos to forget the *gringa*.

"Sorry Marco, I have to cuff you or I'll get in trouble," Jim said.

"What is the basis of this decision to charge first degree? I want to see the medical examiner's report and the results of any tests on Marco's clothes."

"You'll get everything in discovery. It'll all be in my supplemental police report."

"I need this immediately for the bond hearing. This is unfair. When will the report be ready?"

"The report has to be typed and approved by my captain. It'll be a while, and let me remind you that there is no bond for first degree murder."

I looked away as Officer Forrester led Marco out a side door and into a squad car.

Chapter Twenty-Seven

I returned to the office directly from the jail. My head and throat hurt from watching as Marco was printed and photographed and led away. The worst experience of it all was the humiliation of seeing Marco led out of the squad car at the entrance to the jail where a gaggle of media buzzards happily photographed the "perp walk". I knew it would be on the evening news and the internet.

I called Carlos to warn him to break the news to Marco's parents and to Angie. Then I had the awful job of letting Catherine know and instructing her about tomorrow's bond hearing. I knew she would want to be present, but I tried to dissuade her. The media would take pictures of her and she had to think of her kids and what this would mean to their treatment at school.

I heard the door to the reception room open, and a woman's voice called out, "Hello?" I hurried out and saw Jay Washington's mother standing in front of Catherine's empty desk.

"Mrs. Washington, did we have an appointment?" I asked

"No, ma'am, I just came by to give you a check and see how you were coming with Jay's case."

"You didn't have to come in person to pay Jay's fee. That was very thoughtful."

"You haven't answered me. What about Jay's case?"

"Of course, I'm working on it. Please have a seat. I've picked up the file from Mr. Fieldstone. He didn't really understand the ins and outs of a criminal case, so I have a lot of work to do."

"What will you have to do?"

"I will need to take depositions of all the witnesses that the state has listed. That means I will need sworn statements from the alleged victim and her parents. We will have to go to trial in this case. The state has offered a plea to Jay and I fully understand that he has rejected it. There is no other way."

"Maybe you can shake the truth out of that girl."

"It won't matter as far as the law is concerned, because the law says that even if a minor consents to sex with an adult, it's still considered sexual battery. So right now our best shot, our only shot is that a jury will see things differently than what the law says."

"Oh, like I saw on *Law and Order* one time. They called it jury no-something."

"Jury nullification. But remember that the ultimate decision about a trial or a plea belongs to Jay. He's my client and it's his life. If a jury finds him guilty, the judge can sentence him very harshly. I will be having discussions with Jay as often as possible so he understands the risks."

"I can't believe this is happening to my son. He's such a good young man. I'm afraid this will kill his father." Mrs. Washington's shoulders slumped as she walked to the door.

"Wait, Mrs. Washington. There's one other thing. Mr. Fieldstone would like to stay on the case only as a second chair, like an assistant. He wouldn't be charging any fee or questioning any witnesses."

"Why would you let him do that? I don't trust that man."

"For only one purpose. He's acquainted with the judge, James Luongo. That could mean that the judge would be more agreeable to listen to our side."

"What's going on here? So this is how the justice system works? And the big football game is coming up and I'm so afraid for Jay. People at church told me that there was going to be a bunch of demonstrators. Maybe this will turn out to be a race riot."

"Please stay calm, Mrs. Washington. I'll get this sorted out. In the meantime you need to help Jay keep his spirits up." I yelled after her, but she moved out the door without turning back.

I returned to my desk and tried to clear up the mail, the e-mails, and the messages that were accumulating without Catherine's capable hands. How was I going to handle all these huge cases without her? I put my head down on the desk for a minute. The next thing I knew my watch said five o'clock. I had dozed off and now I felt like I had a fever.

Chapter Twenty-Eight

Carlos drove up just as I was unlocking the door to my house. Sam came loping out to meet me with his usual greeting, paws on my shoulders and a wet tongue on my face. This time the wetness felt good on my burning cheeks.

My cell phone rang as I unloaded my purse on the living room sofa. I fumbled for the phone in the pocket of my suit jacket.

"Mary, honey, are you okay? I just saw Marco on the TV being led off to jail. He looked like a possum in a pumpkin patch."

It was Mother. When she gets excited she reverts to her southern accent and expressions.

"Mother, where are you? I've been so busy I never checked with you to see if the condo is okay. Are you coming back here tonight?"

"Don't worry about me. The condo is great and I'm going to stay here tonight. I picked up a rental car and got my suitcase at your house this afternoon. Tomorrow if you can meet me at the rental car agency, I'll turn in the car and you can drive me to the house in Boynton Beach. If you can help me a little, we can pack what I need and I'll drive my car or dad's car back down to Miami. Dad can't wait to get out of the hospital."

"Okay, I'll work everything out. I have to be in court for Marco's bond hearing in the morning. I guess Jonathan or William or the girls couldn't go with you?"

"I need you. Besides, they've already given up a lot of their schedules when you were on that extended vacation in Vermont. You sound kind of strange, sort of nasal or husky or something. Are you okay?"

"Sure," I lied. "It's just been a long day. I'll call you tomorrow."

Carlos was standing in the doorway. "Mary, your face is flushed," He put a hand on my forehead. "You're running a temperature. Do you have a thermometer?"

"No, it's just a cold coming on. My throat's a little sore."

My phone rang again. Carlos took it out of my hand. "Go get in bed. I'll take care of this."

I handed the phone over and gratefully retreated to the bedroom, cranked up the air conditioner and fell into bed.

Sometime later I heard Carlos in the kitchen. I fell asleep again and when I woke, Carlos was standing by the bed with a bowl of soup in his hand. "I found a couple of cans of soup in your cupboard. God knows how old they are, but at least it smells good. I fed Sam so don't worry about getting up. That phone call was from Catherine. Her parents are on their way down from Daytona to stay with her, and she said her mother might be able to help you out in the office until she gets her act together."

I guzzled down the soup. It was great to have someone else take charge for a change.

Chapter Twenty-Nine

Sun creeping through the bedroom curtains and crawling up the quilt that laid in a heap over my feet tipped me off that it was morning. The sheets were soaked so I must have sweated out the fever. My throat felt like someone had scrubbed it with steel wool, but the rest of me was good to go.

I came out of the shower and saw Carlos dressed in his best business attire.

"I went over to the coffee shop at the Hyatt down the way and got you some coffee and orange juice. Sorry to rush out. Today is the day the Chinese investors are arriving."

"Oh, I'm sorry I forgot. The mess with Marco took it right out of my head. And you know I have to drive my mother up to her house after I finish in court and at the office."

"I'm going to be tied up with these guys all day and through dinner. They want to look at the two blocks of old buildings east and west of Biscayne Boulevard. I have an option on some of that land."

"What do they want with it? It's almost a slum."

"That's why they want it; to tear everything down and build a hotel and stores and they hope the state will okay a gambling casino. If I can help them, I'll get the job of building a whole new village."

"It sounds great for you, but gambling in the middle of downtown? I don't know."

"I don't care if they want to build an elephant park in the middle of downtown I've got to keep my crews working, and you should be glad too. Crime follows gambling. You'll get new clients."

"My God, Carlos, I don't want to ruin the city just to make a living."

"I'm not as altruistic as you are, my love. Let's not argue about this now. You have your hands full with Marco's hearing, and remember

Catherine is going to bring her mother to your office later to see if she can help you. I'm out of here. *Ciao* for now."

I pulled out my red suit and hoped that it would emit power just like the woman at Nordstrom said. Sam cooperated by eating, taking care of business in the yard and settling down on my bed. I knew he would transfer to the sofa as soon as he heard my car pull out of the drive.

I downed some of the orange juice and coffee on my way out. The juice burned with each swallow as if it were a poison cocktail.

The courthouse was mobbed. The line to get through the metal detectors stretched down the steps and curled along the curb. I finally made it to the front but as soon as I walked through the detectors every bell and whistle began clamoring.

"Step to the side ma'am. We'll have to use the wand."

"I can't understand this. I put all my metal stuff through the x-ray machine."

A heavy-set woman appeared with the magic whistling wand which she began pushing over my body. "Here's the problem. Your jacket has these huge metal buttons and that metal chain."

I removed the jacket and the creeping wand moved over my blouse in total quiet.

"Next time skip the fashion statement and wear something real plain," the wand lady said.

The specially outfitted courtroom where first appearance hearings are held was almost full. Defendants are no longer trucked in from the various jails. Instead they stand before TV cameras that show them on closed circuit in the courtroom. They can see and hear the judge and lawyers and sometimes family members but it's not the same as actually being in the room. So much for justice trumping convenience.

I spotted a seat in the second row and grabbed it before I noticed a cameraman and reporter in the front row just to my left. "Hey, you're the lawyer for the guy who murdered his girlfriend's husband. Can we get a statement from you?"

Before I had a chance to say no statement accompanied by bashing him with my briefcase, the bailiff called us to order. The bond hearing judge was taking her seat. I recognized retired judge Susan Weil. She had once been known as "hang 'em high Weil."

"Oh, great," I muttered to myself. "Yeah, she's still the same," the attorney next to me whispered.

The monotonous calling of the list of arrestees began with the usual drunk tank occupants. Some of them looked as if the alcohol or drugs still hadn't worn off. Even these regulars weren't disposed of quickly. Judge Weil insisted on the clerk running computer checks again even though their record or lack thereof was in a printout in the file. In fact, she caught a couple of glitches that had failed to show probation holds. The computer missed them but Judge Weil recognized them from past sentencings.

At least I knew she wasn't senile.

I spotted Louise Margolis enter the courtroom and ask to approach the bench. Louise was an assistant state attorney from the homicide division. She also was a classmate from law school. This could be a break for Marco if she was here on his case.

A minute later the bailiff announced "State versus Marco Perez."

I hustled up to the podium and was joined by Louise.

"Louise Margolis for the State."

"And Mary Magruder Katz on behalf of Marco Perez." I handed a notice of appearance to the clerk who passed it to the judge. "I don't see my client on the screen, Your Honor."

"I'm taking this case out of order to accommodate Ms. Margolis. Guards, get Perez up to the front pronto." The judge's order caused scurrying of personnel on the jail side of the camera.

A few minutes later, as the audience of family and attorneys shuffled their feet and sighed, the guards pushed a man in an orange jail suit in front of the camera. It was Marco, but it was hard to recognize him. He looked disheveled and had a bandage on his forehead, and black circles under his eyes.

"Mr. Perez, you are charged with the murder of Brady Aynsworth. How do you plead?"

"My client enters a plea of not guilty and asks for fifteen days from the time of an information or indictment to file motions. Judge, may we address bond for my client?"

"Judge, the status of this case is no bond," Louise said.

"But, Your Honor, the charge at this time is just what the detectives have placed on their arrest warrant. The state must make its own determination of what they will charge. This could be a lesser degree or even no charge at all. In the meantime, Mr. Perez has no criminal record, not even a driving citation. He is the owner of Pit Bull Investigations and is licensed by the state as a private investigator."

"There's a first time for everything, Judge, and for right now this man is looking at a first degree murder charge. We have twenty-one days to file our charging document, or even forty days if the state convenes a grand jury. The state asks the court to keep him on a no bond status until his next appearance at least." Louise gave me a pleading look.

"Judge, I'd like to inquire of my client how he got the injury to his face, He has a large bandage on his forehead and what looks like two black eyes," I responded.

"Go ahead, Mr. Perez, answer your lawyer's question," the judge said.

"I was recognized by another inmate. I was the investigator in a domestic violence case which led to his arrest, and he took exception to my presence with his fists," Marco answered.

"You see, Judge, it isn't safe to hold him here. He can post a large bond and be kept on house arrest with reporting to an officer as many times a day as you order. He has lived all his life in Miami and has a business here and many relatives. He's not going to abscond, and I need his help investigating this case. We don't even know what evidence led the police to arrest him."

"Just a minute, counsel. Catch your breath while I have the clerk run her computer again about your client. Mr. Perez, didn't you testify in the case in the juvenile court when Tommy Rose, the little nine year old boy, was abused by his father?"

"Yes, Judge, I believe you were the judge in that case," Marco said.

"You represented the child, didn't you?"

"I was asked to conduct an independent investigation for the attorney from Lawyers For Children. I did that for free. It was a very sad case."

"I remember it well. The state child welfare workers wanted me to return Tommy to his parents. I was about to do that when you came to court with your report. You were the only one who uncovered the past of the father under another name with a record of child abuse. You saved me a lot of embarrassment of returning a child to someone capable of killing his own child. I'll never forget that case."

"You have a very good memory, Judge," Marco said.

"Very well, Ms. Katz. One million dollar bond and full house arrest with an ankle bracelet. An immediate home investigation to take place by the house arrest officers. Ms. Katz, they will contact you for entry into the house."

"Note my objection for the record," Louise said.

I smiled at Marco, gathered my briefcase and moved quickly out of the courtroom followed by Louise and the reporter and cameraman.

Just ahead I spotted the women's restroom and retreated. A second later Louise followed me.

"Mary, I can't believe Judge Weil let your client out. How are you anyway? I heard you opened your own office," Louise said.

"It's been a long time since I've seen you. Guess we'll be seeing a lot of each other. I forgot to find out which judge is assigned to try Marco's case."

"Well, you won't believe it. It's Sylvia Cohen-Cueto. Remember her from law school? Well, she was just Sylvia Cohen then."

"She was two years ahead of us and thought she was a genius. It'll be like a reunion in that court room." I said.

Chapter Thirty

I was on my cell all the way back to the office, calling Catherine with the good news about Marco, and also to start lining up the many Martin and Perez relatives to gather the money for the bond.

By the time I reached the office, Catherine was there with her parents in tow. She was on the phone and had a list on a yellow pad sitting in front of her.

"Mary, you are a genius. I am so thankful that Marco will be out of that place. I was just talking to Marco's parents. They will put up their house and land as collateral for the bond. Everybody is chipping in with cash so we have almost the $100,000 dollars for the ten percent cash."

"Call Alice Puckett at Bonds Are Us and alert her about this bond. She needs to coordinate with the court regarding any restrictions and you can start feeding her the information about the properties. Too bad Carlos is tied up today with the Chinese guys."

"I didn't know he was busy. I called him and he said he'd get anything we needed."

I realized that we had ignored Catherine's parents who were waiting patiently on the two visitor chairs thumbing through the outdated magazines in my tiny waiting room.

"Mr. and Mrs. Larsen, it's so good to see you," I said extending a hand to each of them. "I know Catherine is happy to have you here."

"Please, Mary, I told you last time we were in town, we are Patty and Doug to you. I can't believe anyone would think that Marco could do harm to someone, although I must admit, I have no sadness over Brady's death." Patty stood up replacing the "Smart Eating" magazine she had been perusing.

Patty Larsen was an older heavier version of Catherine. She was dressed simply in slacks and a print blouse. Doug was the picture of a military man. His grey hair still worn in a crew cut topped off a khaki shirt and slacks and black boots shined to perfection.

"I think whoever shot that jerk did us all a favor," Doug said. "I'd like to have done it myself."

"Dad, you'll get yourself in trouble saying that," Catherine said.

"Well, Mary, let's get started showing me the ropes. Catherine has instructed me about the phones. I'll need a little tutorial about your computer, but I can keep things running for you," Patty said.

"I can't ask you to do that. You're here to help Catherine."

"Doug is here to help with the boys and whatever else Catherine needs. I want to help you. You've been a good friend to Cathy, and I love running an office. I worked on many of the bases we were stationed at. It's just like running a household."

"I sure could use the help. I still have to meet with the house arrest officers and take them to wherever Marco is going to be staying. And then I have to go with my mother to Boynton Beach to help her pack enough to stay in Miami for a while."

"What do you mean where Marco will be staying? His home should be acceptable or my apartment is near his office," Catherine said.

"You must understand that house arrest is just what its name means. He cannot go to his office, or to the grocery, or anywhere. He'll be wearing an ankle bracelet that is attached to a landline telephone. If he goes one foot beyond those boundaries, he will be right back in jail. He'll need help getting his mail, food, everything. Maybe the best place for him will be with his parents. They have a big house and yard. You and the boys and Franco and Carlos can visit him and keep his spirits up." I looked at Catherine who looked shaken.

"I think Mary is right," Patty spoke up. "That big family of Marco's will be in and out of there. Mrs. Perez will love that, but it would be confusing in your small apartment."

"I'll call Mrs. Perez and then I'll set up the inspection of the house by the officers. It's settled," I said.

"Shouldn't we ask Marco if this is okay?" Catherine asked.

"We need to decide what's in Marco's best interest right now," I said.

Patty started collecting files and papers from Catherine's desk. "I'll get these things in order and then I'll take care of those dreadful dead plants on the window sills. We'll have this office shaped up in no time," she said as she bustled into my office.

Oh no, I thought. I've just been adopted by another mother.

Chapter Thirty-One

By mid- afternoon, arrangements had been made with the bonding company. The community control officer had been dispatched to the Perez house. Mrs. Perez was ecstatic to have her favorite son moving in. Angie Martin, her sister-in-law who is Carlos's mother was already over there going over grocery lists and recipes.

Patty Larsen was whipping the office into shape including dusting and vacuuming. I sat at my desk for the first time that day and realized that I still had the sore throat and aching joints. I called Mother to find out where to pick her up and then went home to feed Sam and load him into the Explorer. The car looked nearly brand new after Franco did his magic. Carlos's trip back from Vermont was hard on the old SUV but I was in no condition to buy a new car or anything over $20. Thank goodness for Franco.

Mother was waiting outside the rental car office in the Gables. Dressed in jeans and a white shirt with her hair pulled into a ponytail, she looked like a young girl. She was as enthusiastic as a teenager too.

"Isn't this all too wonderful?" she asked as she hopped into the SUV. Sam nudged her neck and she didn't even push him away. "I mean Dad will soon be out of the hospital and the condo is great; an ocean view and close to shopping and old friends."

"I'm glad you're happy," I said as we headed for the freeway.

"What's wrong with your voice? Are you getting one of your famous colds?"

"Why are they famous?" I dodged her question.

"You always get them when you're stressed out and they last and last and you usually end up losing your voice."

"I'm fine," I said. I turned on the radio to the easy listening station and soon Mother dropped off to sleep. The rest of the lengthy drive was blessedly peaceful except for the elevator music.

We pulled into the entry gate of my parents enclosed community as the sun was setting. After going through the security routine with the guard whose uniform looked like a ship captain's, we drove through the winding streets fronting the very green golf course. Sprinklers were spraying the whole area even though water was becoming a premium.

Mother and Dad's house was one of dozens of red tiled roofs and stucco types with fake Greek columns at its front. Behind the house a gate opened to a man- made lake. Everything about "Tropical Homes" was man-made or faux, a fancy word for fake. It had all been plunked down at the edge of the Everglades and belied its name. Nothing was truly tropical about it. All of the plants required constant watering throughout the long dry period that is winter in South Florida.

"Someone must have been hired to keep up the lawn and plants. Everything looks fresh and mowed. Who looked after everything while you've been away?" I asked.

"The association has workers that insure that nothing mars the landscape. It's in the rules and we pay plenty for it," Mother said.

"You always had a lovely garden at our house when we were kids. Do you have one here?" I looked around as we got out of the car and saw nothing of the orchids and bromeliads that had surrounded our porch.

"No, we can't plant anything that isn't in the master landscape plan for the community."

We unloaded Sam and Mother unlocked the front door. It was clear that no one had touched the inside of the house. It smelled stale and airless. Newspapers were scattered about and coat hangers were seated on the front hall bench.

"I left in a hurry when Dad had the attack and I was only back once to pack a few things. Jonathan drove me up here and he was in a hurry. You know I went in the helicopter with Dad when they moved him to the hospital in Miami."

"Don't you have cleaning help here, or a neighbor who could have helped out?"

"I use a cleaning service sometimes, but I didn't call them to come. A couple of friends called and offered to look after things, but they are both so nosy and gossipy that I didn't want them poking around in here. Of course, Dad's golf friends called when he first went to the hospital and they asked what they could do. I asked one of them if they had a cleaning lady they could recommend, and, guess what? They never got back to me."

"We're here now, and I'll help you. I put my arm around Mother's shoulder and felt her relax."

I followed a sickening odor into the kitchen coming straight from the refrigerator. "Wow, I guess you forgot about cleaning out some food when you and Jonathan came up here. Give me some garbage bags."

Two hours later the kitchen was passable. Mother had packed her favorite cookware and recipes, some of her clothes and Dad's clothes and golf clubs, their toiletries, and a stack of books and magazines.

We began loading Dad's Cadillac SUV. Mother started her prized Mustang convertible that would remain behind.

We collapsed in the family room. I felt grimy, sweaty and exhausted.

"You can't drive back to Miami tonight, Mary. You're way too tired and I know you're coming down with some bug. Stay here tonight and go back in the morning. Let me fix you something to eat."

For once, I didn't argue a bit. I put my feet up on the sofa and closed my eyes. Sometime later, Mother tapped me on the shoulder. She was carrying a cup of tea, and a plate of stew.

"Here, dear, I had this in the freezer, and please take these." She handed me four tablets.

"These are guaranteed to knock out what's ailing you."

"What are these?" I looked at them with some suspicion and then I recognized them as one of Mother's cure-all homeopathic remedies that she had fed us since Jonathan, William and I were teenagers.

We settled down with our plates and gobbled in silence like two starving refugees.

I began to perk up once the food and pills were downed.

"Mary, dear, I don't mean to pry, but—"

"Yes, you do. Just admit it," I said.

"Okay, I'm prying, but only because I love you. What's happening with you and Carlos? Are you going to get married? You seem so happy now that you're back together."

"I don't know. I can't see why things can't stay just as they are. I'm happy with our, what would you call it, arrangement."

"Isn't this the same arrangement you had with Frank?"

"No. I never felt relaxed with Frank and his Harvard crowd and his socialite parents up in Palm Beach. It's different with Carlos. And I like Angie and J.C. and all the cousins. They know how to have fun."

"Then what's stopping you from making it permanent?"

"Do we have to have this conversation tonight when we're both tired?"

"Yes, we do. I never see you to talk, just the two of us. I just want to understand why you can't commit to someone who loves you and makes you so happy."

"Okay. I'm scared. I'm afraid that if we were married, everything would change. We'd be pushed to have kids and I'm not sure I want any. Kids would be pushed to choose some religion and have loyalty to one ethnicity or another. I'm scared that I might end up resenting Carlos instead of loving him. Maybe he'd expect me to stop practicing law and that would kill me or kill the marriage."

"Wow, that's a lot of fear. I think most of these fears are just out of the realm of reality. Your dad and I have made it all these years with different religions and backgrounds and you three kids turned out great."

"I don't think we all turned out so great. We got pushed from one set of grandparents to the other. Summers were taken up with pleasing everybody but myself. Three weeks in North Carolina with the Magruders and their constant dragging me to church. Then three weeks at that Jewish camp in Georgia. By the time I got home the whole summer was over and I felt like I was the middle in a tug-of-war. I've watched you give in to Dad about everything, including moving to this retirement place that you don't like at all. I don't want to get caught in that same trap."

"Oh, Mary, I feel heartsick that I'm the one who is stopping you from a happy marriage. I never knew that your summers were unhappy. You're wrong about Dad and me. We've loved each other since we met as teenagers. My nature is so different from yours. Maybe it looked like I was always letting Dad have his way, but in return he never stopped me from going to church, or celebrating my holidays and his. I never wanted for any material thing, and I always knew that I had your father's complete love. We have so many friends that got divorced over infidelity. I never worried about that."

"What about this move to Boynton Beach? You didn't want to come up here. I see that now."

"I felt Dad deserved that reward for all the days and years he worked so hard. I was at home enjoying you children, playing tennis, doing volunteer work. How could I refuse to let Dad enjoy some leisure? And now I think Abe is going to see that he can enjoy himself even more back in Miami."

I was suddenly jarred by my cell phone buzzing in my pocket. I saw from the caller ID that it was Carlos, and I realized I had never called him to say that I was staying overnight here.

I touched the answer button. "Where are you? It's eleven o'clock. Are you on the road? I just got in, and where's Sam?"

"I am so sorry. I meant to call but we got so busy getting things done up here. Sam is with me and I'm going to stay overnight with Mother and come back in the morning. How did it go with the Chinese guys?"

"Thank God you're not driving at this hour. It didn't go so well with the investors. I probably just wasted a day and an expensive dinner, but I'll talk to you tomorrow about it. You get some sleep. I was just worried. Call me in the morning."

"Carlos was worried. I forgot to call him," I told Mother who had politely stepped out of the room. "We better get some sleep."

"Of course, but one other thing. You are a different person than I. You are strong and smart. You'll never have to worry about Carlos making your decisions for you. Please, promise me that you won't let anything about me or my life stand in the way of a marriage and family."

I didn't answer. Instead I went into the guest bathroom and turned on the hot water. Nothing like a good soak in a bubble bath to mull over a mother-daughter talk that we'd never undertaken before tonight.

Chapter Thirty-Two

I woke early, feeling less like a flu victim and more like myself; exhausted but able to get out of bed. After a quick cup of coffee with Mother who bestowed a bottle of her magic capsules, I hit the road.

The lights were on in the office as I drove into the parking lot. Sam hopped out of the passenger seat and bounded into the office. Patty was seated at Catherine's desk playing with the computer. The smell of freshly brewed coffee filled the room.

"Okay, I think I've got the hang of this computer. Marco called. He was released last night and he wants you to call him ASAP to get started investigating for the real killer. Here are a few other phone messages. Oh, and Carlos called to see if you were back. Better call him. Now put me to work. What's on the agenda?"

I felt exuberant. Patty was almost as perfect as having Catherine back. I gave Patty a list of witnesses to subpoena for depositions in Jay Washington's case, along with forms for her to follow.

"I need these set quickly, so get them to our server right away. The trial date is so near. And call the Assistant State Attorney and let him or her know the dates. See if they'll agree to having the depositions in my office instead of in the courthouse or their office."

"You're a smart cookie, Mary. Home turf is always best, just like in football. One of those phone messages is from Franklin Fieldstone. He wants to know if you're going to let him second chair Jay's trial."

I had to talk to Carlos about Frank's offer, and the sooner the better. Just as I dialed one of Carlos's three cell phones, I heard Carlos announcing himself to Patty in the waiting room. In a second he entered my office. He was dressed in his work boots and jeans, giving him a macho, sexy look that clouded my brain momentarily.

I got up and threw my body against him, but before things got out of hand, Sam shoved himself between us and encircled Carlos. Sam is a herding dog. It's hard to resist going where he wants his people to go.

"Okay, boy." Carlos pulled Sam away and sat down on the edge of my desk. I plopped down next to him.

"Marco is so relieved to be out of jail. He's got his top investigators at Pit Bull ready to get to work on his case. You better call him."

"I plan to go to see Marco later. What happened with your Chinese guests?"

"They aren't willing to pay any amount close to the going rates. Seems they feel entitled to get all their investments at a discount because in their words 'they're keeping our country afloat with loans from their country.' Don't worry about this. You have enough of your own worries now."

"Yes, and I need to talk to you about one of them. It's my football player case."

"Did you get the file from that Fieldstone asshole?" Carlos's face began to redden.

"I got the file, but there's more and I don't want you to start freaking out. Frank wants to stay on the case as second chair. I wouldn't even consider it except for the fact that the judge is James Luongo who just moved over to criminal from the civil court, and Frank has won at least one big case in front of him."

"So what! You're the great lawyer who can win big criminal cases."

"Judges who have been on the civil bench think only big pricey law firms are believable. That's why I think it will get the judge to at least listen to my case. You know I have nothing to go with in this case. I explained to you that the law says underage victims can't give consent even when they rip their clothes off and demand sex." I realized I was trying to raise my voice but my sore throat made me sound like Sam barking.

Carlos started to answer but a coughing jag drowned him out. I couldn't stop coughing.

"Hey, have you picked up the flu bug?" Carlos took my arm and led me to the sofa. He grabbed a glass of water poured from the carafe on the table.

"I guess I have something. I'll take some more of Mother's magic pills," I said as I tried to regain my composure. "I'm being upfront with you so we don't get into a mess like we did over Margarita. Don't you understand? You have nothing to be jealous about. What can I do to stop you from going into these rages?"

"There is one thing you can do. Marry me. If there isn't anyone else you want to be with, why can't we get married?"

"I just can't get into a discussion about something so serious right now. Please, be patient with me a little longer."

"I've worn out my patience quota. I want to hear reasons from you. If you don't love me, say so, for God's sake. If it's something in your past, tell me that. If there's something about me that I can change, tell me that, but I have no more patience." Carlos raised his voice to a reverberating pitch.

"I have some real reservations. I want to talk about them, but now's not the time; not with Marco in such trouble and Jay's case looming and your dad facing a possible indictment and my dad just coming out of the hospital and this damn sore throat." I felt tears welling up and that started the cough again.

Carlos felt my forehead. "Mary, you have a temperature. You need to see the doctor. Okay, all talk is off the table for now, but once all this mash-mash clears up, I want a total talk about this."

"I think you mean mish-mash," I said trying not to laugh and cough simultaneously.

Chapter Thirty-Three

The rest of the day was filled with aggravating telephone calls. Patty reported that the state refused to have the depositions in Jay's case in my office.

"What's the name of the prosecutor?" I asked.

Patty thumbed through a pile of papers on her desk. "Oh, here it is. It's Fred Mercer."

"Oh, not him again. Get him on the phone for me, Patty."

Mercer was the head of the public corruption unit. I had tangled with him in June when he tried to indict Judge Liz Maxwell. That turned out to be a big win for me and a loss for Fred that he couldn't forget. Then he surfaced once more when I beat him again in Franco's case. He charged Franco with bribing a cop, but he never even produced a witness. Now here he was again in a sexual battery case. Maybe he was determined to prosecute every case I defended.

Patty buzzed me to say that Fred was on line one and he sounded angry.

"Hi there Fred. What are you doing in sex bat? That doesn't sound like public corruption." I tried to sound friendly but my hoarse voice sounded gruff.

"I have been transferred to help out an overwhelmed division. If you're calling about the depositions again, may I remind you that depositions in criminal cases must be held in the office of the state or in the courthouse. I'm not going to waive criminal procedure rules just to accommodate you. And let me also tell you that I intend to prosecute this case to its just conclusion."

"Listen, Fred just because you and I have appeared as opposing counsel in previous cases, please don't take out your past anger on my client. I'll take the depositions in the courthouse. That probably makes it easier to be near a judge to settle any questions regarding your victim's failure to answer."

I settled for the courthouse, hoping that the austere venue would scare the alleged victim and her family into telling the truth. Even if this young hot-to-trot girl gave a total confession, I knew Fred would never drop this case on his own.

My next call was to Frank to tell him he could stay on the case in name only.

"That's great, Mary. Just tell me anything I can do, besides smile at the judge," he said.

"There is something you can do," I said, recalling Mrs. Washington's fear that there would be trouble at the university football game. "I want you to contact the powers that be at the university to provide as much security as possible at the homecoming game. Some groups are going to demonstrate against Jay being allowed to play while his case is pending."

"I can't do that. I advised the university to suspend him after he was charged. They refused to listen to me. The coach convinced the university board that it would look racist because a white baseball player was allowed to play after being arrested in a D.U.I. I think the real reason is that they didn't want to lose a big game."

"Listen, Frank, if you want to help me in this case, you'll have to act like a defense attorney and remember the client comes first, not your prejudices. If you don't warn the university of the trouble that may boil over at the game, you aren't doing your job for them or for Jay. If you want your name on this case, do what I instruct you to do, or stay the hell out of my business and my law practice."

"Okay, okay, Mary. I'll do what I can."

"Fine. Let me know who you talk to and what security they will provide." I slammed down the phone.

Next I called Marco. His mother answered the phone and spent minutes thanking me for bringing her "baby boy" home. When she let Marco have the phone, he sounded annoyed.

"I thought you were coming over here. Where are you?"

"I'm sorry, Marco. I had planned to come there but I have a flu bug or something and I thought it best to call. Which one of your Pit Bulls do you want to work with me on your case?"

"I want to investigate my case myself. No one's as good at this as I am."

"You can't work your own case. First of all, you're on complete house arrest. How can you do the work when you can't be out of your house? Are you wearing your ankle bracelet?"

"Yeah, I'm wearing it, but you can go back to court and tell the judge that I have to do my investigation myself."

"Listen to me, Marco. You are so lucky to have gotten out. The state intends to charge you with first degree murder. One complaint from you and you'll spend the next six months or even a year sitting in the Dade County Jail. You can be in constant contact with whoever you want to cover this case. You can be the director from home. Now who do want me to work with? Or maybe you want a different lawyer."

"Oh, no, Mary, don't desert me. I'll do what you say. Talk to Reuben Porter. He's great at undercover work. You'll just need to keep an eye on him. He's a cowboy."

"Meaning?"

"Meaning he goes a little beyond what's legal."

I hung up and decided not to make or receive any more calls for the day. The phone gods were not in my corner.

Chapter Thirty-Four

I took two more of mother's magic pills and threw some sticky cough drops from the back of my file cabinet into my briefcase. I told Patty I would be at Pit Bull Investigations for the rest of the day.

I wasn't sure what was in those pills but I felt slightly dizzy as I pulled the Explorer out into Dixie Highway traffic.

Marco's office was only a few blocks from my office, but traffic was slowing to a crawl. I took a side street, circled through the Grove and over to Grand Avenue. Traffic was at a stop here too. Out of the corner of my eye, I spotted Uncle Sly's Barbecue Restaurant. I realized I hadn't eaten much. Maybe that's why I was dizzy. I pulled into the parking lot.

The usual assortment of men was congregated outside the restaurant. This corner is one of the places where out-of-work day workers wait for trucks that need extra hands on a job. Mostly they are roofing companies or lawn mowers, euphemistically called landscaping companies. I was surprised to see so many men still waiting around so late in the day.

The restaurant was pretty full even though it was past the lunch hour. I grabbed a stool at the counter.

"What'll you have, lady?" A burly Black man with a white apron smeared in barbecue sauce asked.

"Are you Uncle Sly?" I asked.

"Nah, Uncle Sly passed ten years ago. I'm his great nephew, Jackson."

"I'll have a barbecue sandwich. Do you have any soup?"

"We sure do. We got Aunt Fanny's chicken soup and you sound like you really need it."

"I'll take that too. I thought only Jewish aunts made chicken soup for a cold."

"Now see there, honey, the Jewish aunties are taking the credit. Who do you think gave them the recipe?" Jackson belted out a peal of laughter.

"Jackson, why are there so many people outside and what's got the traffic tied up?"

"Where you been, honey? Don't you know the President is in town campaigning with Senator Gorham. They're coming right by here. Maybe they'll even stop in for some barbecue. There's an election in a few days."

"I can't believe I forgot. I've been super busy. I'm a lawyer and I've got some tough cases.

"You represent anyone from around here?"

"I'm Jay Washington's lawyer and Marco"--

Before I could finish my sentence Jackson reached across the counter and grabbed my hand which he pumped up and down furiously.

"You must be Mary Katz. I'll be damned. Doreen get out here," he hollered.

A young woman came out of the door behind the counter wiping her hands on an apron.

Jackson pointed to me. "This is Jay Washington's lawyer."

Doreen smiled and shook my hand too. "So pleased to meet you. We all love Jay around here. I'm so glad you're helping him. He has such a great future and he's a good young man, never in trouble. Where's your order? This lunch is on us. What's your name?"

"I'm Mary Magruder Katz."

"Mary Katz?" a deep male voice said behind me.

I turned to see a tall Black man. Muscles bulged below his short sleeved polo shirt. He was as handsome as a model or a movie star.

"Yes, that's me, and you are?"

"Reuben Porter. Marco told me to get over to see you but I couldn't get through the traffic."

"I was on my way to your office and got stopped by the traffic too. Pull up a stool and let's have lunch and a meeting right here at Uncle Sly's."

Chapter Thirty-Five

As soon as the President's limo paraded down the avenue followed by many dark SUV's, the crowd began to thin. Multiple Secret Service agents stood around on the sidewalk talking into the lapels of their navy suit jackets.

"I don't know who they're jiving in those uniforms. You can spot them a mile away, the not so secret agents," Jackson said.

"How come you didn't go outside to wave to the big guy?" Jackson asked Reuben.

"Been there, done that," Reuben said. "It seems like every couple of weeks either the President or some cabinet member disrupts our lives by tying up traffic or closing down the airport. If they want my vote, they should stay the hell out of Miami."

"I hear ya'," other diners answered or nodded their heads.

I was busy devouring my soup and barbecue. The food burned my nagging sore throat but was so delicious I forgot about everything else for a few minutes. Reuben had piled into a rack of steaming ribs. We ate in silence. Finally I suggested that we move to a table in the corner and start planning how to help Marco.

"What do we know about Brady Aynsworth, other than the fact that he was the deadbeat who ran out on Catherine?" Reuben asked as he pulled a pen and pad out of his pocket.

I was having a hard time trying not to stare admiringly at Reuben's hard body and handsome face.

"So you know about Brady and Catherine. Well, I have the name of the woman he was living with recently. She lives somewhere in Ft. Lauderdale. Her name is Renee Francis and Marco learned that she had a drug arrest for a small amount of something. Brady had some arrests for drugs too, but I don't think either Renee or Brady was convicted. That's a starting point."

"I'll put on my drug dealer outfit and nose around the suspect neighborhoods up in Broward. I'll start digging, starting with this Renee chick," Reuben said.

"I have to ask, did you ever play football?" I was still staring at his muscles.

"Sure did, at Alabama in 2002."

"Why not Miami?" Now I was as nosy as my mother.

"They didn't offer me a scholarship. My mom was kind of mad at them because she wanted me to play close to home so she could go to the games, but she made it up to Tuscaloosa a few times. She wanted me to be a pro and play for the Dolphins. That dream ended when I tore my ACL and the next year I came back to play and had a concussion, so here I am working for Marco and digging up dirt on people instead."

"I'm sorry I asked. I didn't mean to bring up something unpleasant. I paused for a minute and saw that Reuben's expression was unchanged. Then a thought hit me.

By the time we left Uncle Sly's I had hired Reuben to help me with Jay's case. An ex-football player had complete sympathy with the plight of a younger football hot guy.

Chapter Thirty-Six

The office was quiet on my return. Patty was watering the plants again. They were probably going to drown before Catherine returned.

"Your mother called and left her new number at the condo. She's very worried about you. You better call her. She's got her hands full getting ready to get your dad from the hospital. She shouldn't have to worry about you too." Patty stood in the doorway to my office, her hands on her ample hips looking accusingly at me.

I felt immediate anger rising in my head and flooding my already hot cheeks. "Patty, the last thing I need right now is another mother. I know you mean well, but please don't give me orders. I'm not your child. Just give me my messages and I'll decide how to dispose of them."

"Of course, here are all your messages," Patty said as she slapped a group of messages on my desk and flounced out of my sight.

The first message was from Carlos announcing that he had made an appointment with Dr. Andreas for five o'clock today. "Do not cancel this. The doctor is staying late to see you," the message read in capital letters.

There was the message from Mother that also said Carlos was setting a doctor's appointment for me. The third message was from Frank who stated that he had already filed his notice of appearance as "your humble helper." I hoped he hadn't used that language on his notice.

The next message referred me to my e-mails. Patty had written that there was an e-mail from Dash Mellman who was waiting for an answer. Dash was the attorney in High Pines, Vermont where I had spent the month of October. I remembered that he had also sent me a letter that I never did open. I guess I put it aside on purpose, not wanting to remember that I had led him on, even had a brief one- nighter with him. I didn't need any extra guilt this week.

I found the letter and opened it.

"Dear Mary,

I hope you are well and happy back in Miami. Everyone here misses you, and that includes me.

I have a client who is trying to settle the estate of his uncle in Miami. He is the sole relative, and it should be an easy matter to resolve. He is in need of counsel and I suggested that he contact you. Hope you can help him. His name is Matt Bernard. Let me know if you can make time for him.

Fondly, Dash."

The e-mail repeated the letter and asked for me to acknowledge that I would provide help for his client. I quickly hit reply. "Glad to help. My brother, Jonathan Katz, specializes in trusts and estates. Attached is his contact information. Best regards to you, Daisy, and everyone there. Unless your client or his uncle is accused of a crime, Jonathan is better able to help than I."

My mind wandered back to High Pines, the lack of traffic, and the rural landscape. I guess I would always wonder what life would be like if I hadn't returned to Miami.

"Mary, it's 4:30 and Carlos just drove into the parking lot to pick you up for the doctor appointment. I'm trying not to nag, but did you call your mother?"

Patty wasn't going to stop nagging. I had to get Marco out of this murder case and get Catherine back at her desk.

Chapter Thirty-Seven

"You didn't have to take me to this appointment, Carlos. I'm not disabled. I just have a bug or a virus or something."

We were seated in Dr. Andreas's waiting room. The receptionist was engrossed in a lengthy chat with an over perfumed, dripping with jewelry, woman who had two young girls by her side. The conversation was entirely in Spanish and moved so quickly that I could only make out a word or two. They interrupted each other frequently adding to the mix while the two girls rolled their eyes and tried to get out of the grasp of the excited woman.

"What are they arguing about?" I whispered.

"The girls are supposed to get shots against cervical cancer, some new innoculation. Apparently, one of the girls made the appointment herself and the mother is outraged. She is screaming that the shot is only for sexually active females. She just said her daughters aren't whores."

"I caught that word."

"The doctor's receptionist is trying to explain why the inoculations are a protection in later life, but the mother isn't buying it. She thinks it's like being on the pill. Mary, where are you going?"

I moved over to the reception desk. The nameplate said Sadie Lorenzo.

"Sadie, please tell this lady that I am a lawyer and I know these girls need this protection. Tell her it's like an insurance policy and then buzz the doctor and tell him Mary Katz is waiting for her appointment," I said.

Sadie relayed the message. The mother and daughters moved to the side and continued arguing with each other. In a minute we were ushered into the doctor's office. After a round of pleasantries and inquiries about how my dad was doing, the doctor motioned me to his examining room and told Carlos he should have a seat. Carlos tried to follow us into the exam room, but Dr. Andreas closed the door firmly.

After listening to my chest, observing another coughing fit, looking into my ears, eyes, throat and taking several swabs and a blood sample, he told me to get dressed and return to his office.

I felt a little dizzy as I jumped down from the examining table. The next thing I knew I was laying on the floor with the doctor, Carlos, and a nurse standing over me.

"What am I doing here?" I mumbled.

"What indeed?" the doctor said as he felt for my pulse. "You are a sick little bird. You have a strep throat and I think you have an infection in your larynx. You need complete bed rest for a few days and I want you to fill the prescriptions that I gave to Carlos. Lots of fluids and no talking on the phone or rushing off to court."

"You've got to be kidding. I'm in the middle of at least two important cases. I can't just go to bed. I missed work almost all last month." I was scrambling to get up but realized I was very dizzy.

"If you don't stay in bed for at least a couple of days, your next trip will be to the hospital. Your clients can wait two days or even three," the doctor said. "And don't visit your dad until you get rid of this infection."

Chapter Thirty-Eight

The next morning I awoke from a restless sleep filled with nightmares about being late to court and arriving in court without any files. I lay in bed looking out the window at a gaggle of Ibises pecking out seeds or grubs or whatever it is they munch. Sam jumped up, front paws anchored on the window sill and barked his "get out of here" bark. The birds took off, their giant white wings swooshing through the cloudless still air. I couldn't believe that at ten o'clock on a work day, I was engaged in bird watching. My unread Florida Law Weeklies were spread across the quilt unopened, unread, and unappreciated. My head and throat still had a dull ache.

My office was being manned, or womaned by a substitute assistant; Marco's murder case and Jay's sex battery case were languishing. I couldn't keep lying around like this, but I felt like I had been beaten into submission by a germ. My pity party was interrupted by the buzz of my cell phone on the nightstand. Reluctantly I pressed the answer button and heard a male voice I didn't recognize.

"Mary, I called your office and your secretary told me I could call you at home. Sorry to hear you're under the weather. It's Reuben Porter. I had a little news on Marco's case."

"Oh, Reuben, sorry I didn't recognize your voice and I didn't look at the caller ID." I snapped back into attorney mode, sat up and reached for my note pad.

"Well, last night I went up to Broward County and started nosing around. The name of that girl, Renee Francis, in Ft. Lauderdale and that address, you know, that you gave me."

"Yes, the woman that Brady was supposed to have been living with."

"That building was abandoned. It was condemned by the city. I asked some of the street people if they knew Renee and one of them gave me an address in Hollywood on Taft Street. I followed up on that. It's a heavy drug area, by the way. I found the apartment and Renee Francis answered the door herself. I think she thought I was a buyer, so she let me in."

"That's great, Reuben. What did you find out?"

"After she realized I wasn't a customer, she got a little crazy. Thought I was an undercover cop and went for her gun. I think she was a little out of it, coked out."

"My God, Reuben, I didn't mean to send you into a shoot-out." For the moment I forgot about my aching throat trauma. I was sitting up in bed, my feet dangling over the side ready to jump up as if I were facing Renee and a gun.

"Not to worry. I'm used to it. You should see how violent a straying spouse gets when he gets caught with his girlfriend during my surveillance. Anyway, back to Renee. I pulled my gun out of my waistband and told her to chill, that I was only there about Brady Aynsworth. She said 'that piece of shit, I never want to see that fucker again.'

"I assured her that she wouldn't have to, he was dead. Someone offed him and I was representing a guy who had been accused of doing the job."

"Do you think Renee was the one that shot Brady? Now we know she wasn't afraid to use a gun."

"I don't think so. Once she heard why I was there and that Brady wasn't gonna bother her, she got all friendly. She invited me to sit down and offered me a shot of vodka or a line of cocaine. I started talking about Brady and she opened up. Told me she threw him out a few months ago. Seems he was cutting into her profits snorting up her inventory. She said he was going downhill fast. She got him a job in the service department at the auto mall where one of her regular customers worked. Brady knew a lot about cars after his work at the race track in Homestead. That's where he walked away from his wife and kids."

"Yes, I know all about that part of his life. Catherine, his ex-wife, is my paralegal."

"He only kept the job a few weeks. He used his first paycheck to purchase some product from one of the pill mills in Ft. Lauderdale. Renee finally kicked him out and moved her operation to Hollywood. The last she heard he had moved in with a prostitute who worked out of the Seminole Reservation off of 441 and Sterling Road."

"Did you get her name?"

"Renee thought she was called Sheila Bird, but she also thought that might be her street name. I'm planning to go back up there tonight and nose around where some of the pro's hang out. I'll call you tomorrow and let you know what I can find."

"Does Marco know about all this?"

"Yeah, he calls me every thirty minutes. He's a wreck."

"I'll talk to him. Gotta go. My call waiting is clicking."

I clicked onto the new call and heard Carlos's excited voice.

"Mary, who are you talking to? You're supposed to be resting your voice. I'm going to come right over and remove your phone."

"If I'm not allowed to talk why are you calling me?"

"Because you're not to be trusted to follow orders. Don't you want to get well?"

"I feel much worse when I'm not involved in work. Anyway, I didn't call anyone. My investigator called me to report on some stuff in Marco's case. Don't you want me to get him out of this homicide charge?"

"*Mi amore*, I only want you to be one hundred percent well again, so we can discuss, well everything." I clicked the 'end call' button. The pressure from Carlos and even my own family made red hot anger begin to take over. Why can't things stay the way they are? Carlos and I just got back together. What was wrong with just being lovers?

I got out of bed and whistled for Sam. He was standing patiently by the backdoor. I had forgotten to take him out. As I opened the door, a flash of fresh air hit me. Sam began a run around the fence circling faster on each round. I breathed in air that wasn't humid. It was November in

Miami. Summer was over and winter had begun. Who says South Florida doesn't have a change of seasons?

I pulled a folding chair out of the garage and plopped down in the dappled sunlight near the Norfolk Island Pine tree. Sam flopped down next to me, panting from his run. We both nodded off for a few minutes of peaceful appreciation of the weather, the only thing that changes when it wants to.

Chapter Thirty-Nine

By noontime, I felt the beginning of being semi-healthy. I showered and dressed in jeans and a tee shirt, and was about to go out for some lunch, when Sam barked excitedly, drowning out the sound of the doorbell.

I opened the door and found Chicky standing on my front step, holding a bag with the logo of Havana Harry's Restaurant. Sam sniffed the bag and wagged his tail. He was no restaurant connoisseur. He loved them all. Chicky, Carlos's sister who runs the Corona Boutique, looked gorgeous and fashionable as usual.

"Chicky, what are you doing here? Aren't you working today?"

"I'm entitled to a lunch hour and Carlos is worried about you. Mama was going to come over but I thought you might enjoy my company a bit more. I picked up lunch. There's nothing like Harry's chicken soup." Chicky moved past me and set the food bag on my dining room table. She began unloading cartons and bags. "Where are your spoons and forks?"

"This is great of you. I was just going to go out and get some soup," I said as I helped set the table and took in the aroma of authentic Cuban soup and rice and black beans, a Cuban staple. Growing up in Miami means appreciating a variety of ethnic cuisine.

We settled down at the table and I realized I was actually hungry.

Chicky, whose real name is Celia, was living in Buenos Aires until last June when she returned from hanging out in smoky tango bars to run the boutique of my former client, Luis Corona. Carlos's mother credited me with getting her daughter back to Miami, so I scored one point in spite of the fact that I am and will always be the *gringa*.

"I haven't had a chance to see you since you got back from your hideout in Vermont," Chicky said as she started to clear the table.

"I know and I'm sorry. With Dad in the hospital and Mother moving back here and trying to get my office up and running, it's been a bit hairy."

"Don't apologize. I just wanted to be sure you're okay, not just from the flu or whatever but I mean okay about Carlos. The two of you belong together. Listen, Mary, I don't want to be butting into your life. I just want to see Carlos happy. Margarita put him through hell. When you left town, he went back into depression."

"I understand you care about your brother. I just don't want to lose my independence. It scares me when you tell me that his feelings are tied to my being here. Can you understand that I've been on my own for a long time? I don't want that to change, even though I love Carlos."

"You need to think about what you just said, Mary. If you aren't willing to share your life than you shouldn't get married. I'm no authority because I haven't met someone wonderful but I keep hoping. But I can see from my own parents and my brother in Argentina that being married is sharing and giving to someone if you love them. Anyway, I'm glad we're friends, no matter what happens."

"I'm glad too. I value your friendship," I said.

I really meant this. When I first met Chicky I thought she would be like her mother, a tiny woman who exuded nervous excitement. Chicky was tall and dark like Carlos and his dad. Her exotic looks belied her common sense approach to life. Like all of the Martins, family was important to her, so I understood that she wanted to protect Carlos.

"Mary, I wanted to ask you about something else. I don't know if you can answer without divulging a lawyer confidence or whatever you call it. Is my father in a lot of trouble? I can see that he's very worried and I know he has to go before some kind of jury."

"It's the grand jury. I can't really discuss his role in the bank investigation. I don't know where the federal investigation is going. I can only tell you that I will do everything in my power to make sure that he's not in trouble. There are no guarantees, but remember J.C. is a very smart man."

"Federal investigation! That sounds scary, but I trust you. You are a very smart lawyer. I remember how you found Luis when we had all given up last June. Carlos admires your legal skills. That's why I know your fear of Carlos interfering with your career is only in your imagination."

As I watched Chicky drive away, I decided she had delivered more than my lunch. She brought me added pressure to make a decision that continued to elude me.

Chapter Forty

I must have nodded off for a while. The cell's alarming jangle woke me. I've got to change that sound, I thought.

Patty's chirpy voice cleared the sleep out of my brain. "Mary, you sound better. I thought I'd better remind you that the depositions in Jay's case are set for next week. The first one is on Tuesday. Do you want me to change them?

"What day is this? I've completely lost track."

"It's Friday."

"Where did this week go?" I mumbled.

"It's been a week all right. Brady's death, Marco's arrest, and your germ. It's no wonder you don't know what day it is."

"Who is set on Tuesday?"

"The arresting officer and Jay's coach. The so-called victim and her father are set for the week after that. They called and couldn't make it this coming week; something about the Veteran's Day holiday weekend. They were going out of town, so I changed them. Is that okay?"

"Yes, that's great. It'll give my investigator time to do some leg work on the case. How is Marco and how is Catherine holding up?"

"Marco is a wreck. Catherine has pulled herself together. She and the boys go to see Marco every evening, and Catherine insists she's coming back to work on Monday. She wants to keep busy. We'll probably stay a few more days and then go home for a while. I'm thinking that we'll want to be back here for the trial."

I thanked Patty over and over for stepping in and running the office, but I couldn't wait to get Catherine back. We had become a team, and it's hard to play when your defense is missing, and that reminded me. I still hadn't gotten to use my Florida Panther hockey tickets that Carlos gave me for my birthday. I didn't even know how many games they had already lost.

I had been so out of it that I didn't even know how Mother and Dad were or if they were settled in the condo. My cell phone was still in my hand. I punched Mother's cell number in my contacts. She answered on the first ring.

"Mary, sweetheart, how are you? You'll never guess where we are. Walking on the beach. It's a gorgeous day. Are you still contagious? When can you come over?"

This was typical of mother; a dozen questions without a pause.

"I am feeling better, but more important, how is Dad? And the condo, is it what you wanted?

"Dad is doing great. The doctor wants him to get some exercise, so the beach walk is just the ticket now that the weather has changed. The condo is fun but a little cramped, but Abe loves being here seeing old friends who keep dropping by. Now here's the real news. Uncle Max and Aunt Myrna are going to come back from New York and rent a condo for the winter, and Grandma Katz is coming for a quick visit to see for herself how her baby boy is doing."

"When is she coming?"

"For Thanksgiving."

"Well, that's all great news. As soon as I'm one hundred percent over this infection, I'll be over there."

I put the phone down and pictured the whole Katz family together again on the beach. After Grandpa Katz died suddenly of a heart attack, my grandmother was totally lost. She had worked at the market for a good deal of her life. Now her sons, my dad and uncle, took over and began expanding. She felt left out and stayed home most of the time. That is, until one of her friends persuaded her to go on a cruise.

She had never had such a posh vacation. The cruise went from Miami through the Panama Canal and up the Pacific coast of Mexico ending in Los Angeles. Seated at her dinner table was a widower named Ronald Morgan from San Diego. By the time the ship docked in Los Angeles, they were inseparable. Two months later, after visits to meet each other's families, they "eloped". Now Bertha Katz is Bertha Morgan living in a house overlooking the sea in La Jolla, California, with a closet full of designer clothes and an engagement book filled with parties, movie premiers, and travel plans. My brothers and I call her Grandma Rich Bitch, behind her back, of course.

I was still remembering the metamorphosis of my grandmother when the phone rang again, and Patricia said Jay Lincoln was on the line, and she was putting his call through to me.

"Hey, Mary, it's Jay. I just wanted to remind you that the homecoming game is this Saturday at noon. I have a few tickets and I'm going to leave two for you at the Will Call window at the stadium. Can you come?"

"Sure I will, Jay. Have you heard anything about a demonstration at the game?"

"Oh, yeah, everybody knows about it."

"Are you worried?" How about your mom and dad? Are they upset?

"I'm not worried. Just some crackers jiving. There's gonna be some of the brothers making some noise too."

"You mean rival crowds demonstrating?"

"I guess you could call it that. My head's only concentrating on the game. A lot of scouts are coming from the NFL."

University of Miami Homecoming, Veterans Day weekend, and two rival groups demonstrating at a University of Miami vs. Florida State football game; couldn't happen anywhere but Miami.

Chapter Forty-One

I knew I should be resting my voice, but Jay's call filled me with anxiety. Florida State and Miami are serious rivals. A win by Miami or a loss by Miami could mean ugly crowds of beer swilling, fist throwing fans. Adding to the mix are the demonstrators for and against Jay Lincoln. All of it spelled Trouble with a capital 'T'. I called Frank's office and got a voicemail stating that the Fieldstone firm was now closed for the weekend. It was after five and it was homecoming weekend so no one was sticking around to accommodate any late-calling clients. I had forgotten that big corporate clients didn't work after five on Fridays.

Frank had promised to talk to the university about beefing up security at the game. That was really the only job I had assigned him. I needed to know whether he followed through or ignored me as he usually did when I worked for him and was his girlfriend. I still remembered his cell phone number.

"Mary, it's good to hear from you. I was just on my way to have a drink with Buddy Lipscomb. You remember him, the CEO of Lipscomb Industries. Why don't you join us over at the Ritz?"

"This isn't a social call, Frank. I just learned that there are going to be rival demonstrators at the football game tomorrow. Did you instruct the university about additional police?"

"What do you mean rival demonstrators? Miami and FSU always have that kind of thing."

"No, I mean crazy, foaming at the mouth crowds for and against Jay Lincoln. I told you to alert the administration. Have you done anything?"

"I talked to the head of campus police. He said he's aware that feelings could be running a little high. They'll keep an eye on things. I wouldn't worry too much. Now that the games are played in Dolphin Stadium, there are officers from Miami Dade and the city that are always out there."

"Frank, do you live in Miami or under a rock? Don't you understand that this could turn into a race riot? Jay said a group of African-Americans will be out there, and the man who is head of CRUMS, Luis Marina, told the Herald that at least 500 people would be demonstrating."

"Yes, so?"

"So the so-called victim is Hispanic. Jay, the accused, is African-American. Don't you get it? This could blow up into a county-wide riot."

"Oh, yes, I see what you're saying. Well, I'll make some calls as soon as I get to the Ritz. Not to worry."

"Frank, you are an idiot!" I said as I clicked off. Thank God I broke up with Frank. Carlos would know what to do. He lived in the real world.

I was still holding the phone in my hand when it rang. The ringtone that sounded like a fire alarm knocked me back on the bed. The caller ID announced Lucy's name and number. Lucy is my oldest and best friend who made my runaway trip to Vermont possible by loaning me her summer house. We met in the fourth grade and lived around the corner from each other in Miami Beach. I realized I had neglected her since coming home.

"Lucy, I'm glad you called. I've been in bed with a strep throat or I would have called you this week."

"Not to worry. I knew you were sick when I called your mom to check on your dad. That's not why I'm calling, Did you see today's Herald? You're a busy girl."

"I haven't seen the paper. What's in it?'

"Just a picture of you on the front of the local section with a story about the Miami quarterback and his rape charge and that there may be the potential for a mess at the game tomorrow. By the way, the picture isn't all that great. It says you're Jay Lincoln's lawyer."

"Yes, I am, but why would they put my picture in the story?"

"They can't put the victim's face in there and I guess they thought you were better looking than Jay. And Jay's picture is in a big spread on the sports page, so they were left with you."

As I finished Lucy's call, Sam's bark reverberated through the house. It was his greeting bark and a minute later Carlos walked into the bedroom. He was carrying a copy of the Miami Herald under his arm.

"Your picture is in here," Carlos shook the paper at me. "It's the picture from Luis Corona's case. They shouldn't have exposed you like that with this talk of a riot."

"Yes, I know about the picture. Lucy just called. Carlos, Jay is leaving us tickets for the game at the stadium. I have to go. I've got to talk to someone about the police being prepared for this demonstration at the game."

"You shouldn't be going but I understand. I'll be there with you and I've already started making some calls. Marco is getting some of his guys to be out there too. We'll get through it."

I threw my arms around Carlos and held him so close that Sam couldn't get in between us. Having a boyfriend you can depend on makes life livable.

Chapter Forty-Two

Saturday morning sun flooded the house with enormous heat. For some unexplained weather phenomena, the humidity had returned. The thermometer outside the bedroom window shouted eighty-two degrees. The clock said nine a.m. By the start of the game, it was sure to be at least ninety. I remembered an article in my criminal justice magazine that stated people were more easily angered when the weather was very hot.

Carlos was still sleeping as I shut the bedroom door and went to the kitchen. Carlos deserved breakfast prepared for him after all his fussing over me while I was sick. I started a pot of coffee and pulled eggs, milk and bread from the fridge. I was in the process of cracking the eggs into a bowl, when I felt Carlos's arms encircle my waist.

I turned to him and felt his lips part mine. In a minute or an hour, time stopped as he took my arm and led me back to the bedroom.

"It seems like I've been missing you for such a long time. I thought I'd lost you when you left last month. Then your mom was here with you when you got back and then Marco was arrested and you got sick. Now it's our time together, *mi Amor,* come to me."

I felt his lips and hands on my breasts. Then we were touching each other and making love for an eternity. Or maybe it was just a few minutes, but time felt suspended. As we stayed in each other's arms, I thought I never wanted to leave this warm safe place. For the first time, I thought of the good things that would happen if I did marry Carlos.

Chapter Forty-Three

All good things must end. Reluctantly, we realized that the game was at noon, due to television's schedule, not the university's desire for an evening game with cooler air. The hint of fall had receded and the humid summer air wasn't what the sports announcers labeled football weather.

We showered and dressed in our Miami Hurricane shirts. I pulled my thoroughly frizzed hair into a ponytail and tied it with orange and green ribbons. We gulped down the coffee that had been standing for an hour and set off for an interminable ride through game day traffic. Both I-95 and the Palmetto Expressway were wall-to-wall cars creeping north to the stadium. Buses with the Miami logo filled with screaming students filled the slow lanes as we passed them. I almost felt like I was back in college again until I looked in the mirror and saw my pale skin lacking its usual suntan and the dark circles under my eyes.

"Where can we park?" I asked as we neared the stadium.

"Marco had some parking passes. His business provides security to some of the VIP's at games. Look for lot 'H'," Carlos said as he threaded the Escalade through a sea of people walking, drinking, and tail-gating.

We saw the stadium looming straight ahead, and then we saw the signs; signs being waved in the air by two distinct groups. Uniformed police and giant plain clothes guys were doing their best to keep the two groups apart. On one side was a sea of dark faces with a smattering of whites holding signs that read: "Not guilty 'til a jury says different," and "stand by the U, Jay is our quarterback," and "Miami's first black quarterback brings out the racists."

Meanwhile the other group held their signs aloft that said: "no cheers for a rapist," and "keep our Latinas safe, get rid of Jay Lincoln," and "Jail Jay Lincoln."

There were a few unprintable signs as well, but the police were confiscating those; that made the groups scream about their First Amendment Right to free speech.

Carlos pulled around the melee and eased the car into the parking lot. Police directed us to a place at the front of the lot. As soon as the air conditioned car stopped and we opened the doors, the humid air hit us like a steam bath. Standing in line at the Will Call window my clothes felt as if I had just removed them from the washing machine. The rattled clerk at the window had a hard time spelling Magruder Katz. It was clear he needed remedial reading help.

Finally, tickets in hand, we made our way to our seats. They were on the fifty yard line on the shady side of the field. I realized that my flu episode had left me weak and feeling shaky. I tucked my arm into Carlos's to steady myself. Carlos smiled at me and I felt even weaker. That smile always affects me especially as I thought about our romantic morning.

"Mary, you're here. Jay said you'd be sitting with us." As we found our seats, I saw Lorena Lincoln, Jay's mother seated next to us. Lorena introduced us to Horace, Jay's father, a handsome large framed man. I saw Jay's resemblance instantly. I introduced Carlos to them and then we all stood for the Star Spangled Banner sung by a glee club of students who perceived our national anthem as a blues song and seemed to have revised some of the lyrics.

Florida State fans across the field had begun what would be hours of their Indian chop hand sign. FSU's nickname is the Seminoles. They never changed their name or mascot, a native American dressed in war paint on a horse with a flaming arrow, even though most other schools were cajoled into ridding themselves of overt Indian stereotyping. The Seminole Tribe comprised the only real native Floridians. Their history of love of this tropical area includes stories of their preservation of the natural wonders of Florida. They also are the richest tribe having bought the Hard Rock hotels, casinos and restaurants, so I guess they didn't object to FSU trading on their name. It was good for business.

On our side of the field, flag bearers raced around the perimeter bearing hurricane warning flags, being that Miami's nickname is The Hurricanes. Our mascot is Sebastian the Ibis, a wading bird prevalent in South Florida. He wears a head with a massive beak and is dressed in Miami colors of orange and green and bears a giant "U" on his shirt which causes the fans to scream, "it's all about the U" while making the "U" sign with their hands. So much for higher education.

"The police must have kept the demonstrators from coming into the stadium," I said to Carlos.

Lorena leaned over apparently overhearing my remark. "Yes, thank you Jesus," she said. "I just hope Jay hasn't seen any of the signs outside."

A great roar went up as the teams came through the tunnel onto the field through a cloud of manmade smoke. Both bands struck up their fight songs, players got in place and the refs in their zebra shirts opened the game.

Miami won the toss and elected to receive. On the first play, Jay was totally bottled up by FSU's humongous defensemen. He elected to keep the ball, tried for a run and promptly lost three yards. A great cheer went up and I realized that some of it came from the Miami side of the stadium. It dawned on me that some of our own fans were against Jay. A sick feeling came over me. Lorena put her head on her hands covering her face. Horace put his arm around her.

Within a couple of minutes on the scoreboard clock, Miami had gone three and out and kicked the ball. On second down, the FSU quarterback threw a pass down field directly into the hands of a Miami defenseman who, in spite of his hefty body, ran the ball back for a Miami touchdown.

When the first quarter ended, the score was Miami-7, FSU-0. Carlos stood up and stretched and I heard him say something in Spanish under his breath.

"What's wrong?" I asked.

"Look in the upper deck," he said.

I stood and saw a canvas sign hanging from the railing. "Jay Lincoln, our rapist quarterback. Kick his butt." I knew the TV cameras would pick this up. I also knew there would be fistfights. I saw several uniformed cops coming down the aisle toward the sign bearer. I sat down feeling very sick.

At halftime the score was Miami-7, FSU-3. More signs were popping up and the police were now ringing the field. Carlos had gone out to the refreshment stand and returned with hotdogs, fries and cokes, for the Lincolns and us. I couldn't look at the food but gladly gulped down a coke. I couldn't wait for this game to be over. Our community couldn't escape the ugly blot that was being shown to a national TV audience along with the obligatory shots of South Beach and oceanfront hotels that are actually twenty miles from the stadium.

The second half began with Miami kicking off to FSU. A speedy special unit receiver grabbed the ball on the twenty yard line and was off to the races. Nobody laid a hand on him and he spiked the ball in the end zone and began a victory dance. The excessive celebration gave FSU a penalty setting them back five yards for the extra point kick. The crowd went wild as the kicker flicked the ball wide right. The score was now Miami-7, FSU-9.

For the next quarter and a half, the score remained the same until deep into the fourth quarter, Jay faded back to pass but instead began an end run around startled defensemen. Thirty yards later, Jay fell across the line with an FSU tackle hanging on his ankle as fans yelled 'touchdown Miami.' But the FSU coach was tearing down the sideline screaming that he was challenging the call. He claimed that Jay never crossed the goal line and had been stopped just short.

It seemed like hours as the officials gathered on the sidelines in heated discussion as the head ref stuck his head into a TV monitor. Florida State fans chopped their hands in their Indian war chant. Miami fans began a chant of their own, booing Jay Lincoln. Screams of 'the rapist stinks,' and 'get him off the field' filled the humid air. On the sidelines, Jay stood with his helmet in his hand and his head bowed. Miami-Dade police officers stood nearby.

Lorena had tears in her eyes, but she sat proudly erect. Horace was standing, his hands balled into fists. "They're going to take that touchdown away from my boy. They better not." Horace screamed at no one in particular. Carlos moved past me and stood next to Horace, talking quietly to him.

At long last, the referee stood at midfield. "The call on the field remains. Touchdown Miami."

The sound of boos reverberated from across the field, but there were also some boos from the Miami side mixed with the cheers of the hardcore Miami fans.

Miami made the extra point kick. The score read Miami-14, FSU-9, with two minutes remaining. The Miami defense held as the crowd counted down the seconds. As the final whistle blew, the team hugged each other, and we all stood for the Miami Alma Mater.

Chapter Forty-Four

The crowd surged toward the exits. We hugged Lorena and Horace. The heat was still oppressive as we were enveloped with the crush of people trying to get on the escalators and coming down the ramps moving toward the parking lots.

We finally shoved through the turnstiles only to be stopped again by a wall of people. Then we saw what had stopped them. The two groups of demonstrators had begun to advance toward each other. Signs were being grabbed and thrown to the ground and stomped on. Some signs were being used as weapons to hit opposition demonstrators. The police were unable to separate the groups and some officers were retreating from the melee realizing they were outnumbered.

Carlos guided me back toward the stadium and tried to get us around the battle. More demonstrators had appeared from the parking lot carrying signs with the CRUM acronym. Now we were surrounded and unable to move at all. I held onto Carlos as I stared into the look of rage on the faces of the CRUM members. Their screams filled the air with sounds that seemed more like the roar of wild animals.

The screams were mostly unintelligible. A word here and there in English and Spanish could be understood. Then I recognized one sentence. "That's her. That's that lawyer." Two men were looking at me.

I heard Carlos yell, "Mary, get down," as he threw his body over me, pushing me to the concrete, and then I heard the shot.

Chapter Forty-Five

"Carlos, Carlos, are you okay?" I screamed over and over. All I heard was a moan.

I couldn't move. Carlos lay on top of me. I felt as if I were seeing and hearing everything from outside my body. A frightening scene emerged and washed over me. The shot must have hit Carlos and he was unable to move. Maybe he was—no, I couldn't think such a thought. I screamed "help, someone help us." The crowd noise was deafening. I didn't think anyone could hear me. Then I heard sirens and someone yelling for people to move back.

I felt Carlos being lifted off of me, and a male voice giving orders. "Get that ambulance over here now. Ma'am, are you hurt? Can you tell me where the pain is?"

I sat up and saw the brown uniforms of Miami-Dade officers surrounding us. Carlos was lying beside me. Blood covered his shirt. I looked down and saw blood on my arms and hands.

"I'm not hit. It's Carlos. Is he? Is he?"

"He's alive, but he's been shot. The medics will be here in a second. They're getting through the crowd. Can you give me your name?"

"I'm Mary Magruder Katz and"…Just then I heard Carlos trying to speak. I moved close to him.

"Did you get the bastard?" Carlos said.

"Don't try to talk," the officer said just as sirens announced the arrival of the ambulance.

"Ms. Katz, you have blood all over the back of your shirt. You better get checked out."

The medics, a man and a woman, were rushing toward us with a stretcher. They began an examination of Carlos, listening to his heart, checking the bloody area under his shirt, attaching things to his arms. They moved him to the stretcher and then into the ambulance. The officers helped me into the ambulance, the doors shut, the sirens roared and we were careening down the road away from the stadium and onto the freeway ramp.

"How bad is Carlos? Can you tell anything? Where are you taking us?" My voice sounded far away as if it were coming from some other person.

The woman medic began examining me. She pulled up my shirt and looked at my back and sides. She placed a blood pressure cuff on my arm.

"I'm okay, just tell me about my boyfriend, please."

"He has a gunshot to his chest. It appears that it missed his heart, but we don't know if it hit his lungs or any other organ. We'll be at the hospital in just a few more minutes. We're going to the trauma unit at Jackson Hospital. They are the best equipped to handle gunshot victims."

I reached into the pocket of my jeans and was amazed to find my cell phone was still there. I hit the phone icon, found J.C. and Angie's number and placed the call. Carlos's parents would never forgive me if they heard their son had been shot from some stranger. Luckily, J.C. answered.

"Mary, what a mess at that game. Are you on your way home?"

"No, J.C., and you'd better sit down."

Chapter Forty-Six

The medics wheeled Carlos into the trauma unit where multiple nurses and doctors materialized and began hands-on work over Carlos. Someone pushed me into a wheel chair and began wheeling me into a separate curtained area.

"No. I need to stay with Carlos," I yelled .

"We need to examine you first," a woman in green scrubs said as she restrained me from leaving the chair. "We'll keep you informed as soon as we get information about your friend. We need to make sure you weren't shot. You have a lot of blood on your shirt and your face."

I read the woman's badge, It said Dr. Lois Alonso. Dr. Alonso removed my shirt and placed a hospital gown over my shoulders. She began a full scale look at my body, prodding fingers here and there. She sponged blood from my back, hands, and face.

"It looks like you weren't shot, but you have a nasty scrape on your forehead, and left hand." She cleaned the scrapes with alcohol and placed a bandage on my head.

An officer accompanied by another doctor parted the curtains. Dr. Alonso motioned for them to come in.

"Ms. Katz, I'm Sergeant Cantor, Miami-Dade County Police. I was the officer at the scene, do you remember? I need to get some information from you. He pulled out an I-Pad and a stylus, and began asking Carlos's name and address, then mine, then occupations.

"I'm going to need to take a full statement from you as soon as possible. I'll be back to talk to you in a few minutes. This is Dr. Evans," the officer said. "He's a surgeon and has news for you about your friend."

Dr. Evans asked what my relationship was to Carlos. When I told him I was his fiancé, he frowned. "I'm going to need next of kin permission to do some surgery, unless the patient himself is aware and able to sign some documents. Does the gentleman have a living will? A document that tells us his end of life requirements ?"

"I know what a living will is. I'm an attorney. What do you mean end of life? You better tell me exactly what the surgery is and what his wounds are. I need to know now." I got off the examining table and shook my finger directly in the face of Dr. Evans.

We all turned as the curtains parted and an older man entered. He was dressed in rumpled slacks and a University tee shirt. His outfit threw me for a second and then I realized it was Doctor Andreas, the Martin family physician. He treated me in June when I was hit on the head in my own office parking lot, and again a few days ago for my sore throat.

"Doctor Andreas, how did you know we were here?" I grabbed him and gave him a hug.

"I got a message from J.C. I was just driving into my driveway from the game. I had already heard on the radio that there was a shooting, but until I heard from the Martins, I didn't know it was Carlos who was the victim."

"Doctor Evans, this is Doctor Andreas. He treats all of the Martin family. Please tell us what is happening to Carlos," I said.

"Well, Ms. Katz here is only a fiancé, so I can't let her sign these papers."

"Carlos's parents will be here any minute, but this is ridiculous. These two young people are as good as married and I know that will be taking place soon. Please give us your diagnosis. I've been treating Carlos since he was sixteen years old." Doctor Andreas was showing his impatience.

The curtains parted once again and J.C., Angelina, and Chicky entered. By now, the enclosed space was teeming with people and making me claustrophobic. The curtain opened a bit more and someone peered into the space but there was no place else to stand.

"Mother, what are you doing here?" I recognized the worried face that was looking at us.

"Angie called me. I made some excuse to Abe and got right over here. I didn't want to upset him."

"Look, folks, I've got to get my patient into surgery. Will you all please move across the hall to the visitors' room. I will talk to you briefly and then I've got to get scrubbed and get to work." Doctor Evans propelled us across the hall. I moved awkwardly still in the hospital gown and bare feet.

"Carlos has a bullet lodged in his chest cavity. I believe it entered through his back. We've done x-rays and stopped the bleeding. He's a lucky guy. The bullet missed his heart. He has at least one broken rib. We don't know if his spleen is damaged. I may have to remove it, but not to worry you can live without a spleen. He lost a lot of blood, so we will be transfusing him. I may need one of you, a parent or sibling, to donate some blood. The nurse will be in to talk to you about blood type. I also need his parent, is that you, sir?" he said pointing to J.C., "to sign these documents giving us permission to treat your son and do the surgery. We also need all of the medical insurance information. I believe we found his insurance cards in his wallet. I'll have the nurse give you his watch and other valuables we found."

"Can I please see him before they move him to surgery?" I asked.

"He's been calling for Mary. Is that who you are?" Doctor Evans asked. "Doctor Andreas, do you want to observe the surgery?"

We all answered yes together. A nurse appeared and motioned me to follow her. She led me to another room in the back of the trauma unit, Carlos was on a gurney, with numerous tubes and wires protruding from everywhere. He was very pale and his eyes were closed.

"Carlos, can you hear me?" I asked.

"Mary, thank God. Did you get hit?"

"No. I'm fine, thanks to your quick thinking. You saved my life. I am so sorry that I got you into this."

"I know you'd do the same for me. I love you."

"Oh, Carlos, I love you so much," I said.

"We need you to step out now, ma'am. We need to move the patient upstairs," the nurse said.

As I stepped into the hallway, a thought stabbed through the fog in my brain. This hospital sojourn was the reason marriage makes a difference. According to Jackson Hospital, without that piece of paper called a marriage license, Carlos and I had no rights when it came to life and death decisions about each other.

Two attendants wheeled Carlos down the hall to the elevator. I shuffled back into the visitor's lounge where the family sat staring at the green walls.

Mother stood up and took my arm. "Mary, sit down here. You look a little shaky and you're shivering."

"She needs a shirt and some shoes," Chicky said. "I'll find out what they did with her clothes and I can go down to the gift shop and see if I can get a clean shirt down there. It'll give me something to do."

I let mother guide me toward a sofa. The room began to spin and then everything went black.

Chapter Forty-Seven

The next thing I remember is someone forcing some smelly thing at my nose. I opened my eyes and for a minute couldn't remember where I was. I looked at a collection of anxious faces surrounding me. Then everything came rushing back, the shooting, the hospital, Carlos lying in the trauma unit.

"Oh, Mary, you fainted, just like a *Cubana machada*. You darling girl. Let's get you up." Angie was trying to lift me off the floor.

A nurse pushed her away. She put a cold towel on my forehead. "Don't try to get up just yet," the nurse said. "I better have a doctor come in and have another look at you."

"No, please, I'm okay. I'm just scared about Carlos."

Angie, who is a tiny woman, shoved the nurse away and helped me to the sofa. "We take care of our own," she said.

I started to cry when I realized that Angie had totally accepted me into the Martin tribe. My tears made everyone gather around me, hugging me until I felt claustrophobic again.

The overwhelming attention of so many relatives caused me to control my emotional outburst.

"I know everyone wants to help so I'm going to lean on you for a bit. Can someone call Franco and see if he can go to the stadium parking lot and pick up Carlos's Escalade? Tell him it's in lot H. He'll know how to start it without the keys.

"Someone needs to go to my house and feed and walk Sam. Mother, could you call Catherine and see if she can go there? She has a key and someone needs to let her know what happened. She'll need to let Marco know before he hears about this on the evening news."

Chicky spoke up. "I am going to get you some clothes before you freeze in here. The air conditioning must be set at fifty degrees. And I will bring back coffee and sandwiches for us. Ciao," she said as she left the room.

"Mary, you should go home yourself. You've just gotten over your flu bug. You need to rest," Mother said.

"I'm not leaving here tonight. I will stay with Carlos when he comes out of surgery. I'll go home when I know he's going to be one hundred percent again."

Chapter Forty-Eight

I was dressed in a shirt that said "Jackson Hospital Honeys." Chicky made a donation to some charity in order to get me a shirt. We were drinking coffee and trying to pass the time waiting for word of the surgery. We took turns looking at our watches and cell phones as the minutes dragged by as if they were being held back by heavy chains.

The door to the waiting room opened and Sergeant Cantor appeared. Behind him was a plain clothes detective.

"Ms. Katz, this is homicide Detective Vincenti. We really need to ask you some questions while everything is fresh in your memory. I'm sure you understand how important it is for us to get on top of this investigation. We want to catch the shooter and right now you are our best source until the victim is able to talk to us."

"The victim? Oh, you mean Carlos," I said. I couldn't stand to think of Carlos as a victim. "Okay, I understand. I'll try."

Detective Vincenti motioned me to follow him. We walked down the hall to a small room that seemed to be a supply area. Some folding chairs were set up next to a wall of shelves filled with medical supplies. A woman in grey slacks and a white shirt sat on the chair facing the door.

"This is my partner, Detective Vivian Suarez," Vincenti said.

Vivian and I stared at each other. She looked familiar.

"Mary Katz? My God. I haven't seen you since high school. Remember me? Vivian Naranja?"

I couldn't believe this well- muscled, statuesque woman was scrawny Vivian, who opted out of every gym class and hid behind horn-rimmed glasses.

"Of course, Vivian, I just didn't recognize the last name."

"It's my married name, Suarez. Maybe you remember my husband, Sammy Suarez."

"From the Suarez spas and gyms? I see his name everywhere."

"It's okay that you didn't recognize me, Mary. You've been through a lot today, and I've changed a lot with Sammy's help."

Detective Vincenti interrupted. "This is good that you know each other. Maybe you'll feel more comfortable talking with Vivian."

"Yes, that will be fine," I said as I took a seat across from Vivian.

"Mary, tell me everything you can remember leading up to the shot that hit Carlos Martin. He's your fiancé?"

"Yes, well, we're together. We were trying to get through the crowds leaving the stadium after the game. The groups of protesters were everywhere and they were fighting. Carlos tried to get us back toward the stadium but we couldn't move. More and more people were shoving into us and pushing us toward the CRUM people and their signs. I heard someone scream something like, "there she is," and then Carlos screamed at me to get down and he fell on top of me and then I heard the shot--."

"Okay, Mary, it's okay. Just take a deep breath."

I felt the tears coming down my cheeks and I was having a hard time catching my breath. Vivian handed me a Kleenex.

"Now, how many shots did you hear?"

"One, I think. No there was a second one but it wasn't as loud, or maybe Carlos was blocking the noise some. He was completely covering me."

"Did you see the gun or the person with a gun?"

"No, it all happened so fast. I wish I could have seen more. I know how important it is to be a thorough witness."

"I know you're a lawyer. I've seen your name and picture in the paper. In fact, I saw your picture in the paper about this case."

"Wait, that's what the guy said. He said, there she is. There's that lawyer. Right before Carlos said to get down."

"Mary, as soon as Carlos is able to talk to us, please call me." She thrust a card into my hand. "We've detained a number of CRUM members for questioning. We'll get this bad guy."

Chapter Forty-Nine

The time on my cell phone said ten o'clock. I was sitting in a reclining chair next to Carlos's bed. The battle over my decision to stay with Carlos overnight was won by sheer stubborn determination. The doctor explained that he had to remove Carlos's spleen. The bullet broke two ribs and the impact shattered his spleen, but his heart and lungs were fine. He was still out from the general anesthesia, just moaning a little.

I was wearing my terry cloth robe that someone brought me from home along with clean jeans, shirt, bra and panties. Mother found me a carton of soup. The surgeon assured me that Carlos would soon be completely recovered, so I drifted in and out of sleep.

At six a.m., nurses shuffled in and out of the room, checking blood pressure, temperature, IV drips, and assorted other medical stuff. The hospital was coming to life and so were Carlos and I. It was Sunday morning. The bells from the Baptist Church where my grandparents first came to teach in Miami played a hymn that I remembered hearing. The sun shone on the tops of the oak trees ringing the parking lot. It was a new day.

Chapter Fifty

Three days later, Carlos was released from the hospital. A caravan of Martins and Katz's were on hand, carrying out the balloons and flowers dropped off by cousins, and workers from Carlos's construction crew. Franco was waiting downstairs in the Escalade. I was in the Explorer having dashed from the office to be there for the happy occasion. Angie had arranged for a practical nurse and her housekeeper to be on hand all day at Carlos's Pinecrest mega mansion. Sam and I would be there every night.

We were passing out boxes of candy to the many nurses who fussed over Carlos. An orderly wheeled him out to meet the car, but Carlos refused the ride in his car and hoisted himself into my Explorer. "I always go home with the date that brought me," he said, as the crowd on the sidewalk laughed and cheered. I couldn't stop smiling, knowing that this ordeal was behind us. Soon we would just be Mary and Carlos again, fighting over all the silly stuff that makes us a couple.

We pulled into the circular driveway behind the wrought iron gates at Carlos's house. The two women sent by Angie rushed into the brick courtyard and helped Carlos out of the car and into the house.

Soon he was propped up in bed with a lunch tray on the bedside table.

"Carlos, I hope you won't be angry if I leave you and go back to work. I'll be back before dinner. I know you're in capable hands. I wouldn't leave if Jay's case wasn't looming and Marco is a total basket case about you and about his case."

"I know, and don't forget about my dad and his grand jury visit."

"Of course I haven't forgotten J.C. We'll talk tonight. You rest this afternoon, but you also need to call Detective Vivian Suarez as soon as you feel up to setting an interview with her. They need to find out who put that bullet into your chest."

Chapter Fifty-One

I sped back to the office to prepare for the depositions in Jay's case. Catherine was back at her desk and had jockeyed around every calendar item while Carlos was hospitalized. Early next week I would be deposing the detective who arrested Jay, and the father of the teen-age alleged victim in the case. Catherine had also managed to reset the depositions more than once.

As soon as I finished preparation for those depositions, I would be meeting with Reuben, the great investigator, who was working on Marco's case and Jay's case. My work was piling up but I couldn't think about anything while Carlos was in the hospital. Through all of this, I was consumed with guilt over ignoring my dad who had his own health problems.

Catherine was waiting by the front entrance as I arrived.

"How's the patient? And how are you? You look frazzled. Is Carlos being difficult?"

"No, he's following orders, and that's scaring me. He hasn't said a word about getting back to work or even leaving the house or his bedroom. That means he's not feeling at all well yet."

"Mary, be thankful for that. In a day or so, he'll be pissing off everyone, and climbing the walls. I've pulled together all your notes on Jay's case. Everything's in the file on your desk but it isn't much. I took the liberty of telling Reuben to come over in a few minutes. I thought he might have uncovered something to help you in Jay's depositions."

"Catherine, you are so smart. I am so happy you're back. I promise you, I'll get Marco out of this and you'll live 'happily ever after.'

"Life's never a fairy tale, Mary. I'll settle for happy occasionally."

The thin file in Jay Lincoln's case took less than ten minutes to peruse. If Reuben didn't have any news I would be flying blind in the depositions.

Another thought rattled my already addled brain. Frank Fieldstone would be attending the depositions as my second chair. I could imagine his "I told you so" expression when I couldn't find anything to dispose of this rape charge. Everything in Jay's life would be altered. Instead of a pro football career, he would be having a prison career, and he would be on the sex offender list for the rest of his life. All because of a fifteen year old girl who went beyond being a groupie.

I looked up and saw Reuben standing in the doorway. His huge frame filled the entire space.

"How is Carlos doing? And I see how you are, exhausted," Reuben said as he took the chair across from me.

"Carlos is home from the hospital but he's a long way from being himself."

"Marco asked me to see what I could uncover about that CRUM group. The cops are sure that one of them was the shooter, but no one in the group is talking, at least not yet."

"I want to get the creep who did this, but right now I need to concentrate on Jay's case. Do you have anything new?"

"I've been nosing around Coral Gables High School. I was able to identify this Jennifer person from her yearbook picture. She sure doesn't look like fifteen. She looks like a Victoria Secret model. She hangs with another female all the time." Reuben looked at his notepad. Her name is Candy Gomez. Gomez is a big, sort of horse-faced girl. She follows Jennifer all the time. Probably has a thing for her. I figured if I could get something on Candy, maybe you could use that to get her to give us the dirt on Jennifer, but so far I haven't come up with anything."

"Do you have an address for Candy? I could subpoena her for a deposition. That might be enough to scare her, or maybe I can rattle her with questions at the deposition. At least it's something. Where does she live?"

Reuben looked at his notes again. "Four-eighty Compere Street in the Gables."

"That's amazing. That's one street over from my house. She's practically in my back yard. Sam and I will walk by there tonight. Now what about Marco's case. Anything new that you've found?"

"Not a lot to report. I went back up to that area on Sterling Road in Broward County looking for Sheila Bird. Talked to a couple of the pros who were on the street. That part wasn't hard. One of them flagged me down. Anyway, they knew Sheila but they said they hadn't seen her for a while. One of them said she may be living back with her family on the reservation."

"Any names or addresses for her family?"

"I talked to a guy I know from the Hard Rock casino and he said Sheila's father or uncle or some relative ran the small casino. He thought his name was Oscar. I checked the cross directory and found an Oscar Songbird, manager of one of the Seminole casinos. I don't know if he's related to Sheila, but here's the address of the casino. I think it's right near the Seminole tobacco shop on the reservation. You know, where the Indians sell cigarettes cheaply."

"I think the better label is Native American, and the reason they can sell at a discount is they're a separate nation so they sell without adding on the state and U.S. taxes. I'll follow up on this lead. Thanks Reuben."

I walked Reuben out and then stopped at Catherine's desk. "Catherine, please prepare a subpoena for Candy Gomez for a deposition on the same date as the other witnesses. Here's the address. I plan to serve her myself tonight. Tomorrow I'm going up to the Seminole reservation to follow a lead in Marco's case. Why don't you come with me?"

Chapter Fifty-Two

Carlos looked more like himself when Sam and I arrived. He was out of bed, dressed in shorts and a tee shirt sitting on the patio with an open briefcase in front of him and a sheaf of papers in his lap.

"What's all this?" I asked while trying to hold Sam back from leaping on Carlos.

"These are reports from my foreman on the apartment building site and the minutes from the city council meeting about the development plans for the downtown site. Don't lecture me. I've got to get back to work or at least up to speed on my projects."

"As long as you work from here, I guess it's okay, but no going out to the site until the doctors clear you for driving and moving about. Still, I feel relieved to see you up and about."

"I called Detective Suarez. We talked on the phone and she'll stop by tomorrow to record my formal statement. I was able to give her a little description of the guy who had the gun. I got a quick look at him and his gun. The detective said they were questioning a number of members of CRUM, but I didn't see a sign in his hand, just a gun."

Angie's housekeeper had prepared dinner before she left. I warmed up the chicken and rice that smelled delicious. My flu bug seemed to have flown away while I concentrated on Carlos. Maybe the brush we had with the gun shots scared the bug away. However it happened, my usual appetite was back.

While I was clearing away the dishes, I told Carlos about Candy Gomez.

"Would you be okay for an hour or so if I run back up to the Gables and see if I can talk with her? I can take Sam with me. She lives right in my neighborhood."

"I'll be fine and you can leave Sam with me. I like his company, but don't work all evening."

The drive back to the Gables took only a few minutes. The rush hour traffic was dying down. I left my car in my own driveway, took my briefcase with the subpoena and walked down one block to the Gomez address. The house was a low stucco ranch like most of the houses in the neighborhood, but I remembered this house having walked by it with Sam many times. The house was on a double lot with a half basketball court next to the house. I often heard kids playing under the lights as I walked by. There was a trampoline in the back yard where I could see kids jumping and laughing. I often wondered how many of the kids lived there or if they came from adjoining houses.

Tonight the house was quiet but there were lights on in the front window and by the front door. I rang the bell twice before I heard a voice say "Okay, I'm coming. Stop ringing already."

"Oh, I thought you were Sandy," a tall young woman dressed in a warm-up outfit said as she opened the door. The warm-up jacket said Duke University. "May I help you?"

"Are you Candy?"

"No, that's my little sister. If you're selling something or collecting for something—"

"Neither." I interrupted her. "Is your sister at home?"

"What do you want with her?" the door-answerer was getting spooked and started to close the door.

I stepped through the door quickly and found myself in a comfortable living room. "I have a subpoena for Candy Gomez. I need to serve her. Would you call her, please." I handed the young woman my card. She examined it and frowned.

"Candy, come in here. What have you been doing?"

"What's the matter with you, Sophia?" A voice called from the back of the house.

A few seconds later a girl who fit Reuben's description of Candy entered the room. A young teen-age male accompanied her. He was carrying a huge bowl of popcorn. Sophia handed Candy my card. "This attorney says she has a subpoena for you. Her card says she defends criminals. What have you been doing?"

"Candy Gomez, this is a subpoena to appear for a deposition at the criminal courthouse as a witness in *State vs. Jay Washington.*"

"Look Ms. Katz, Candy just turned sixteen. My mom will be home in a few minutes. What is this about?"

"Who are you and who is this young man and how old are you?" I asked in my best courtroom voice. I watched Candy's reaction. Her hand was shaking holding the subpoena.

"I'm Sophia Gomez. I'm twenty and this is my brother, Raymundo. Ray is seventeen. Can you please tell us what this is about."

"You are of adult age, Sophia, so I don't need to wait for your mother to arrive. Candy, I believe you are a witness in the case listed on your subpoena. I represent Jay Washington. I believe you are a close friend of Jennifer de Leon."

"I think you'd better leave now," Sophia said. "You need to speak to my parents."

As Sophia held the door open, a car pulled into the driveway. An older heavier version of Candy pulled herself slowly out of the car and retrieved two grocery bags from the back seat. Sophia ran out and took the bags from her mother. She spoke in a whisper to Mrs. Gomez, or who I guessed to be Mrs. Gomez. They hurried into the house.

"This is my mother, Ms. Katz. I told her about the subpoena," Sophia said.

Mrs. Gomez took the subpoena from Candy's trembling hand and looked it over. "What is this about? I can't have my daughter going to the criminal courthouse in the middle of a school day. What is she supposed to be a witness to? I'd like to call our family lawyer."

"Mrs. Gomez, I'm not here to upset anyone. Candy is a close friend of Jennifer de Leon. In fact she's Jennifer best friend, isn't she? And Jennifer has accused my client, Jay Washington, of sexual battery. If you don't want Candy to come to the courthouse, I'm willing to interview her right here, right now with you present."

"I guess that would be better. I don't know if Candy is Jennifer's best friend, but they are friends, and I have told Candy repeatedly that I wasn't happy with that friendship," Mrs. Gomez said.

"What was it that you didn't like about the friendship?"

"Excuse us for a minute kids. Come into the kitchen with me, Ms. Katz," Mrs. Gomez said.

I followed her into a kitchen filled with a long wooden table and six chairs. I could imagine family dinners around that table filled with noisy kids. I felt a minute's remorse for my surprise visit upsetting their evening routine. Then I thought of Jay and his parents and their misery caused by Jennifer.

"Let's sit here for a minute, Ms. Katz." Candy's mother gestured to the table I was still looking at. "Candy is a good girl. She's not very mature; isn't interested in boys or dating. Her life revolves around athletics. She plays soccer and volleyball. Her friends are mostly teammates, but for some reason in the last year she's got a thing for this Jennifer person. Jennifer is a complete opposite to Candy. She's into clothes and makeup and partying. I found out that Candy went to a party at Jennifer's house. She came home after her curfew of midnight and, I'm sorry to say, she was drunk."

"Are you sure they were at Jennifer's house?"

"What are you getting at?"

"Jennifer was hanging out at the university on several occasions in the last year and she had a friend with her." I saw the shock on Mrs. Gomez's face.

"Are you sure or is this something Jennifer made up?" Mrs. Gomez asked

"I'm absolutely sure, but you need to talk to Candy about this."

"I plan to do just that. After the drunken episode, I called Jennifer's father to see if he had been at home the night of this party. Her mother split on them when Jennifer was nine or ten and I don't think her mother is in touch with her from what Candy tells me. I guess her dad is doing the best he can as a single parent. There is a younger boy who is twelve. It's a lot for a man to handle."

"What did you find out when you talked to the father?"

"He claimed that to his knowledge there wasn't a party at their house, but then he said he had been out of town on business. He claimed the house was in order when he got back."

"Does the father travel a lot?"

"I'm not sure. He works for a grocery distribution company. That's all I know, but I'm about ready to tell Candy that she can't go anywhere socially with Jennifer anymore."

"Mrs. Gomez, are you aware of the case against Jay Lincoln, the University of Miami football player?"

"Well, just what I've seen on the TV news. What has this got to do with my daughter anyway?"

"I'm Jay's attorney and the victim of the alleged sexual battery is Jennifer de Leon. She brought this charge against Jay in August and alleges that the incident occurred last May. I am hopeful that Candy can shed some light on this; that she may have information that will help me in my case. Jennifer was accompanied by a friend when she hung out on the campus on different occasions. Candy seems to be the friend that Jennifer is usually seen with. That's why I subpoenaed her. I'm willing to speak to her informally tonight with you in the room."

"Oh, dear, this is very upsetting. Let me talk to her for a few minutes and then you can interview her. If she knows about this crime, I want her to be honest with you."

"That's what I want too."

Chapter Fifty-Three

I waited in the kitchen. I heard Mrs. Gomez tell Candy to go up to her room; that she wanted to talk to her. The minutes ticked by and I thought about Carlos alone at home. I pulled out my cell and called him. He picked up after five rings.

"Carlos, are you okay? You sound a little off."

"Yeah, I fell asleep. Where are you? What time is it?"

"It's not quite eight. I'm still at the Gomez house. I may be another hour. Are you sure nothing's wrong?"

"I was having some pain so I took one of the pills the doctor gave me. I guess it knocked me out. I'm okay. Just do what you have to. I'm going back to sleep."

All kinds of worries rumbled through my mind. I hadn't completely realized what a slow recovery Carlos would be making. Carlos was always Mr. Energetic, working on a construction site, then going to the gym and still wanting to go out for drinks and dinner and then home for some great sex. This was going to be a different Carlos, and I wondered how long it would be before he was the human example of the energizer bunny.

Mrs. Gomez and Candy were staring at me while I stared at my cell phone. I hadn't heard them come back into the kitchen.

"Candy is ready to talk to you now. It seems Candy has been giving me some misinformation about where she's been going with Jennifer. I've instructed her to be absolutely truthful with you." Mrs. Gomez pulled out a chair and seated herself at the table.

Candy sat down next to her. Her face was crimson and she twisted her hands together. I wasn't sure if she was scared of me or of the sure punishment that would be meted out by her parents when they heard about her escapades with Jennifer.

"Candy, I'm going to take some notes. If what you tell me is relevant to Jay Lincoln's defense, I may have to call you as a witness at his trial. If you are a witness, I will have to list your name on the witness list that I give to the prosecutor and he will have the right to take a statement from you. Do you understand this?"

"Yes, ma'am, I guess so." Candy answered in a barely audible voice.

"How long have you known Jennifer de Leon?"

"Since the beginning of ninth grade. We were on the same class schedule, and she came to watch me play soccer."

"Did you see Jennifer apart from classes and school functions?"

"We started going to the mall and movies on weekends and she invited me to her house and to sleep over."

"Did you accompany Jennifer to the University of Miami campus?"

"Yes."

"How did you get there?"

"The first time we walked over there after school. It isn't that far."

"How many times were there?"

"A lot."

"Tell her the number of times," Mrs. Gomez said. "And I'd like to know too. All those times you were supposed to be studying or working on a school project."

Mrs. Gomez face was contorted with suppressed anger.

"Maybe five times last winter and spring. And the time after the football scrimmage."

"You said you walked to the campus. What was the reason you went there, and what did you do when you got there?"

"Jennifer said it would be good for us to see what it was like at college. She said the boys at school were immature jerks and that it would be more fun to date college boys. We hung around outside some of the fraternity houses. Jennifer would start talking to boys out on the lawn and make it sound like she was a student there."

"What did you do? Did you get in on the conversations?"

"Not really. I just sort of hung around. Sometimes I would watch a tennis match or a volleyball game until Jennifer was ready to leave."

"Did you go to the campus at night too?"

"Yeah, Jennifer got us a ride over there once with some guy she knew who went there. He was her neighbor. He left us off there but we couldn't find him to go home so we hitched a ride over on Lejeune Road."

"My God," Mrs. Gomez muttered.

"Once we got my sister Sophia to drop us at the library on the campus. She was home for winter break. We told her we were working on a project for school."

"Did Jennifer ever mention a boy named Jay Lincoln?"

"She talked about him all the time."

"What did she say about him?"

"She said he was hot and she was sure he thought she was hot too, and that she was going to be his girlfriend. She cut out stuff from the paper about his football games."

"Do you know if Jennifer ever sent him pictures of herself?"

Candy looked at her mother and then down at the floor. There was a long pause.

"Candy, answer Ms. Katz's question," Mrs. Gomez said.

"Well, she did but that was after the fraternity party," Candy said.

"What fraternity party?" Mrs. Gomez raised her voice to a new level.

"You're just going to kill me," Candy answered.

"I want to know exactly what you're talking about," Mrs. Gomez was half way up from her chair.

Candy and her mother appeared to have forgotten that I was in the room and trying to take a statement.

"Okay, but don't tell Dad," Candy said.

"I'm not making any deals. Now let's hear the whole story," Mrs. Gomez said.

"I'd like to hear the whole story too," I said, trying to interject myself back into the conversation.

"I'm sorry Ms. Katz. This is all so shocking. You think you know your kids and then, well." Mrs. Gomez's voice trailed off.

"Please call me Mary. I feel like part of the family. Don't apologize. I'm the one who's sorry for intruding on you, but maybe it's for the best. We can both hear the whole story and I can help my client. Candy, tell me about the fraternity party you mentioned. Was it a university fraternity? When did it take place."

"It was last spring. Jennifer told me that she had arranged to get us a ride over to the campus on a Friday night. She said we should put on some cool outfits and she would do my makeup and hair. I said what am I going to tell my parents and she said to come over to her house to get dressed and tell them she was having a party at her house."

"Okay, tell me where you went when you got to the campus."

"Jennifer said to just follow what she did when we found a party to hang out at. First we hung out with a group in some student building, but Jennifer said it was lame, so we walked around some more, and heard a lot of music at this fraternity house. We went in and just walked around saying hi to people like we belonged there. Jennifer spotted Jay, the football player and started talking to him. Some guys started talking to me and I danced with one of them and then they started offering me some drinks. When I looked around Jennifer was gone and by then I was starting to feel kind of dizzy and then I felt really sick so I went outside to look for Jennifer. I got sick over in some bushes. Finally I saw Jennifer making out with that guy."

"You mean Jay Lincoln?"

"Yes, Jay. I finally got her attention and she left Jay and came over to me. I told her I had to get home, that it was already past my curfew. We couldn't find the kid that drove us over, so Jennifer called her housekeeper, Jonelle, to come and get us. She said she had an agreement with Jonelle not to tell. I think she gave Jonelle money to shut up."

"Did Jennifer ever talk about Jay at any other times after that or see him again?"

"She talked about him all the time. She said she was going to hook up with him sooner or later. Then one day we were at her house after school and she showed me something in her phone."

"What did she show you?"

"She had taken a picture of herself without her bra and she said she sent it to Jay. I told her she was crazy. She said she was crazy about

Jay and they were going to hook up soon and that he thought she was a freshman at the U. I tried to tell her she was gonna get herself in a lot of trouble, but she just laughed at me."

"When was the next time you went with her to the campus?"

"I didn't go again. She was beginning to scare me a little. I liked her a lot, but then I had spring soccer and volleyball practices were every day after school, so I didn't have time to hang out so much."

"Is there anything else you know about Jennifer and her crush on Jay?"

"Well, right before the end of school, I went over to her house to help her with her science stuff. She begged me to help her before the final exam. I guess I asked her if she was still so crazy about Jay. Then she told me all about them having sex and how she found out he had another girlfriend while he was with her and he'd be sorry. Then she said he wasn't as hot as she thought and she was through with him. I was surprised, but then I saw her getting in a car with another guy after school, so I guess she was through with him."

"Who was the other guy?"

"I don't know. He looked too old to go to high school."

"Do you know anything about Jennifer pressing criminal charges against Jay?"

"She never said anything to me but I didn't see her over the summer. I was away. I got to be a junior camp counselor. This year at school we were still friends but she wasn't around after school. I think she might have gotten in trouble with her dad because I saw him pick her up after school a few times. He was never around much the last school year."

"Is there anything else you can think of about Jennifer's relationship with Jay?"

"Not really. Well, yeah, my brother told me he heard that Jennifer was the one who had accused Jay Lincoln of raping her. I didn't believe that she would have done that, but now you're here and telling us that you're Jay's lawyer. I really don't know what to believe."

Candy looked at her mother. She got up and put her arm around her mother's shoulder.

"I'm so sorry, Mom."

"Ms. Katz, Mary, can Candy be excused? She's told you a lot even though she knows how upset I am."

"Yes. Of course. Candy, thank you for being truthful with me. I need to remind you that you may have to give a similar statement to the state attorney, but don't worry about that now," I said.

I glanced at my watch and made as quick an exit as I could, leaving Mrs. Gomez to deal with her daughter, all the while wondering how such a great kid could have gotten mixed up with such a messed up kid as Jennifer de Leon.

I pulled my car into the brick courtyard in front of Carlos's house. The house was quiet as I let myself in and turned off the alarm system. All the Pinecrest houses seemed to be connected to alarms and video surveillance cameras. I guess they weren't necessary in my neighborhood. There weren't enough goodies to steal.

I tiptoed into the bedroom and heard Carlos snoring. Sam was on the foot of the bed. He lifted his head and acknowledged me and then went back to watching over Carlos. I was too keyed up to think of sleeping after listening to Candy confirm everything that Jay related to me in our initial interview.

I went downstairs again and entered the kitchen where I did what any harried lawyer would do. I extracted a pint of chocolate chunk ice cream from the freezer and prepared to demolish it.

Chapter Fifty-Four

A few hours of sleep later I awoke trying to remember something important. I grabbed my phone and beamed up my calendar. At the top of today's events was the item, nine-thirty Carlos doctor appointment. Then I realized Carlos was not in bed.

I found him in the kitchen drinking coffee and reading the morning Herald. A pot of the dark brew bubbled on the electric coffee maker filling the kitchen with a tantalizing aroma. Carlos was dressed in shorts and a tee shirt. He looked like his old self.

"Today's the day for your checkup. Did you remember?'

"Yeah, but you don't have to go. Franco can drive me."

"Absolutely not. I want to be there. This is one day the office can wait," I said.

Two hours later, we were leaving the doctor's office with nothing but good news. Carlos was allowed to drive short trips and could return to his office for a few hours a day. Life was returning to normal or what passed as normal for us. The doctor did caution us to remember that Carlos would not be able to fight off infections normally because of the loss of his spleen.

By the time I dropped Carlos back at his house and reversed course to reach the office, it was nearly noon. Catherine greeted me with the usual fistful of messages and e-mails. I put them on the desk without even looking through them.

"Catherine, the most important item today is to go up to Broward County and try to talk to Oscar Birdsong. If he is the father of Sheila Bird, maybe he can lead us to information that will help Marco. I'd like for you to come with me. Maybe he'll be intimidated by two women staring him down. Can you get home a little late for the boys?"

"I'll call Franco to pick them up and stay with them if we're late. He's been asking what he can do to help Marco. I'll go call him and then we can leave. What about all those messages and e-mails?"

"Is anything important?"

"Your brother, Jonathan called and said he needed to talk to you, and Frank Fieldstone called for the fiftieth time to make sure he knew when the depos. were set. I gave him the schedule again."

"I'll call Jonathan while you call Franco." I dialed Jonathan's private number and he picked up on the first ring.

"Mary, thanks for calling back. I feel like a heel. I haven't been around while Carlos has been recuperating. How's he doing?"

"He's better and starting to get back to normal. I know you're busy."

"I thought the best thing I could do for you would be to keep tabs on Mother and Dad while you were taking care of Carlos, and that's another reason I feel like a heel. I made such a big deal about their moving back to Miami. I was just so stressed out with the office and Randy and the kids, but anyway, you were right. They are keeping busy. I'm checking on them more than they're calling me."

"I'm glad to hear a good report. How does Dad feel and what are they up to?"

"He's still tired from the surgery, but they're seeing some of their old friends and playing bridge and going out to dinner. Next week he's going to play nine holes of golf. I called for another reason too.

Remember the estate settlement you sent me from your friend in Vermont? Well, I think I need to send it back to you or work on it with you. It turns out the deceased was under indictment for Medicare fraud and some other federal charges and the estate is tied up with the feds trying to take all the assets."

"Wow, sounds complicated. Can it wait a few weeks? I'm swamped."

"I'll try to drag my feet with some motions until you have time to get involved."

Chapter Fifty-Five

We were on the freeway on the way to the Seminole Gaming Casino in search of Shirley Bird.

Catherine stared out the window at the scenery as if there was something interesting about the warehouses, billboards, and rumbling trucks we were passing.

"Catherine, have you eaten anything today?" I asked,

"I guess not, but I don't have much appetite since Marco was arrested."

"Let's stop for some lunch. You need fuel to have enough energy to handle everything; your kids, your job and trying to keep Marco from going stir crazy."

I pulled off the highway at the next exit and saw an ad for an ice cream and sandwich shop on Dania Beach. It turned out to be on a street of quaint shops and had a small town look about it. The sign outside said it was established in 1958, making it an antique in South Florida where the restaurants go in and out of business faster than South Florida women change hair color.

We ordered grilled cheese sandwiches and chocolate sodas, enough cholesterol to satisfy a craving for fat for a month. As soon as our waitress left, I saw Catherine drumming her fingers on the marble table, a sure sign that she was debating whether to tell me something.

"Catherine, what is it?" I asked as I covered her perpetual motion hand with mine.

"I am worried about something awful. If I tell you, will you promise that it's just between us and never to be used in Marco's case?"

"Of course. What is it?"

"It's my dad. Do you think he could have been the one?"

"The one? What one?"

"The one who did Brady in."

"Are you kidding? Your dad is as straight arrow as they come."

"I know, but he hated Brady. Never wanted me to marry him, but of course, I wouldn't listen. And when I told him on the phone that Brady was back and the problems I was having with him, he went into a rage. And he spent his life in the military, so he has a lot of guns, and he won every marksmanship award. He even told the detective that he was glad Brady was killed and he wished he'd done it himself."

"There, you see, he said it wasn't him, just that he wished he'd done it." I pondered what Catherine had just told me. Doug Larsen couldn't be the shooter, or could he? The thought that Catherine and I could be caught between defending her fiancé or her father was too bizarre to contemplate.

"Catherine, we will find out who did this. You need to stop conjuring up foolish worries.

Let's go find Oscar Songbird and see if he can lead us to a real killer."

Chapter Fifty-Six

Even though it was still early afternoon, the parking lot adjoining the casino was already half full. This was the smaller Seminole casino, not the glitzy Hard Rock Resort and Casino that had changed the lives of the Seminole Indians. The advent of casino gambling on the reservation meant that every member of the tribe shared in the enormous profits that came from the gambling enterprise.

The history of the Native Americans in South Florida was one of sadness. The Seminole and Miccosukee Tribes were pushed from the land they loved, their chief died of heartbreak on a reservation in the west, and they fought to regain the land they now held in Broward County in the midst of an urban area. Even those who don't like gambling don't begrudge the money it has brought to the tribe who lived in poverty for many years.

I anticipated that this would be a quiet time in the casino, so we could speak to Mr. Birdsong. Instead we found a smoke filled hall also filled with older people gazing in rapt attention at the slot machines that growled and grumbled. Occasionally, bells rang and someone let out a whoop of joy. It appeared business was great.

I approached the caged window where chips were purchased. An elderly Indian lady sat on a high stool behind the cage.

"How many you want?" she asked.

"No, I don't want to play. I want to see Mr. Birdsong. Where can I find him?"

"Why you want to see Oscar?" The woman frowned. Her weathered face looked wary.

"We're friends of his daughter, Shirley, and we can't get in touch with her, so we thought we'd come by and see Oscar," I said. I smiled at the gatekeeper.

The woman didn't say Shirley wasn't Birdsong's daughter, so we hadn't wasted our time.

"Wait here. I'll call someone," she said.

We watched her pull a cell phone out of her pocket. She turned her back to us and spoke into the phone in a native language. She put the phone back in her pocket and faced us again.

"You wait over there. Someone will come for you." She gestured to a bar with some empty stools.

We sat watching the slot players until a young man approached us.

"Please come with me," he said and motioned us to follow him. He led us through two double doors and into a hallway. At the end of the hall, he unlocked another door with a combination. We followed him down another hallway filled with portraits of Indian men, some in tribal head-dresses. The young man stopped in front of a dark wooden door and knocked. He opened the door for us and we entered a regular looking business executive-type office; large desk, a sofa and chairs, a computer desk, and family pictures. Behind the desk and rising to greet us was an older handsome Native American man dressed impeccably in a grey suit, blue shirt, and striped tie.

"You are the girls who were asking about Shirley? Please have a seat."

"Yes, we were wondering where she is. She hasn't answered her phone or anything." I said.

"Well, where do you know Shirley from? You don't look like you were working with her in her last occupation," Mr. Birdsong said.

"Okay, look. Don't throw us out. I'm a lawyer and this is my paralegal, Catherine Aynsworth." I handed Oscar my card.

He looked at it and then at us. "Aynsworth? Not that rat Brady Aynsworth. I think I'll have to ask you to leave."

"Wait, Mr. Birdsong, Brady Aynsworth is dead. Someone shot him on the street in Coconut Grove. Catherine is his ex-wife from many years ago. Brady came back to her home and began harassing her the week before he was murdered. Now her fiancé is accused of the murder. I have traced Brady to his last known address which was with your daughter.

Shirley Bird. We think she might have information that would lead me to the real killer. Please don't throw us out. You're our last lead to try to stop an innocent good man from being wrongly convicted."

Oscar looked at us and then out the window. He didn't speak for several minutes. His phone rang and that made all three of us jump. Oscar finally answered the jingling noise. Without hearing who was on the line, he said he was busy and clicked off. Then he buzzed an intercom and told someone to hold all his calls and messages.

"First, let me say that Shirley is my niece, not my daughter. I guess I am the closest thing she has to a parent. My brother and his wife had big problems with alcohol and Shirley came to live with me when she was twelve. When she graduated from high school, she went to work off the reservation. That was my mistake, letting her go on her own. She wouldn't go to college and she was hired and fired from a variety of jobs. She worked here for a year, but she took off again. Eventually, some tribe members found her living in a drug house with that Brady person. She was working the streets and Brady was feeding her drugs bought with her earnings. I guess he was feeding himself that stuff too."

"I am so sorry," Catherine said. "He seemed to have a way to fool women, including me when I married him."

"Finally, Shirley hit the bottom. She was sick and destitute. She reached out to me. It broke my heart to see her like that. I threw Brady out and brought Shirley home. We tried working with her ourselves, used the sweat tents, but nothing worked. I was able to get her into a rehab center and that's where she is. Thank God I had the money to pay for the facility. She may be there for a year getting clean and getting her life back."

"Can we go and see her? Maybe she knows who would have killed Brady."

"There are probably dozens of people who would have gladly shot Brady. I wish I had done it. No one can visit Shirley yet; not even me and my wife. Those are the rules at the rehab center. They said they'd let us know when we could see her. I got to talk to her once on the phone. That's been the only time and only because she was threatening to leave."

"There must be a way to find out what she knows," Catherine said. "Please, Mr. Birdsong, I can't stand it if my fiancé gets convicted. I suffered so much because of Brady. I have two sons and Marco is the only father figure they've ever known. Please, help me."

Catherine was trying to stifle the tears that wouldn't be stopped. Oscar came around the desk and put his hand on Catherine's shoulder.

"I am so sorry. I don't know if there's anything I can do, but I'll try. I'll talk to the head of the rehab facility and see if I can talk to Shirley. I promise I'll let you know."

"Thank you Mr. Birdsong. If I can ever help you or the tribe with any legal matters, I would do it for free," I said.

"Well, you never know. I'll remember your offer, and I'll get back to you." Oscar walked us down the hallway and back into the smoky, noisy casino.

Chapter Fifty-Seven

It was late afternoon by the time we fought our way through the traffic moving through Broward County. Dade County was even busier with two accidents tying up the freeway. I dropped Catherine at her apartment and took a maze of side streets back to the office.

The afternoon mail was in the doorway. I shuffled through the pile of bills and ads for office supplies and computer accessories. I was about to toss a law review from the St. Thomas Law School, a crosstown rival of the University of Miami when the cover article caught my eye. *Romeo and Juliet Laws and Their Effect on Those Accused of Sexual Acts Against Minors.*

I opened the book and began to read devouring the words as if they would disappear from the page before I absorbed them.

"Consensual sexual conduct has become more prevalent particularly where one of the participants has reached the age of seventeen but the other has not. The older teen is technically guilty of rape as any consent between the partners, even if freely given, does not meet the standard of law since it is given by a minor. Romeo and Juliet Laws, passed in several states serve to reduce or eliminate the penalty in cases where the couple's age difference is minor and the sexual contact is only considered rape because of the lack of legally-recognized consent.

"The Florida Romeo and Juliet Law recently passed is designed to protect individuals from the sex offender list. The victim in the case must be between fourteen and seventeen, a willing participant, and no more than four years younger than the defendant. The offense must be the only sex crime on the offender's record. In the case of a conviction for this crime a judge was bound to add the offender's name to the sexual predator register, barring him from many occupations and causing him to adhere to a number of conditions, such as never living in a residence with children. The new law gives the court leeway to keep the defendant from the sexual predator register. Some states have gone further with these new laws and provide for reduction or elimination of penalties."

I tucked the law review article into my briefcase. At least I had a way to keep Jay from being labeled a sex offender for life. More research might bring other relief. Now all I had to do was show that Jennifer not only consented, she arranged the whole sexual encounter. The depositions were crucial. I would have to bring more than my 'A' game.

My cell phone rang as I locked the office door. "Mary, where are you? We're waiting to have dinner and your parents are here. They agreed to stay for dinner."

"I'm on my way Carlos. I'm getting in the car now. It's been a very productive day,"

Chapter Fifty-Eight

Sam met me at the door. He dropped a large bone at my feet. It looked like it belonged on some part of a cow. Sam was clearly enjoying his stay at the Carlos mansion where he was spoiled by everyone and he had Carlos all to himself most of the day.

I hurried into the dining room where Carlos sat at the head of the expensive bleached oak table flanked by Mother and Dad. The house-keeper was loading plates with lamb, rice, and vegetables. It all smelled wonderful.

Carlos got up, kissed me, and guided me into the chair nearest to him. I sensed from his kiss that he was feeling much better.

"Your parents stopped by to see how I was doing and I persuaded them to stay for dinner. Gisela offered to stay. You know she cooks enough for an army." Carlos smiled at Angelina and J.C.'s housekeeper who was like a second mother to the Martin siblings.

"Mother and Dad, this is great. You both look so good, especially you, Dad. You've got color back, even suntan, and Mother you are absolutely glowing."

"Why wouldn't I be. Dad is getting healthier by the day and we're having so much fun staying on the Beach," Mother said.

"Hope, why not make this permanent? Stay here in Miami. What do you think about it Abe?" Carlos asked.

He squeezed my leg under the table. He was definitely feeling better.

"It's sure something to consider. You know all the years we spent in Miami Beach I was so busy working that I never got to enjoy this place," Dad said.

"Mary, did you remember that your Grandmother Katz, well I guess she's Grandmother Morgan now, and Aunt Myrna and Uncle Max will be here for Thanksgiving. It will be wonderful to have the whole family together, and Carlos, we want your parents and Chicky to be with us too."

"It'll be something, that's for sure," I said, imagining the continuing questions about my unmarried status.

Chapter Fifty-Nine

The next morning at the office as I was clearing away the e-mail ads that had surfaced overnight, an unsolicited Facebook request grabbed my attention. Why hadn't I thought to look for a Facebook page for Jennifer de Leon? All teenagers have them. In fact, all lawyers have them. It seems anyone who is alive and breathing has one.

I surfed to Facebook and put in Jennifer's name. Up popped her picture, profile, timeline, messages, comments. Everything I ever wanted to know about Jennifer. There was a picture roll of at least twenty pictures. Several showed Jennifer in a bikini at the beach with various people including Candy. The caption under one said "feeling hot, how do I look?" In that photo she had lowered the bra straps of the bikini. Under another one, the caption read "Jay L. don't you wish you were here?"

I switched to the comment section. She was having a running conversation with someone named Armando. She asked him when they could meet. He countered with "What will we do when we meet?"

The next message described what she wanted him to do to her. "How long can you go?" she asked, and "Do you like oral? I do!"

In one of her comments to her 256 followers she described how it felt to be drunk on beer and pot. The details were nausea inducing. This was a treasure trove of damning information, but would it be admissible at trial? At least it could be used to confront Jennifer and her father to show that she couldn't play innocent sweet sixteen.

I called to Catherine. "Come and look at what's on my computer." Catherine and I poured over the contents. "See if you can find any other goodies of Jennifer's on the internet while I rewrite my notes and questions for the deposition. Print out what you can or take screen shots with your phone." And call Jay Lincoln and remind him I need that nude selfie Jennifer sent him."

Frank Fieldstone was wrong. Every case is winnable if a lawyer digs enough.

Chapter Sixty

In the midst of the chaos that served as my desk, I pulled out a pad of notes and realized they were notes about J.C.'s case. I had totally neglected him even after Carlos's reminder about his dad's case. I grabbed the phone and called all his numbers; home, bank, and two cells. All of the male Martins liked having more than one cell.

Every number answered with a voice mail message. I left word for him to call me on every one of his phones. Within minutes my cell rang. I still hadn't changed the jarring ringtone that made me jump out of my chair.

"Mary, I haven't wanted to bother you with my problem. I know your hands are full with Marco and Carlos's recovery."

"Your are never a bother, J.C. We need to go over the documents that you've located and plan for your grand jury testimony."

"Well, about that, Mary. I may not need to testify. I may have taken care of that."

"You what? What did you do?" Fear gripped me as I pictured all the ways J.C. could have made his situation worse.

"We should talk in person whenever you have time. I want to visit with Carlos anyway so I can come by the house."

"That would be fine. Can you come this evening?"

"Angie and I are invited to the opening dinner at the performing arts center. It's one of the charities we support, but it doesn't start until seven. Can we meet at five?"

"Yes, of course, I'll leave the office early, and bring any of your documents, e-mails, anything that you've gathered about this case."

The suspense of waiting to hear if J.C. was doing anything illegal made the rest of the afternoon crawl by. Carlos and his father never met a law that couldn't be bent. Like Carlos selling land he didn't yet own back in February. They needed to be kept on a short leash and monitored like

Sam who always pretended to be innocent no matter what shoe or rug he shredded.

I left the office at 4:30 to be sure to arrive on time. Usually I stopped at my house in the Gables on the way to Pinecrest in order to check on my house and to pick up more clothes and Sam. Sam had begun staying with Carlos full time so I blew off the house check and headed straight to Carlos's house. The whole arrangement was wearing thin, but until Carlos was completely recovered and back to his normal schedule, the current arrangement needed to continue.

As I idled in traffic on Dixie Highway my mind wandered to the questions of where we would live if I gave in to everyone's push for marriage. Carlos was sure to want to establish our joint home in his mega mansion. I loved my Coral Gables pad even if it was small. It's cozy and I am proud that I bought it on my own and had never missed a mortgage payment. Only twenty more years and it would be paid off. I know there are dozens of gay and lesbian couples who would give anything to have that marriage license. It's just these nagging questions like housing that keep me strung out.

A cacophony of honking horns broke into my thoughts as I realized I was sitting in front of a green light. Several cars pulled around me into the right lane almost causing collisions. One driver gave me the Miami traffic salute; middle finger raised.

I passed through the electronic gate and into the brick courtyard in front of Carlos's house at exactly five o'clock. J.C.'s black Mercedes was already there. Franco's truck was also there. I locked my car although it seemed superfluous what with the locked gate, but Carlos made a great fuss if I left it unlocked.

Sam greeted me at the door with his usual leap and tongue washing. Right behind him was Angie. She must have come along with J.C. and was dressed for their charity function. Her black satin dress was adorned with a gold sequined flower. She was decked out in multiple jewels that made the ornate flower fade in comparison. These included a gold and diamond bracelet, a three strand pearl necklace with a diamond center-piece, long diamond earrings, and an emerald and diamond ring. The effect made me want to don sunglasses.

Just behind Angie was Franco dressed in his usual mechanic's overalls and carrying a tool kit. I wondered how J.C. and I were going to have a lawyer-client conference.

"Mary, darling, I hope you don't mind my coming along with J.C. I thought it would be easier to start downtown from here instead of J.C. coming back to the Grove to pick me up, and I wanted to have a look at my *Carlito* to see how he's progressing. I know you and J.C. are supposed to discuss some business deal of his."

"Of course, I don't mind," I lied. "Hi, Franco, do we have a non-functioning car?"

"Carlos started his Corvette today, and it has some problems, so I thought I'd swing by and take a look. How's your Explorer?"

"My car is great after you tuned it up from its trip to Vermont."

"Come out in the garage with me while I look at the Corvette." Franco motioned me to follow him.

"Tell J.C. I'll be right with him," I called as we went through the kitchen and into the garage.

"Mary, I want to find out how you're doing with Marco's case. My parents are worried and Marco is going *loco*. He's back to smoking a pack a day and he looks like a skeleton." Franco lowered his voice, although I doubted that anyone could hear us. The garage with its three portals was as solid as a steel bank vault.

"I'm getting new information about everyone involved with Brady the last few months. The police are dragging their feet producing the reports that I need, but I am staying right on this, Franco. I know it's hard on everyone, but these cases take time to develop. Is there anything you want me to do that I'm not doing?"

Franco looked embarrassed. "No, no, I just wanted to get up to date. We all know you care about Marco. It's just hard to see what's happening to him."

Franco began opening the Corvette and examining its complicated insides. "This car is aging. Before he got shot, Carlos was looking at a Porsche. I guess he'll decide when he feels better. And he had his eye on a great SUV for you. I think it's a Cadillac."

"What? I don't need a new car. I love my Ford. You mean he was going to buy me a car without even asking me?"

"Oh-oh. I think I spoiled his surprise. It was going to be for your birthday. Don't you have a birthday soon?"

"Yes, this month, but I don't want to be surprised."

"Ay, Mary, don't tell him I ratted him out. And you do need a new car. That buggy's got 80,000 miles on it."

I left Franco to his puttering and went back in the house to swallow the anger that was building. I was not about to allow Carlos or anyone else to make decisions for me, like when to buy a new car and what to buy. Carlos just didn't get it. I'm not Margarita, a silly airhead who likes being treated like a child.

"Mary, how are you dear?" J.C. was standing in the doorway of the kitchen staring at me.

"J.C., I didn't see you standing there. Let me get my briefcase and we'll get started on your case right away."

"Are you feeling okay? You look a little flushed."

"I'm fine, just a little surprised about something Franco told me. Let's go into Carlos's office where we can talk quietly."

Chapter Sixty-One

J.C. and I were seated facing each other on the leather sofa in Carlos's little office. Papers were strewn over his desk and blueprints were spread out on the table. The sofa was the only clear area in the room.

"Mary, you probably won't be happy with me for pushing ahead without your knowledge. You know Angie and I have a long time friendship with Congressman Manny Madrugo. I had dinner with him at the yacht club two weeks ago and told him about the bank being investigated. He was aware of it, but he didn't know I had been subpoenaed. He volunteered to set up a meeting with the federal prosecutor and me and I gave him the go-ahead to do that."

"When is the meeting?"

"We already had it a few days ago."

"Didn't the prosecutor ask you if you had a lawyer?' Did he read you your Miranda Rights?"

"He didn't ask and I don't remember anything about my rights."

"Tell me everything you do remember about the meeting."

"I brought some documents with me and I shared them with him, so we started at that point after he read through them."

"My God, J.C. what were the documents?"

"After you explained to me about the procedures that banks need to have, I started looking through the files. I read the minutes of the board meetings and I found one meeting where we discussed the procedures. One of the board members, Vivian Surliss, asked if we were monitoring the investment customers, checking their backgrounds. She wanted information about bank procedures. The president told her that we had a whole checklist that someone went through to see the background of the new clients. I copied all the pages of the minutes from that day.

"Then I found some e-mails from the bank secretary to me asking me to tell the clients that I solicited that they would have to open more than one account to deposit their cash receipts. I answered her asking why I had to do this, and she said that those were orders from the president."

"What else?"

"I brought a list of bank clients that were referred to me. The prosecutor thanked me and I asked if I still had to go to the Grand Jury. He said maybe just as a witness for the government or maybe not at all, and that with this new information he was going to postpone the grand jury date. He also asked me to be on the lookout for any other memos or e-mails that concerned how large cash deposits were to be handled."

"J.C., do you realize that you have now become an informant for the government? That you may have to testify against your friends at the bank?"

"So be it. I never took this job to get into trouble with the government. I love this country and so does Angie. We became citizens years ago. I'm not going to put my family into disgrace just to protect someone who manipulated me."

"Supposing the feds don't believe you and think you were part of the bank's illegal scheme and you were just making up this testimony to clear yourself? Before you gave aid to the prosecutor, you should have obtained immunity from prosecution for yourself. I wish you had discussed this with me before you did all of this. If you didn't have faith in me as your lawyer, I could have obtained any number of attorneys to help you."

"It's not about faith in you. It's that I have always taken care of this family. I've been in many businesses here and in Argentina. I know what I'm doing."

"Well, now I know for sure where Carlos gets his macho personality. You can't always be in charge, J.C. Sometimes you have to rely on others to help you in areas that are unfamiliar. I'd like your permission to meet with the prosecutor and try to establish immunity for you."

"I know you just want to help me, but I know what's best for me. I haven't done anything wrong so why should they want to prosecute me?

I have a good feeling about this prosecutor so I don't want you to speak to him now."

""I hope you're right. Listen, J.C., you read the papers. Wrongly accused people are sitting around in prison cells. At least please keep me informed of any other meetings or communications from the feds or the bank."

J.C. patted my hand and rose from the sofa just as Angie opened the door. "Come on you two, Carlos and I are into our second cocktail already."

J.C. kissed me on both cheeks and took Angie's hand as they went down the hallway to the family room. I zeroed in on the cocktail part of Angie's statement. Carlos wasn't supposed to drink while he was on pain pills. Great, now we had two Martin men who knew better than everyone else.

Chapter Sixty-Two

After a sleepless night worrying about Carlos's failure to follow the doctor's instructions and J.C.'s failure to understand the serious nature of playing ball with prosecutors, I gave up attempts at resting. I was up at six, showered and dressed and in my Ford Explorer on the way to the office.

The car reminded me of the anger I felt at Carlos for deciding when I needed a new car and what kind of car that would be. How could I consider marrying a guy who still didn't get the fact that I make my own decisions? He showed a lack of respect for me as a person when he overlooked my own abilities. And wasn't that exactly what J.C. did when he went running off to the prosecutor totally ignoring me as his lawyer?

I was brought out of these thoughts in an instant by a truck that tried to change lanes and nearly sideswiped me. I was still a little shaky from that encounter as I fumbled with my keys to unlock the office door.

"Are you Mary Katz?" a voice spoke out of the semi-darkness of early morning.

I jumped and dropped the keys. The figure of a tall male emerged from the shadow of the stairwell that led to the upstairs offices.

"Who are you? Why are you looking for Ms. Katz?" I backed toward the outside door.

"Don't be scared. I'm not here to hurt anyone. You are Mary Katz. I recognize you from your picture."

"What is it you want? The office isn't open yet."

The male came closer and I saw that he was young, maybe eighteen or so, and dressed in jeans and a University of Miami sweatshirt.

"Do you need to hire a lawyer?" I asked. He was close enough to hit me or shoot me and he hadn't, so maybe he was just a kid in trouble.

"No, I don't think I need a lawyer. I just have some information for you. I didn't want to phone or text. Please, can I talk to you for just a minute?" He looked out the door as he spoke and I saw that he was nervous.

I gambled and unlocked the door to the office. I motioned him to follow me as I turned on all the light switches. I could see him fully now. He was tall and heavy but with a baby face. His huge hands were shaking. I pulled out the visitor's chair next to Catherine's desk and motioned for him to sit. I remained standing just in case I had to run out of the office.

"Please, tell me your name." I said.

"I'd rather not."

"Well, can you tell me what the information is about that caused you to be at my doorstep before seven in the morning?"

"It's about the shooting at the football game."

"Okay, were you involved in the riot?"

"No, ma'am. I'm actually on the team."

"The football team?"

"Yes, ma'am. I didn't see the shooting, but I know who did it."

"Why didn't you go to the police instead of coming here?"

"I'm too scared to go to the police," he said. He continued to eye the door as if he thought someone was following him.

I almost laughed, looking at this giant kid, who could probably maim anyone who threatened him.

"See, I feel terrible because I should have warned someone before someone got shot, but I tried to stay out of trouble. I don't want to be involved now either, but I just couldn't wait for someone else to get hurt and not try to stop it from happening."

"Stop exactly what from happening?"

"From you getting killed," he said.

Chapter Sixty-Three

I sat down in Catherine's chair. Now I was the one who was scared. Maybe I was looking at the person who shot Carlos instead of me, and he was here trying to finish the job. He had a backpack that he hadn't removed when he sat down. It looked heavy enough to house a large gun.

"Why don't you take that backpack off and sit back and try to relax," I said.

He removed the backpack and placed it on the floor.

"Why don't you start from the beginning about what you know. You can start with telling me your name," I said.

"I don't want to give you my name. I just want you to know that you need to be careful. You are Jay's lawyer. Jay isn't the only quarterback on the team. He beat out Roy Carter to be the starter. Roy is the backup. That's what started this mess. Roy is from Clarksdale, Mississippi. He hates Jay for getting the number one position and he also hates him for being Black."

"Okay, but what has this got to do with threatening me?"

"Roy was so psyched when Jay got arrested. He figured Jay would be kicked off the team, but he wasn't. Then he thought Jay would be convicted or he would have to plead guilty, but then he got you for a lawyer and he told everybody that you were this smartass lawyer. Excuse me ma'am. You know what I mean. He was bragging, saying you told him no plea. He was going to trial and win. So Roy got it in his head that you were the reason that he wasn't going to get rid of Jay and grab the quarterback job. And the more Jay talked the crazier Roy got.

"Roy's got more than one gun. I know because he's one of my roommates. He knew about the demonstration at the game. He even talked to the head guy from CRUM, and he told me he was going to get rid of Jay's N-loving lawyer."

"Did he tell you that he fired the shot that hit my fiancé?"

"No, but the day of the game, he wasn't in the locker room. He didn't dress. Coach said Roy was real sick and his parents wanted him to see a doctor at home. He was gone until a couple of days ago. But now he's back and he's acting crazy. Not going to class or practice and last night when I came back from practice, he was cleaning one of his guns. So that's why I left before he got up and I figured I'd wait at your office to tell you to watch out."

"Why didn't Roy take out Jay if he wanted to be rid of him? Why come after me?"

"Roy would be the first enemy of Jay the police would look for. He's too smart for that."

"This was a really brave thing that you've done. Please, tell me your name. I promise I won't tell anyone else who gave me this information. You have nothing to be afraid of."

"Sure I do. Maybe the police will charge me with withholding information or something, but I'm really scared of Roy. I have to live in that dorm room."

"The police won't charge you. In fact, I want them to protect you. They can do this undercover. And Roy wouldn't know it was you who tipped them off until he's off the street and sitting in a jail cell."

"No, it's better to be, what do you call it, anonymous."

He picked up his backpack and bolted out of the office just as the first rays of sun shone over the parking lot.

Chapter Sixty-Four

When Catherine arrived at the office, I was still sitting at her desk staring out the window.

"You look like the Mona Lisa without the smile. What's going on?"

"I had an early morning visitor who stopped by to tell me who shot Carlos and was gunning for me. Just the usual morning."

Catherine listened in amazement while I filled her in.

I went into my inner office and called Carlos.

"*Mi Amore,* where are you? I got up at seven and you were gone. Are you okay?'

"I'm fine. I'm at work. I got some news a few minutes ago. I'm pretty sure I know who shot at us at the game. I'm going to call Vivian Suarez and give her these leads."

"Are you in any danger? Shall I come over there?"

"No, I'm fine. I'm actually worried about you. Why were you drinking with your parents last night when the doctor said no alcohol while you're on the pain pills?"

"That's just it. I haven't taken any pain medication for a day and a half. I feel good and I'm going to the office for a few hours."

"I'm glad to hear it. Just the office, don't do any car shopping."

"What? You sound funny."

"We'll talk tonight," I said as I clicked off and dialed the Miami-Dade Detective Bureau.

By ten o'clock Detective Vivian Suarez was seated in my office, note pad open as I gave her a play by play recap of the anonymous visitor and his information.

"We've been going in the wrong direction questioning the CRUM demonstrators and doing background checks on several of them. If this story leads us to the bad guy, wow!"

"Vivian, we have to find the name of this source and get him protected. Roy Carter sounds like a maniac."

"It shouldn't be hard. If he's Roy's roommate, the university has his name and he told you he's on the team. You may be able to pick him out from a team picture. I can get back here with a photo later today. Mary, don't you think you need some police protection yourself?"

"Oh, no, that'll scare off the few clients I have."

Chapter Sixty-Five

I was still thinking about my mysterious visitor when Catherine buzzed on the intercom to remind me that I had the first two depositions set tomorrow morning in Jay's case.

"The arresting detective is set for ten o'clock at the Justice Building. The girl's father is set for eleven. I have all your notes typed up from your talk with Candy Gomez and the ones from Reuben. They're in the file."

I searched my disorganized desk, found the file and began planning my questions. Two minutes later the intercom buzzed again.

"Mary, Oscar Birdsong is on the phone. Can I listen in?"

"Catherine, that's not a good idea. I know how important this is and I promise I'll let you know exactly what he says."

I pushed the outside line button. "Mr. Birdsong, thanks for getting back to me. Were you able to speak to Sheila? Does she have any idea who would have wanted Brady dead?"

"That's pretty funny. I wanted him dead. Sheila wanted him dead. In fact, I think everyone who knew him wanted him dead. The question is who actually can take credit for it."

"You are right. Did Sheila give you anything you can pass on to me?"

"I was able to visit Sheila yesterday. She looks a lot better. She's still struggling through her rehab. The first time I've seen her smile in a long time was when I told her Brady was dead. The rehab director would only let me stay for a few minutes. After we talked a little, I asked her if she knew who might have been the one to kill Brady. She said maybe she could guess, but she wouldn't say what that guess was, and I couldn't push her. She's still very weak. I gave her your card and she promised she would write to you. She said maybe this could count as one of her steps to recovery. You know this rehab center uses the twelve step program.

One of the steps is making amends with those you have hurt so maybe she thinks helping you and Brady's ex-wife is one of those steps. I hope this will be of some help and please, let me know. Come back to the reservation some time and I'll show you some of the programs we've started for our young people."

"Thank you Mr. Birdsong, for trying to help."

"Next time we talk, please call me Oscar." He clicked off

I stared at the phone and listened to the dial tone that sounded like a lonely cry. Now all we could do was wait for the mail, but I felt this lead was only another dead end. I would have to get Reuben beating the bushes again, and Catherine's hopes would be crushed again.

Chapter Sixty-Six

At six o'clock I packed my briefcase for tomorrow's depositions and locked the office. Just as I was unlocking the car, an undercover police car pulled into the parking lot. Of course, everyone knows it is a police car because all the detectives drive dark colored Ford Crown Victoria models. They might as well have police in large letters on the sides and roof.

Vivian Suarez jumped out waving an envelope at me. "Wait, Mary. I need you to look at this."

I walked over to her as she opened the envelope and spread a large photo on the hood of her car.

"See if you recognize the guy who came to see you today."

I looked over the picture. It showed the football team dressed in their orange uniforms trimmed in green with Miami across their chests.

"Vivian, do you mind if we take this over near the light pole? It's hard to see in this half-light."

"Let's get in my car and I'll turn on the inside lights. Take your time."

We sat in the car as I looked at the huge array of players, kneeling, sitting and standing in three rows. The uniforms made them look more alike than different. They all looked huge.

Finally I saw my visitor standing in the back row, taller than the rest of the row of heads, but with a baby face.

"That's him." I placed my finger over his face.

"Yep, that's one of the two roommates of Roy Carter. His name is Brett Fieldstone. He's a sophomore ."

"Fieldstone? Is he from here?

"From Palm Beach."

"Oh, my God, he's Frank Fieldstone's nephew."

"Does that matter? We've got him under protection. He doesn't know it, but we will be getting him out of that dorm room tonight. He's going to be called to the Dean of Men's office, so it'll look like he's in some trouble. Meanwhile we are getting a search warrant to serve tonight to get those guns and compare them to the shot that Carlos took, and anything else we can find as evidence."

"Are you sure he's really the shooter?"

"We've been tracing his whereabouts over the last two weeks. He never was sick or at home, His parents didn't know anything about his being ill and he wasn't in Clarksdale. We found a girlfriend at the TGIF restaurant across the street from the campus. We brought her in for questioning a little while ago and that's where Roy was staying after the shooting until he turned up at school again. She has an apartment in South Miami. So, yes, it looks more and more like he's our shooter."

"You sure have worked fast. Does the university know about this?"

"They've been very cooperative. They want to make sure no one else gets hurt. This has been enough of a black eye. I guess some parents don't want their kids to go to that stadium again. And it's bad for recruiting new students. Now where are you headed?"

"Home for the rest of the night. Carlos is there so don't worry about me. Just get this guy off the street."

I waved to Vivian and headed back to my car for the drive to Pinecrest. I just wanted to be going to my own house in the Gables. I promised myself that tomorrow night I would move back there and Sam and I would hunker down in peace and quiet.

Chapter Sixty-Seven

Carlos was on one of his cell phones as I came into the house. Sam barked his usual greeting, leaping into the air and racing around me in circles.

"Mary, please, shut him up. Can't you see I'm on the phone?"

I saw a heap of mail in Carlos's lap and scattered on the end tables in the family room. Sam followed me to the kitchen where I stuffed one of his treats in his mouth to keep him quiet for a minute. I checked the pot simmering on the stove and found a beef burgundy left by the housekeeper. I poured two glasses of red wine and carried them back to the family room.

Carlos was off the phone. His face looked like a storm cloud, but I wasn't expecting the thunder that followed.

"Are you okay?' I asked as I handed Carlos a glass of wine."

"No, I'm not okay. One week I was out of the office. One week I wasn't at work and all hell has occurred. You'd think someone could have called me or come over here to tell me what's going on. But, no, they just let it all pile up and hit me with it on my first day back."

"Well, I haven't had such a great day myself. What happened at work?"

"Just that the apartment complex failed to pass inspection and now I can't get the certificate of occupancy for months. We have to tear out some of the electrical wiring and redo it. This is the first time one of my buildings hasn't passed inspection. And the bank is demanding that I pay some of the bridge loan on the new project, but I can't do that until I can turn over the apartments and collect the rest of the payment. That's all. And then you come in like a tornado with Sam carrying on like you've been gone a month while I try to negotiate with the bank president."

"Hey, Sam is a dog. He doesn't know about phones or banks. Sam and I don't have to hang out here. I would love to go to my own house for a change, but I know you got shot because of me so I've stayed here to help you get better. Obviously, you are at full strength again, so Sam and I will pack up and go home."

"I didn't think you were here because you felt sorry for me or guilty or whatever. I thought you cared about me. If you want to leave, go right ahead."

"I will just as soon as I pack up the rest of this wine and my plate of dinner." I stomped up the winding ornate staircase with its mahogany bannister and began throwing toiletries, clothes, and Sam's collection of tennis balls into my overnight bag.

I loaded the car and came back to get Sam. He wasn't waiting by the door for his trip in the car. He wasn't in the kitchen. I returned to the family room and found him with his head in Carlos's lap. Carlos was rubbing his chest and talking quietly to him. That sight overcame my anger. I went back in the kitchen and sat down at the butcher block table.

It was totally my fault that Carlos was away from his work convalescing from a gunshot meant for me. What I had said to Carlos was mean-spirited and wholly selfish. I felt ashamed. I started through the kitchen door and almost collided with Carlos.

"I am so sorry," we both said at the same time. I put my arms around him and we stood there for a moment until Sam tried to butt his head between us.

"Sit down and let me serve up some dinner. Put all those papers away until tomorrow, and I have a good idea. Tomorrow night we'll move over to my house. You need a change of scene. Everything will look better tomorrow," I said.

Chapter Sixty-Eight

I cleared the metal detectors at the courthouse by nine-thirty, early for once. I had actually managed to cook a real breakfast for Carlos, and helped him load all the mail and paperwork in his Escalade. He left for his office in a decent frame of mind with a slew of solutions to his problems.

The depositions were scheduled in a fourth floor office used by court reporters. As I was unpacking my briefcase, the door opened. I turned expecting to see Annie Miller, my favorite court reporter. Instead Frank Fieldstone entered carrying his Gucci briefcase. I had totally forgotten that he insisted on being present for all the depositions.

"All set for the witnesses? Or would you like me to do the questioning," he asked as he began to pull papers from his briefcase.

"I don't want you to open your mouth. You and I agreed that the only reason you're still on this case is to impress the judge. Here, read these cases and this law review article." I handed him the literature about the Romeo and Juliet statutes.

"Frank, is Brett Fieldstone your nephew?'

"Yes, he's my oldest brother's son. You remember Jack. He lives in Palm Beach right down the street from my parents. You met Jack at the country club at the brunch for my parents' anniversary."

"I remember that Jack had a bunch of little kids, but I guess that was years ago."

"Why are you asking about Brett?"

"I had occasion to meet him recently. I'll tell you about it some other time."

Annie came into the room accompanied by Fred Mercer, my least favorite prosecutor. Annie and I exchanged "good to see you's" while she set up her machine and noted everyone's appearance.

Fred waved his hand at Annie and mumbled "Off the record. Frank, you're remaining of record on this case? Mary, do you intend to persist in this charade of depositions and trial? You know you have no case here. Why are you taking up the court's time?"

"That's my decision and my client's, Fred. My client is not guilty of anything other than bad judgment and that's not a crime. Frank is here in a limited capacity as second chair. Now do you mind if we get started? Where is your first witness, Sergeant Colodny. I believe he's with the campus police."

"Okay, Mary, it's your funeral, or should I say Jay Lincoln's funeral. I'll call the witness. He's in the waiting room."

"I'll get him." Frank was out of his chair and through the door before Fred could move.

Frank is smart, I thought, not giving Fred a last chance at coaching his witness. Maybe it's not so bad having Franklin Fieldstone as second chair. I never questioned his expertise as a lawyer, just as a boyfriend.

In a minute Frank returned preceded by a young cop dressed in full uniform. Annie placed the witness under oath, and we were off to the races.

"State your full name and occupation, please."

"Sergeant Mack Colodny. I am employed by the University of Miami Police Department where I've worked for five years."

"What are your duties there?"

"I am in charge of second squad of evening patrol. We patrol the south end of the campus, and answer calls in that area. I also investigate crimes occurring on the campus, and interact with students and faculty to educate them about campus safety."

"Were you ever asked to investigate an alleged crime concerning Jennifer de Leon?"

"Yes, I was directed to follow up on a report of an incident concerning Ms. de Leon."

"Who made the report?"

"The father of the girl, Tim de Leon."

"Now the de Leon's weren't a part of the university, were they?"

"No, they live in Coral Gables near the campus."

"So they were outside of your jurisdiction, correct?"

"That's right."

"So what was your role in this investigation?"

"I met with Coral Gables P.D., Officer Graves, who told me—

"Objection, Hearsay." Fred Mercer interrupted.

"This isn't a trial, just a deposition, Fred. Objection noted. Continue Sergeant."

"Gables called our department because Mr. de Leon was alleging that Jennifer was raped by one of our students, Jay Lincoln, on our campus. Officer Graves told us that Mr. de Leon was angry and wanted the Gables Department to take action."

"What did you do with this information?"

"I made arrangements with Officer Graves to set up an interview with Mr. de Leon and his daughter."

"Tell me about that interview."

"Can I look at my report about that?"

"Yes, and I will need a copy of that report."

"Just a minute, Mary. I don't think you're entitled to that report. Officer let me look at that." Fred Mercer snatched the report from the officer's hand.

"Are you kidding, Fred? That report and any others should have been given in discovery a long time ago. Frank, were you ever given this police report?" I asked.

"I gave you everything I had in the file, Mary, when you came to my office. I never saw a report from the campus police," Frank said.

I picked up the file and rifled through it, even though I knew no such report was there.

"If you continue to refuse to give me all the police reports, we'll let a judge settle this after the depositions," I said. "Sergeant, go ahead and tell us what transpired when you met with the de Leons."

"Officer Graves and I met with the father and daughter at the university police station. Mr. de Leon objected to coming there. He wanted us to come to their home but we told him to come in and bring his daughter. They came in on August twenty-first [t] at four p.m. I asked the daughter, Jennifer, when this incident occurred. She said it was on May third. I asked her why she took so long to report this. She said she was scared because Jay Lincoln was an important football star and she thought no one would believe her. I asked her for the details of this incident. She said Jay invited her to a party and gave her several drinks. Then he lured her to his dorm room where he raped her. She claimed that she was wasted and didn't know all the details."

"Did you ask her how she knew Jay?"

"No, I never asked that."

"Did you ask her if there were other times she visited the campus?"

"Yes, she said she used the library at the university on occasion."

"Can you describe Jennifer? How was she dressed?"

"She's very pretty. Tall, long blond hair. She was wearing what looked sort of like a school uniform, a plaid skirt and white blouse and flip-flops."

"What age would you judge her to be, just by your first look?"

"I would have said at least eighteen."

"Objection, he's not an expert in making such a judgment," Fred said.

"Judgment of someone's age by appearance doesn't require an expert. It's an everyday observation. But your objection is noted for the record," I said.

"Now did you ask Jennifer how she got home from the campus in her wasted condition?"

"I did, and she said she couldn't remember."

"Okay, anything else about the interview with Jennifer? What was her demeanor?"

"She looked pretty nervous and she looked at her dad a lot. We wanted to interview her alone, but since she's a minor we had to let the parent stay."

"Did you also interview Jennifer's father?"

"Yes, we asked Jennifer to have a seat in the lobby while we talked to her father."

"Please describe that interview."

"Do you mind if I look at my report again?"

"Do you have an independent recollection of that interview?"

"Not completely. It took place three months ago."

"Okay, look at your report. We can take a break while you do that."

"Thanks, I'll go to the restroom and be right back."

"Please remember not to discuss your testimony with anyone during the break," I said.

Fred Mercer was about to follow the officer out of the room, but apparently thought better of it after my instruction. He sat down again and made a pretense of reading his notes.

I motioned to Frank to follow me into the hallway. The court reporter jogged down the hall to the women's bathroom.

"Frank, read these notes of a statement I took from Candy Suarez, Jennifer's best friend. Jennifer lied about everything." I stopped talking as the officer walked past us.

Frank looked surprised as he read the notes. "How did you find this girl?"

"By doing my homework."

Chapter Sixty-Nine

We were once again seated in the room that was fast becoming smaller as the day wore on.

"Back on the record," I said pointing to the court reporter. "Before proceeding with the questions for the officer, I am handing a defense witness list to the state containing the names of Candy Suarez and a private investigator, Reuben Porter."

Mercer stared at the names. His frown telegraphed that he had never heard of Candy.

"Now Sergeant Colodny, do you recall the interview with Tim de Leon after looking at your report?"

"Yes, I do. Actually Officer Graves did most of the questioning of Mr. de Leon since he had talked to him before. Graves asked when de Leon had learned of this alleged rape. He said that sometime in early August he picked up Jennifer's phone to make a call because he had misplaced his phone. He looked through the picture roll on her phone and saw several pictures of some football players. Then he saw a semi-nude picture of Jennifer and he freaked. He called her in and showed her the picture. She started crying and told him about the alleged rape and said that Jay Lincoln had taken the picture of her and e-mailed it to her phone."

"Did you see the picture?"

"No, her father told us he deleted it from the phone."

"What else did you discuss with him?"

"We asked him if he had noticed any problems with Jennifer, if she had been upset around the time this sexual battery was supposed to have taken place."

"He said he traveled a lot on business so he wasn't around that much, but he did say he asked the housekeeper and she hadn't noticed any problems."

"What else did you ask him?"

"We asked him if Jennifer had any boyfriends, and if he knew if she was on birth control medication. That's when he got very angry and said Jennifer was the victim and we better do something about this. We told him it was difficult for the police to investigate this because so much time had passed, that we couldn't gather any physical evidence at this late date. We went round and round and finally just ended the interview."

"Now Sergeant Colodny, you were the officer that arrested Jay in late August in the coach's office, is that correct?"

"Yes, Ma'am."

"And you obtained an arrest warrant from the State Attorney's office, right?"

"That's right."

"What else did you do to investigate Jennifer's allegations?"

"Like what?"

"Well, did you interview any of Jennifer's friends like Candy Suarez, Jennifer's best friend? Or did you question Jay Lincoln, or any of his professors or his coach, or any of his teammates?"

"We didn't talk to any of her friends. We did talk to the coach."

"Didn't the coach tell you that Jay was a terrific young man and never in trouble?"

"He did tell us that. We didn't talk to Jay because the coach didn't want us to. We talked to a couple of his teammates. They said he was a great guy. One of them said Jay had girls falling all over him all the time, like waiting for him after games and practices."

"Was there any other basis, other than Jennifer's statement, that caused you to charge Jay with sexual battery?"

"Listen, I tried to explain to the father that this would end up being a "he said, she said" case and that his daughter would have to go to court and testify."

"What did he say?"

"He said he'd have me fired if we didn't get this guy, Jay, arrested. Then he went over my head to my chief and threatened him with a law suit against the university and Coral Gables if we didn't file charges and get this guy arrested. I got orders to do that."

"How did you feel about this?"

"Honestly, I didn't feel great about arresting Jay, but I thought the prosecutors would investigate and decide whether to follow through with an information or indictment. It was out of my hands, and I sure didn't want to lose my job over this."

"You were the officer who made the arrest of Jay. Who else was present at the arrest?"

"Two other officers from my squad. We went to the office of the coach and explained why we were there. He called Jay in from the practice field."

"Describe what occurred when Jay arrived in the office."

"Jay was in his practice clothes. He was very sweaty. We told him why we were there, to arrest him for a charge of sexual battery." He appeared totally shocked or surprised. He asked us who was he supposed to have battered. We told him the name of the victim. At first, he said he didn't know anyone by that name, but a minute later he said something like, 'Oh, that chick who came to the dorm a while back?'"

"What did you tell him?"

"We told him that he'd have to ask all questions when he went to court. We showed him and the coach the arrest form that showed Jennifer was a fifteen year old. He said, no he never had no relations with any young kid."

"Did you read him his Miranda Rights?"

"Yes, we did and we told him to stop talking to us, that whatever he said would be used in court. We had a hard time handcuffing him. He was so sweaty from practice, and his wrists were huge. Finally the coach said forget the cuffs and told Jay to go with us. He asked if he could call his mom, so we let him do that."

"Did he say anything else to you on the ride to the jail?"

"He just kept saying that he couldn't believe this. He asked where we were going and how he could get out of jail. We explained to him about bail and the bond hearing. That's all I remember."

"That's all the questions I have. Fred, do you have any questions?"

"No thanks. Sergeant, you're excused."

I stood up and stretched, and Annie walked around the room for a minute. I asked if anyone needed a break. No one said anything so I asked Frank to go bring in Mr. de Leon.

While we waited I asked Fred again for the police reports. He hesitated and then said he would have them sent to me later today. I instructed Annie to get that on the record.

Minutes passed, but Frank didn't appear. Finally Fred got up and left for the waiting room. After another few minutes, Frank and Fred came in together unaccompanied by the next witness.

"Where's Mr. de Leon?" I asked.

"Mr. de Leon has disappeared," Frank answered.

"He hasn't disappeared," Fred said. "He left us a note."

"Let me see it," I said.

"It says he has to reschedule," Fred said as he stuffed the paper into his pocket.

"It says a lot more than that," Frank said.

"I want to see it, and I want it included in the record." I motioned to Annie who began tapping on her machine.

Fred retrieved the note from his pocket and passed it to me. I read it into the record.

"I have been here waiting since ten forty-five and I'm not going to wait any longer. It is now eleven-twenty. I am a busy man and I don't know why I have to take time from my business to answer questions from some lawyer who is trying to defend the man who hurt my little girl. We are the victims and it's appalling that I have to sit in this disgusting waiting room. I'm leaving and don't ask me to come back. Tim de Leon"

I handed the note to Annie to include with the transcript of the deposition.

"I plan to subpoena him again, Fred, and if he doesn't appear I will go before the judge and get an order compelling him to appear," I said.

Fred left the room as Frank and I packed our briefcases. We walked out together.

"Good work, Mary. Maybe we can get this case dismissed," Frank said.

Chapter Seventy

I hurried back to the office to plan for the next set of depositions. I found Catherine pacing in front of her desk. She was carrying a piece of paper and alternating looking at the paper and looking out the window at the parking lot.

"What's up, Catherine?" You look like a robot circling the room."

"The letter, it's here." Catherine waved the paper in her hand.

"What letter? Let me see." I eased it out of Catherine's hand.

"I found it when I opened the mail. It's from Sheila Bird.

I began to read, as Catherine looked over my shoulder.

Dear Ms. Katz: Uncle Oscar brought the news of the murder of Brady Aynsworth. I know it's not nice to say about the dead, but I am glad someone got him. He almost wrecked my life. He is the reason I got so hooked on cocaine and pills that I ended up in this hospital place. Uncle Oscar told me about the man who is accused of the murder and he explained that you needed to know if anyone I knew about could have killed Brady. Brady got a lot of threats when he was living with me. They were mostly from bill collectors and he had a car repossessed. He was into his drug contact for big bucks. I don't even know how much, but this guy came to my apartment several times. I only know him by the name *Oso Blanco.* It means polar bear. He was a big guy with a heavy beard and snow white hair. Once he threatened me; told me he'd be back to beat me up if I didn't get Brady to pay up. I told him we didn't have any money, and he said he had ways to deal with that. That's all I know, and I hope it helps you. If I ever get out of here, tell Brady's ex-wife I'd like to meet her. I can only guess that we share many problems. Sheila Bird

P.S. Don't try to answer this. They aren't letting me have mail from anyone who isn't family.

"Catherine, this is something we can work on. I need to call Reuben and see if he can find this *Oso Blanco.*"

"I already left word for Reuben. I hope you don't mind, Mary. He was out on a case but I know he'll call back. He's anxious to get Marco back to the Pit Bull office. It's not going well with him not able to come to work even though he calls there almost every hour."

"It's great that you contacted Reuben. Did anything else happen while I was at the courthouse?"

"Your mother called, Angie called, J.C. called, and your brother William called."

"No Carlos?"

"Oh, yes, but he just said he'd meet you at your house tonight, and he'd bring Sam."

I went into my office and started calling back the family. I started with Mother. Maybe she would short circuit the rest of the calls. Something told me they were all about the same subject.

Mother answered on the first ring of her cell phone. "Mary, I know you're busy but I need your help. It's about Thanksgiving. I'm trying to plan a real family event and Angie's insisting that we have it at her condo or even at their place on the beach in Marco Island."

"What's wrong with that? The beach house might be fun."

"But it's mostly our family. I told you Uncle Max and Aunt Myrna would be here and your grandmother and her new husband, and Jonathan and his family, and maybe William and his family, but I'm not sure about him. I don't want Angie to just take over."

"She's just trying to be helpful. She knows you don't have room in your rental condo. And my house isn't big enough for nineteen or twenty people. I'll discuss it with Carlos tonight, but try to remember how much we have to be thankful for. Carlos could have died from that gun shot."

"You're right Mary. I'll let you work this out."

Just what I needed. A new problem to work out. Maybe Carlos and I should leave town for Thanksgiving and go to some deserted island.

I hit J.C.'s number in my speed dial. "Mary, I promised to let you know if I had any more conversations with the government about my case. I haven't heard any more from the prosecutor I met with. I think maybe he is satisfied with what I told him and I need to go out of town for a few days, but I didn't want to leave you thinking I wasn't keeping you in the loop."

"Well, at least you weren't calling about Thanksgiving. Where are you going?"

"I'm going to Argentina to check on some matters with the cattle ranches. Don't worry about Thanksgiving. I'll tell Angie I spoke to you. It doesn't matter where we have the dinner, just so we're all together with a healthy Carlos on hand."

"J.C. I don't mean to worry you, but just because the government hasn't pursued more from you doesn't mean they're through with you. Please don't meet with them again without my being with you. Did they say anything to you about not leaving Dade County or being available?"

"Not that I can recall. I think someone asked if I was readily available and I said yes, but I have to take this trip. Carlos's brother needs my help. Don't worry about me. You are a born worrier. I gues that's why you're a good lawyer. Ciao for now."

My last family call was to William. "Mary, I hope you won't get your feelings hurt. I really have to go to my in-laws for Thanksgiving. I know we should be with Mother and Dad after Dad's heart attack, but Joanie has her heart set on being with her parents, and I've been working so many hours lately getting the Miami office up and running. I've neglected Joanie and the kids."

"It's fine. This whole family dinner is turning into a pain in the butt. Mother and Angie are vying to be named hostess of the year. And you know how Grandma Katz gets under Mother's skin. It should be an evening you'll enjoy missing."

"Yeah, I just thought maybe I'd be missing some important announcement. Like you and Carlos finally setting the date."

No, you won't be missing anything like that," I said. What made you think that?"

"I guess maybe because Carlos saved your life and took a bullet for you. Why don't you give the guy a break and get married already?"

"Oh, William, not you too. Maybe you can understand. I've been on my own for a long time. It just scares me every time I try to picture what life would be like if I gave up my decision making and had to defer to another person all the time."

"Why do you think that? You've seen how happy Joanie and I are and Randy and Jonathan too. We share our decisions. It's good to have a partner to help decide important things. Why do you assume that Carlos would expect to tell you what to do?'

"I don't know. I've seen how Mother always let Dad lead the way, and I just couldn't do that."

"Listen, little sis, for a smart lawyer sometimes you're pretty stupid. Mother always put on a show that Dad was the family leader. If you ever really examined their relationship, you'd see that she's always had Dad giving in to her. She'd pretend that her idea was actually his. Remember when he bought her that convertible? She kept telling him she wanted a convertible. He told her a convertible was dangerous especially with a car full of us kids. She kept showing him pictures of sports cars and pointing out her friend's MG, much more dangerous than a convertible, and the next thing you know he drove up in that red convertible.

"And just this fall, she's got Dad primed to get rid of the house in Boynton Beach. She's got him convinced that it's his idea to move back to Miami. You've got the wrong idea about them. Look, I know you don't want my advice, but Carlos is as good as they come. Yes, he's got a Latin temper and sometimes he's impatient, but he adores you. You are equal partners in your relationship. I can see that. Think about what you're doing. If you wait long enough, Carlos will drift away. He's ready for a committed, steady home life."

"How do you know that?"

"Because we had plenty of time to talk when Dad was in the hospital and you were off running away to the North Woods."

"Don't worry about Thanksgiving and give Joanie my love."

"I hope you don't think I'm butting in to your life. Just think about what I said."

As I hung up, Rueben stuck his head in the door. "Am I here at a busy time?" he asked.

"No, I'd much rather work on Marco's case than talk to any more of my relatives," I said as I motioned for him to come in. Do you know anything about a drug dealer who goes by the name of *Oso Blanco*?"

"Catherine read me the letter from Sheila Bird. I called a buddy from the DEA who owes me a favor. Not only does he know of him. They've been trying to grab him for a while. I guess he's pretty slippery. He has a network of foot soldiers who do his dirty work, so they never get him engaged in activity. I told my contact the whole story and he said the Bear could have ordered a hit on Brady. His organization has been suspected of murder in another case in South Florida and one in Atlanta. The key is going to be finding someone who'll rat him out."

"You mean get one of his own guys to turn on him? How can we do that?"

"I'm going to try to work with my DEA connection and I have a call in to FDLE too. The Florida Department of Law enforcement may know more about *Oso* ."

"Reuben, that could take months. Marco doesn't have months. The longer this homicide charge hangs over him, the more he stands to lose everything, his business, his home. You know what happens to a guy who gets accused of a major crime. Even when he is fully exonerated, people will always have their suspicions."

"I know, but what other choice do we have? I'll do everything I can." Reuben pulled his big frame out of the chair and attempted a smile as he headed out the door.

Chapter Seventy-One

I filled Catherine in on my conversation with Reuben, and I was honest with her about the time it might take to get into the drug ring and find a snitch.

"Mary, I can't stand this helpless feeling. Isn't there something we can do?'

"Well, now that we know who might have been behind Brady's murder, let's go back over to your apartment building and ask some more specific questions there and in the neighborhood."

"That sounds like you're inventing busy work to keep me from falling apart. Haven't the police already covered all that ground?"

"Not necessarily. The detectives seemed to have zeroed in on Marco. Maybe they did a half-assed job of canvassing the neighbors. And anyway, they didn't know about *Oso Blanco* and his buddies. Let me call Reuben on his cell and see if the DEA has some pictures we can show around. It's better if you and I knock on some doors. People know you and they won't be scared to talk to us like they would be with Reuben who presents a rather imposing figure or the police who lots of people are scared to talk to."

"It's better than doing nothing. Tell Reuben to e-mail any photos to the office."

Catherine was right. We couldn't just sit and wait for law enforcement to come up with something while Marco's life imploded. I decided to go through my file one more time to see if I had missed anything. I reread my notes of what Marco told the detective right after the discovery of Brady's body.

By the time I reached Reuben on his cell, I had a second assignment for him. Marco was able to account for all his time the afternoon of the murder, except for the hours he was on surveillance. He told the detective that he couldn't reveal his client's name due to privacy concerns. What if the client would come forward himself or herself to corroborate Marco's statement? Reuben agreed to get photos and to check all the records for the day of the murder and talk to the client. Maybe all of this was just busy work, but remaining idle sure wasn't freeing Marco.

Chapter Seventy-Two

I left the office at five and found I didn't even mind the traffic. I was headed home to my own house for the first time in over a week. Carlos's Escalade was already parked in front and I heard Sam's excited bark as I unlocked the front door.

Carlos and Sam were waiting in the living room as I came in. I hugged them both.

"Mary, I should have brought Mama's housekeeper over here to take care of dinner and open up the house, but I did what you said and sent her back to my parents."

"Good, we need some quiet time. I'm going to fix us an omelet and a salad."

I got out of my suit and pumps and into my favorite shorts and sneakers and headed to the kitchen. I poured Sam's kibble into his bowl while he danced in leaps that would have made a ballet star envious. As he wolfed down his food, Carlos came into the kitchen laughing.

"Your dog is a liar. I already fed him thirty minutes ago," he said.

"You mean our dog, don't you?" He seems to have adopted you as a co-parent."

We relaxed over wine while I put our dinner together. For the first time in ages, I felt totally peaceful. My Coral Gables house was my refuge. When work piled up or after a bad day in court, being here felt safe and welcoming.

While we ate, Carlos talked about his busy day starting his electricians on redoing the wiring in the apartment complex and the deal he made with two banks to extend his loans. He talked about his new project rebuilding a blighted area downtown. He looked so animated when he talked about his work.

I caught him up on what I was trying to do to get Marco's case dismissed. I knew that no matter what we discovered, it would take a court to pressure the state for dismissal. The state would never drop the case on its own no matter what we were able to show.

"I guess we're both workaholics," Carlos said. "We understand that our work defines us in a special way."

"Yes, I know, and maybe I can explain to you why I keep putting off making everything more permanent between us. I am scared that you wouldn't want me to be as totally involved in my law practice. Maybe you'd think that major decisions in our lives would be yours to make without me and my input."

"Why would you think that?" Carlos frowned. "Tell me what I've ever said or done that would make you think that?"

"Well, Franco happened to tell me that you were looking at new cars for me for my birthday. A new car is a major decision, but you never asked me if I wanted a new car. Then there's the way you were raised. Your mother was a stay-at-home mom for you and your brother and sister, and maybe that's the life you are looking for."

"She wasn't out working, but she was hardly at home. She belonged to all kinds of organizations. She played cards with her friends and went to luncheons and dinners and concerts and the ballet. The day to day tasks were done by our nanny and housekeeper. Of course, she loved us and was there for our activities, but she could just as easily have been working at a steady job. She just chose a different lifestyle.

"As far as the car surprise, I've been worried about your safety. That old Explorer of yours may not be viable for the way you speed around Miami. I wasn't trying to usurp your decisions. I just thought I would be doing something to surprise you and keep you from spending your time running around to bargain with car dealers. If I didn't give this enough thought, this is something I can change. I'm trying hard to understand you completely. You should try to understand my motivations too. What else is bothering you now that we are being honest with each other?"

"We've never discussed children. I think you have your heart set on a family and I'm not sure I want any kids," I said.

"I guess we have backed into having that serious talk I've been asking for. Is this it?"

"It seems to be."

"I never said that the reason for our getting married was just to have children. That would be something we'd both have to want or not. I want a permanent relationship with you because I think we are good together. We have that special chemistry and we make each other happy. Don't you feel that?"

"Of course, I do. I felt it that first time you came to my office last February. And you know how that ended ."

"Yes, by me putting on my pants while your soon to be ex-fiancé stood glaring at us."

"If we decided to be permanent, where would we live? I love this little house and you're used to your mega mansion."

"What if we sold both houses and found the house that would be ours; the place we would both be happy living in?"

"It's something to think about. Carlos, as a start, would you be willing to just move in together and see how we adjust? You know we have had our escape valve with having our own homes. Maybe we should see what it would be like to be together every day. We could go step by step."

"Well, it's better than your running off to Vermont again. But you have to promise that we can have open discussions like this. Don't hide from me. If you don't tell me what troubles you, I can't know how to fix it."

Carlos pulled me up from the table and we headed for the bedroom. This was one place we could always agree on.

Chapter Seventy-Three

Monday morning I was a little late arriving at the office. It was hard to shake off the deepest sleep I had experienced in weeks. Carlos and I spent the weekend being lazy, watching movies on TV and taking walks along the bay front in Coconut Grove.

"This is a great neighborhood," I told Carlos. "It reminds me of how Miami Beach was when I was a kid; people walking to stores and the beach. It's laid-back, not as hectic as Miami is almost everywhere."

As I entered the office on that Monday, it dawned on me that I was only a mile or so from where we walked on the weekend. Practicing law keeps me so busy that I never get to enjoy the rest of Coconut Grove. Life is the office, the courthouses, the clients, and rushing home to feed Sam.

"Reuben sent some pictures," Catherine said the minute I walked in. She held up print-outs from an e-mail and I was pulled back into reality.

There were several shots of the white-haired bear like man. One looked like a booking shot where he looked almost baby-faced in spite of his beard. The next photos were somewhat grainy and must have been surveillance shots. The "polar bear" was shown talking to other men and looked much older. There were shots of three younger men.

"Who are these other guys?" I asked.

"The e-mail said they were known associates of Mr. Polar Bear."

"Do we know the real name of *Oso*?"

"Not that I know of. When can we start taking these around my neighborhood?"

"It wouldn't pay to do it until this evening when people are at home. We'll go right around the dinner hour. Did Reuben say anything else in the e-mail?"

"No, but he did say he'd try to be in touch later today. Oh, Vivian Suarez called, but she said she'd get back to you later."

I sat down at my desk and wondered where to start. J.C.'s case nagged at me. The next depositions in Jay's case were tomorrow, and I still didn't have the pictures Jennifer sent to Jay. I asked him to be sure to get them to me showing that they were sent from her phone to his and not the reverse.

Marco's case was the most disturbing. If I couldn't discover something concrete, there would be no way to free him. It was clear that the police and the prosecutor had no intention of investigating any further.

The intercom interrupted my thoughts. Catherine's voice said that a Dash Mellman was on the line. I realized that I completely forgot to contact him about his client.

"Dash, how nice to hear from you," I said. "I'm totally embarrassed that I haven't gotten in touch with you."

"How are you, Mary? Busy as ever? I don't mean to bug you, but my client is getting very anxious about his uncle's estate. Has your brother been able to start working on it?"

"That's just it, Dash. My brother found out that the federal government seized the uncle's property right before he died. They accused him of Medicare fraud and other related charges. My brother, Jonathan, said this was more my kind of case than his. My problem is that I'm overwhelmed in work right now. If you can wait a few weeks, I can begin to look into this."

"I'll let my client know and see how he wants to proceed."

I pictured Dash in his Victorian house that serves as his office in High Pines, Vermont. Was it only a month ago that I was working in that office? It seemed like a year ago. I sent regards to Daisy, Dash's secretary who was also his mother. I hung up and felt like a heel. Dash was a great guy who cared about me. I walked out on him the minute Carlos came back in the picture. Now I hadn't even followed through with his client's matter.

The intercom buzzed again. "Mrs. Lincoln is here, Mary. She doesn't have an appointment, but I told her to wait while you were on the phone."

I went out to the waiting room and saw Mrs. Lincoln, her head bowed, looking as if she were attending a funeral.

"Mrs. Lincoln? How are you?"

She looked up startled. Then I saw that she had a bible in her lap and she had been reading or praying or both.

"My dear Mary, how are you and how is that fine man of yours? Has Carlos recovered? We were so shocked when he was shot. Have they caught the shooter?"

"Carlos is doing fine and I'm okay too. No one has been arrested yet, but I think the police are working on something now. I'm glad you stopped by. I was going to leave word for Jay again to see about some pictures on his phone."

Mrs. Lincoln reached into her purse and pulled out a cell phone. "Jay asked me to bring this to you. Let me show you." She fumbled with the icons on the phone and handed it over to me.

There, in living color, was Jennifer de Leon. This photo was more explicit than those I viewed on her Facebook page. She looked like a Victoria Secret model but wearing fewer clothes. I could see that the photo came from *Jenn@aol.com* to *Jayftball@miami.edu.org*.

"This is just what I need for the depositions tomorrow of Jennifer and her father. I want Catherine to take a screen shot of this and make a blow-up for me to use as evidence that this girl was chasing after Jay."

"Will it help? Is there anything that will get my boy out of this mess?"

"I'll do everything I can. Please know that and keep praying." I handed the phone to Catherine and walked Mrs. Lincoln out to the parking lot.

As I headed back into the office, a car came speeding into the lot. I turned and saw Vivian Suarez jumping out of her unmarked police car. My parking lot was turning into our meeting place.

"Mary, glad I caught you. We have our shooter thanks to the tip you received."

"Come into the office and tell me everything," I said.

We settled into the chairs in front of my desk. Catherine came in with a pitcher of ice water and glasses.

"Just what I needed. I've been on the go since six a.m. when we arrested Roy Carter and charged him with attempted murder. We've been keeping him under surveillance since we served the search warrant. I was afraid he'd split before we were through getting enough evidence for an arrest warrant. We got him at his girlfriend's apartment."

"You're sure he's the one?"

"Oh, yes. I told you we served a search warrant at his dorm room. We got Brett Fieldstone out of there safely, like I told you we would. When he reported to the dean's office, my partner took a statement from him, where he repeated what he told you.

"I searched the room with two campus officers. We found a Luger revolver fully loaded and a box of bullets. We also took his computer and notebooks. That was all the warrant covered so we couldn't go through his clothes or anything else."

"Did he make any statements?'

"As soon as we got him to our station, he clammed up and said he wanted an attorney. We let him call his parents who told him they had contacted an attorney after we talked to them. They must have known something was wrong when we asked them if Roy was at home that week and was ill. Anyway, they said they'd have the attorney come to our station right away. We waited over an hour and when no one showed, we booked him into the Dade County Jail."

"Vivian, without a statement and just the gun and some lies about where he had been all week, is that going to be enough to charge him with attempted murder? A good attorney could easily create reasonable doubt to a jury, especially since Carlos and I can't identify him."

"You're forgetting that we have Brett Fieldstone's statement. We also have notes he made in his computer showing the location of your office, your home, and a layout of the whole football stadium. Brett told us that the team gets tickets in a particular section of the stadium and that Jay had been bragging that his lawyer would be at the game sitting with his parents. Once Roy knew you'd be at the game in section two hundred, he had the opportunity to mingle with the demonstrators and see if he could spot you. He got lucky and Carlos got unlucky. If he didn't get you there, his next try was probably your office or your home."

"This all sounds weird. It's so unbelievable."

"Well, truth is stranger than fiction, so the saying goes. As a defense attorney, I'm sure you've handled some cases that were even stranger than this. This is just one more for me as a cop. I'm going to show some photos to Carlos just to see if he has any recollection of Roy before the shot."

"When will Roy be in court?"

"Probably this afternoon for bond hearing. It'll be interesting to see who his attorney is."

Chapter Seventy-Four

The afternoon flew by as I prepared for deposing Jennifer and her father. I was ready to gather the photos of the white haired drug dealer and Catherine and head over to Catherine's neighborhood for the show and tell when I heard Reuben's deep voice in the waiting room. In a minute he and Catherine strolled into my office.

"Don't you ladies ever go home? I thought the office would be closed already, but I have to pass this way on my way home. I actually have a little good news."

"Tell us. Did you find *Oso Blanco*?" Catherine looked like a kid waiting for Christmas.

"No, but our whole office is working on it. But we got the calendar and billings for the day Brady got shot. Marco was on surveillance for almost two hours at the Ritz Carlton Hotel and here in the Grove. He didn't want to reveal who the client was that he was working for. It was a confidential matter. All our clients are confidential. I got the name from the file and I went to see her. She's willing to testify that Marco was surveilling her husband. She gave us permission to give her name and to use Marco's activity report."

"That's wonderful. Now Marco has proof that he wasn't lying about where he had been. How did you ever persuade this client to go public?"

"Here's the activity report. When you read it, you'll understand."

Catherine looked over my shoulder as I read.

Notes Re: Case F-2398, Client: Drusilla Lantz

Activity: Took over surveillance of Marty Lantz from investigator Van Luria. Luria advised that subject has been making frequent stops at the Ritz on 27th Avenue. Picked up subject's Range Rover at Bayshore Drive and 17th Ave. at 1:18 p.m. Followed him to 27th Ave. where he parked his

car two blocks from hotel. Subject entered hotel through service entrance at 1:30 p.m. I entered through main entrance and sat in lobby. Spotted subject walk through lobby. He appeared nervous, looking around before entering a corridor leading to several offices. Subject entered a door marked authorized personnel only. He was admitted after ringing a buzzer. Subject is a member of Heat Pro Basketball Team, so he's easy to eyeball. Continued surveillance seated on a bus bench on 27th Ave. where I kept watch on subject's car. Subject returned to Range Rover at 2:25 p.m. Made several calls on cell phone before driving away. Subject was carrying a small briefcase when he returned to his car that he was not in possession of when he exited the vehicle and entered the hotel. Followed subject to Cocoplum Circle where he entered the gated community where he resides. Left off surveillance at 2:55 p.m. Returned to Ritz and went to the office where subject had gone. Buzzed the buzzer and was met by a woman who asked if I had an appointment. I said I must be in the wrong room and asked what office this was. Was told the man I could see seated inside at a desk was Robert Trisko, a jewelry designer who uses these facilities to meet with local buyers when in Miami. Received his card attached to this report. Investigation ended at 3:35p.m..
Investigator: Marco Perez

"I don't understand, why did Mrs. Lantz agree to waive her confidentiality?" I asked.

"I went to see her and showed her the report. I explained that Marco needed to account for his hours because of this ridiculous murder charge. She was sympathetic and began laughing when I showed her the report. It seems that November 2nd is their anniversary. Marty was having special jewelry made for her. He came home that day with a diamond and sapphire ring and necklace that he had ordered for her. She was told by one of her friends that Marty was sneaking out of the Ritz Carlton one afternoon. That's when she hired Pit Bulls to start following him. Of course, Marty is pretty hard to miss. He's six foot four and covered in colorful tattoos. She was pretty embarrassed about being suspicious once she saw the jewelry, and she agreed to allow Marco to share what he did on that afternoon when Brady was killed."

Catherine and I laughed hysterically. We couldn't seem to stop. Now all of Marco's hours were accounted for and we had just enjoyed another weird Miami story.

Chapter Seventy-Five

Catherine and I locked the office as soon as Reuben left. I phoned Carlos to remind him that we were on our way to canvass the neighbors around Catherine's apartment. Carlos answered one of his cell phones. He was at the apartment site checking on the work done that day. We agreed to meet at Tony's Authentic Pizza for a late dinner. I was worried about Carlos working at full steam so soon after his emergency surgery, but I knew my complaints would fall on deaf ears.

We checked in on Catherine's boys before starting our trek. Cory and Phillip were at the kitchen table eating dinner that Catherine had prepared as she did each day before going to work. Her energy was unmatched. The boys' homework was spread out over the rest of the table. I thought what great kids they were after everything they had been through. Catherine was doing a great job as a single parent. We had to get Marco out of this jam. Catherine deserved a piece of a happy life for once.

Our first stop was the bottom floor apartment of the landlady, Mrs. Morehouse. She didn't seem too happy to see Catherine.

"Yes, what is it? I hope you're not here with more disturbing news, or is it to complain about the plumbing in your apartment again? You're lucky I didn't ask you to move after your ex was shot right in front of my building and your boyfriend arrested and the whole story in the news with the address of my building. I run a respectable place."

I decided to intervene and cut off this rant. "Mrs. Morehouse, I'm Mary Katz, Catherine's employer. Marco has been wrongfully arrested. We are going to get his name cleared. All we are asking you to do is look at some pictures and see if you ever saw any of these men hanging around here before Brady was shot. Can you do that for me, please?"

"I guess so. Come in while I find my glasses. I hope this is the last I hear about that damn murder."

She sat down in a sunken and frayed easy chair, put on her glasses and reached for the photos. "I can hardly make out the people in these pictures. How do you expect me to recognize them?"

She turned over the pictures of The Polar Bear and his cronies and turned to the mug shot. She looked a little startled.

"This is the guy who I saw out in front of the building when I took out the trash cans. He even spoke to me; asked me if the Aynsworths lived here."

"What did you tell him?"

"I asked him, who wants to know? What do you want? He said he was from a collection agency and the Aynsworths hadn't been paying their bills. So I said that Catherine Aynsworth had an apartment here and I wasn't surprised if she owed people money. He just laughed and asked when she'd be home. I told him I wasn't sure."

"Was he alone?"

"He got in a car with two other guys."

"What kind of car was it? What did the other guys look like?"

"It was one of them fancy SUV's, a Mercedes I think. I remember now. I thought collection work must pay real good."

"What about the other guys?"

"The windows were so tinted that all I saw was two men's heads. Why do they tint the windows so heavy these days, or is that just in Miami?"

"I don't know about the window tinting. Do you remember what day it was that you talked to the man in the picture?"

"I think it was a day or two before that murder. Hey, are you saying these guys were killers? And I was outside by myself talking to them. My God, Catherine, I just can't have this kind of thing going on here. If it wasn't for your two great sons I'd ask you to move out today."

Catherine glared at Mrs. Morehouse. "Well, you can't make me move. I have a lease and my boss here will take you to court if you try to break it. You'll have to hire an attorney but I won't, so don't even think about it. And I'd love to move but I have to get my boyfriend out of jail first."

"Okay, Catherine, get a grip," I said. "You've been very helpful Mrs. Morehouse." I took Catherine's arm and led her outside before she punched the old lady.

"That old bitch, she never even told me that anyone was asking about me. And I always pay my bills." Catherine's hands were clenched in fists.

"It's okay, Catherine. This is all good. Morehouse can testify that a notorious drug dealer was nosing around here looking for Brady. Let's see if anyone else can identify anyone in the pictures."

I led the way to the 7-11 store on the corner. "Let's see if anyone in here saw any of these guys."

The store was full of people on their way home from work. Several were filling out Powerball cards. There was the usual assortment of construction workers and delivery truck drivers. The man behind the counter was of some Arab background. He was dispensing cigarette packs to a couple of sweat-soaked grimy workmen.

"Do you know the sales guy?" I asked Catherine.

"Sure, that's Mr. Habib. I stop here with the kids for candy rewards."

"Well, here, go chat him up," I said as I handed her the photos.

She pushed her way to the front of the counter. The two cigarette buyers frowned at her.

"Hey, Mr. Habib, how are you? How's your wife? She's not working tonight?"

"Catherine, hi, where are Cory and Phillip? My wife's home with my son and grandson tonight. What do you need?"

"The boys are doing their homework. I know you're busy, but could you look at some pictures for me and see if you recognize any of these guys? It's real important for Marco's case."

"Sure, let me see. Give my best to Marco. He's such a gentlemen. I know everything will be okay for him. Well, I think I saw this guy." He pointed to one of the men in the surveillance photo. "It's a little hard to be sure, but I think this guy came in the store a couple of times. He sort of hung around, watching the people coming in. He made me nervous. I thought he was going to rob me. The second time he did that, stood around like that, I asked him if I could help him. He said he was waiting to meet someone, so I told him this isn't a social club and please to wait outside. Most people who come in the store, they look at magazines or check out the beer cooler. He just checked out the other customers."

"Thanks, Mr. Habib. This could help us."

"Say, wait a minute, Catherine. Manny, come here a minute." He motioned to one of the men waiting to pay for his cigarettes. "Manny comes in the store almost every evening. Show him the pictures."

Manny looked at Catherine from head to toe and grinned. "You can show me anything, honey. What can I do for you?"

"Could you take a minute and see if you recognize anyone in these photos? Anyone hanging out in the neighborhood. Mary, come over here. Mr. Habib, this is my boss, Mary Magruder Katz. She's a lawyer and she's helping Marco."

I stepped over to the counter. Manny gave me the same ogling treatment and then turned back to the photos.

"Holy crap. This is the guy I almost got in a fight with." Manny pointed to the same man that Habib thought he recognized.

"I was standing outside of the store here and this guy kept looking at me. So I says to him, do I know you? And he says, maybe. He's looking for a guy about my height and build named Brady Aynsworth. So I says, no never heard of him. So he says, you're sure that's not you? So I says, yeah I'm sure. I guess I know who I am. So he says, you better not be lying to me or my boss'll make sure you can't lie to anyone else. That made me mad and I grabbed him by his shirt and shoved him against the wall."

"When did this happen?" I asked.

"Maybe ten days ago, maybe two weeks. Anyway, we were about to go at it when another guy got out of a car that pulled up right next to us and told the guy who called me a liar to get in the car right now." Manny looked down at the photos in his hand. "And I think I saw this guy in the back of the car."

He pointed to the photo of *Oso Blanco*. "I remember the white hair and beard."

"This is great, Manny." Please, give me your full name and how to reach you. A phone number or an e-mail," I said.

"Geez, lady, I don't want to be a witness. I mind my own business," Manny said.

"Oh, please, Manny. It'd mean so much to me if you'd just identify these men if it becomes necessary." Catherine gave Manny a flirty smile.

"Well, okay, but I can't promise to go to court or nothing." Manny took the paper and pen I held out to him and hurriedly wrote his name and phone number.

We thanked Mr. Habib and almost skipped down the street to Catherine's apartment house.

Chapter Seventy-Six

After another night of togetherness with Carlos, I felt rested. I was ready to face the de Leons' depositions. I expected attitude problems, lies, and fake tears from Jennifer, but I felt on top of it all. Well, I was only slightly nervous to be honest.

I stopped in at the office and instructed Catherine to set up appointments with Mrs. Morehouse, Manny and Mr. Habib to take their statements with a court reporter. It was essential to nail down their photo ID's under oath.

"Tell them that we'll come to them wherever they want, work or home, at the time that's convenient. I'm pretty sure Manny won't mind seeing you again, Catherine. Once we have those statements and the report showing Marco's surveillance hours the day of the murder, I can draft a Motion to Dismiss the charges against Marco. Maybe then the police will go after *Oso Blanco*."

The traffic going to the courthouse was so light that I thought maybe it was Sunday. Then I realized it was Veteran's Day, November eleventh, and the schools were closed. It dawned on me that some courts were also closed. I hoped this wasn't going to be an excuse for the depositions to be cancelled.

I pulled into a parking place on the street just feet from the front steps of the courthouse, and fed the meter enough coins to cover five hours. No more towed cars were going to be in my future.

No one was in line at the metal detectors. The security lady actually smiled at me. The lobby echoed with my footsteps. The elevator opened the minute I pushed the UP button and I was whizzed up to the fourth floor. Frank Fieldstone stood by the elevator as I alighted.

"This was a clever move, setting the depositions on a semi-holiday. De Leon can't complain about missing work. Fred Mercer can't say he's too busy to spend time here and Jennifer can't say she's missing school," Frank said as he tried to take my brief case from me.

"I can handle my briefcase case. I'd love to take credit for being clever, but I forgot it was a holiday."

"This is like old times, Mary. You and I on a case together. It feels great," Frank said. He put his hand on the small of my back as we walked along to the conference room I had reserved.

"Don't get any wrong ideas, Frank. Remember, you're just here as window dressing, nothing more, and especially not as my boyfriend."

I did remember cases Frank and I had worked when we traveled to New York for depositions and stayed at a sexy hotel across from Central Park. It was winter and we could see the skaters on the pond and the snow sticking to the trees. It had been very romantic, but that was then and now things were very different. I wasn't sure Frank understood that I was absolutely unavailable. I also wasn't sure why I was thinking back to romantic thoughts about Frank.

The door to the conference room stood open. I could see the court reporter setting up her machine. Fred Mercer was seated at the long table reading notes from his file. This room was a big improvement over the stifling room we used for the last depositions. Now I understood why I was able to book this big space. No one else was working.

"I see that you're still persisting in going forward with this case," Fred said as soon as I entered the room.

"Nothing has changed except that I'm more sure that Jay Lincoln is innocent of the charges. See how you feel after we finish these depositions," I said.

"Here's my offer, pre-deposition only. Jay pleads No Contest, and gets a three year prison sentence and five years' probation. I'm authorized to make this offer if your client takes it now to spare the victim from having to relive the events that are probably going to scar her for life."

"You've got to be kidding. The real victim here is Jay who was led to believe that Jennifer was a college-age student with an over active sex drive. He's the one being scarred for life. I know I have to present any plea offers to my client. That's the law, so I will ask you to go outside to the waiting room while I try to locate him by telephone. Please have your witnesses remain in the courthouse. No depositions have been cancelled."

"If your client refuses the plea, how do you intend to go forward with this case?"

"Listen, Fred, I intend to fight these charges all the way to the Supreme Court of Florida if necessary, so get ready for trial. I might even make new law in this state."

Fred shook his head and left the room.

I pulled my cell phone out of my briefcase, found the Lincolns' number in my contacts and hit speed dial.

"It looks like we've got our work cut out for us," Frank said. "I guess we'll be seeing a lot of each other."

Mrs. Lincoln answered after several rings. I heard a car honk in the background.

"Mary, how are you? Is everything okay?"

"Everything's fine. I'm about to take the depositions of Mr. de Leon and his daughter, but the State has made a plea offer and by law I must present it to Jay. Do you know how I can get in touch with him?"

"I do know. He's in the car with me right this minute. We're on our way to pick up my husband and then we're headed to an award ceremony. My niece is getting a scholarship from our Kiwanis Club. What's this about a plea? What does that mean?'

"Mrs. Lincoln, can you put your phone on speaker. I can explain this to you and Jay together."

"Sure, but Jay's not guilty of anything."

"Hi, Mary, what's up?" Jay's deep voice boomed through the phone.

I explained what a plea agreement is and what No Contest meant. Then I told them about three years in prison and the extended probation. I heard the two Lincolns talking to each other, but I couldn't make out what they were saying. It sounded like they were arguing.

Then Jay spoke to me. "Mary, I know I didn't do anything like a crime. I never raped anyone, but I'm scared. What if we go to trial and we lose. How long could I go away for?"

"No one can predict with certainty what a judge will do. It could be a long sentence. You could be placed on the sex offender list and you would be a convicted felon."

"I'm not letting my Jay enter any plea even if no contest doesn't mean guilty," his mother screamed. "Why are you even suggesting such a thing?"

"I'm not suggesting it. I'm just telling you and Jay what the state has offered before I depose this Jennifer person. I have to tell you about any plea offer. It's my job, but I'm not advocating anything, Mrs. Lincoln. Please remember that this isn't my decision or yours. It's Jay's and if things go badly, he's the one at risk, not you or me."

"Mary, are you willing to go ahead with this case, if I don't take this plea?" Jay asked.

"I'll tell you what I just told the prosecutor. I will fight this case all the way to the Supreme Court if I have to."

"That's it then. I know you're a good lawyer. I've got a good feeling about you, so the answer is no, no plea. I'll live with whatever."

"Mary, you go give that girl what-for, you hear?" Mrs. Lincoln said.

"That's what I wanted to hear." I turned off my phone and pulled out my notes for the depositions.

Chapter Seventy-Seven

We were gathered around the conference table; Frank and I on one side and Fred and Tim de Leon on the other. At the head of the table the court reporter, Annie Miller, was seated with her stenographic machine in front of her. We were ready to go.

"Please state your full name for the record and your address."

"I am Timothy de Leon. I live in Coral Gables, but I'm not giving my address. I don't want that on the record."

"Mr. de Leon, you have been sworn by the court reporter so you are testifying under oath. Do you understand what that means?"

"So you're calling me a liar already? I'm not going to be abused by any woman lawyer."

Fred placed a hand on Tim's arm. "Tim, no one is saying you're going to lie. Ms. Katz is just making sure that you understand your oath."

"I understand just fine," Tim said.

"Now Mr. de Leon. What is your occupation?"

"I work for a wholesale grocery company in the sales department."

"Do you have children?"

"Yes, two, Jennifer and Jeffrey"

"How old are they/"

"Jennifer is sixteen and Jeffrey is eleven."

"Does your work in sales require frequent travel?'

"I don't know if you'd say frequent. I call on clients in Florida and Georgia."

"How many nights a month are you away from home?"

"It varies. Probably eight to ten."

"Is it correct that your wife doesn't reside with you and the children?"

"You apparently already know that. Yes, correct."

"Who takes care of your children when you're away?"

"Jennifer is not a child."

"Oh, so you would classify Jennifer as what? A mature young adult?"

"She's a teenager. She can help with Jeffrey, but I also have a housekeeper."

"Are you aware that Jennifer and her friend Candy have made frequent trips to the University campus in the evenings?"

"No. She was there the night she was raped. She doesn't hang out there."

"Do you know Jennifer's friend, Candy Gomez?"

"I think I know which one she is."

"She's Jennifer's best friend, isn't she?'

"I'm not sure of that."

"Can you name another person who is Jennifer's best friend?"

"I don't have to name her friends for you."

"Isn't it a fact that you don't actually know who Jennifer's friends are?"

"I'm not going to answer that."

"Now if Candy Gomez says that she and Jennifer hung out on the campus many evenings last spring are you disputing that?"

"Yes, she's probably jealous of Jennifer"

"Isn't it true that Mrs. Gomez, Candy's mother called you and asked if Jennifer had a party at your home and told you that her daughter had been drinking at that alleged party?"

"She called me and I told her I didn't know anything about a party."

"And the reason you didn't know is that you weren't at home that whole week, isn't that right?"

"Look, I have to make a living. I employ a housekeeper."

"You never questioned the housekeeper about Jennifer having a party or about where she was going in the evenings, did you?"

"Of course not. That would look like I didn't trust my daughter."

"Now, the police reports state that you first learned of an alleged sexual encounter between Jennifer and Jay Lincoln when you saw a picture of Jennifer in her phone, a picture of Jennifer almost completely nude, correct?"

"Yes, that's right."

"Annie, please mark this photo as exhibit one," I said as I passed a copy of the screen-shot from Jay's cell phone.

Fred was on his feet. "What is that? Let me see it."

"Here, Fred, is a copy for you. You don't have to grab the exhibit from Annie."

Annie passed the marked photo back to me. I showed it to Frank who stifled a laugh as he looked at the voluptuous photo of Jennifer.

"Now, Mr. de Leon, please look at exhibit one. Is this the photo you found in Jennifer's phone?"

"Yes, and I was shocked."

"What did Jennifer say when you showed her the photo?"

"She started crying and told me that Jay Lincoln, the so-called football star, had lured her to his dorm room and took pictures of her undressed like that. That's when I learned she had been molested by that jerk."

"So you believe that Jay sent this photo to Jennifer's phone?"

"Yes, of course, that's what she told me."

"Would you look at exhibit one again, please. Do you see the heading at the top of the exhibit and would you read it out loud for the record?"

"Okay, it says, ah, from Jenn@aol.com to Jayftball@miami.edu.org._Wait, this must be one of your lawyer tricks."

"Mr. De Leon, let me show you the actual cell phone this screen shot came from." I pulled Jay's phone from my briefcase and passed it to Fred Mercer and de Leon.

They examined the phone together and the photo. Mercer frowned and asked for the phone to be marked as an exhibit.

"I'd like to return the phone to Jay, but if you insist we can make it part of this deposition." I passed the phone to Annie who slapped an exhibit sticker on the back of the phone.

"Now would you agree that the photo was sent by Jennifer to Jay and not the other way around?"

"That's what it looks like, but I'm not agreeing that's right."

"Now, sir, would you agree that Jennifer is smiling in the photo?"

"Yes, she looks like she's smiling." De Leon rubbed his forehead as he looked at the photo of his daughter.

"Does she look like she's being abused in the photo?"

"Objection, calls for speculation," Mercer said.

"I'll withdraw the question," I said. "The charge against Jay Lincoln was alleged to have occurred in May, correct?"

"Yes, you already know that."

"Please just answer the questions. Your daughter didn't tell you anything about this until August when you discovered the picture, right?

"Yes, that's right"

"So during the summer did you find that Jennifer was upset or nervous or exhibiting any traits that would have alarmed you or caused you to worry about her?"

"She spent part of the summer with her mother."

"Do you discuss your children with their mother?"

"Sure, we communicate some."

"Did she ever tell you Jennifer was acting strangely?"

"Not that I can remember."

"Before Jennifer left to visit her mother or when she returned was there anything about Jennifer that seemed different to you in any way?"

"No, that's why it was such a shock when I found out she had been assaulted."

"Did you ever ask her why she was at the university?"

"She was crying and hysterical."

"I'll take that as a no. Did you ask her how she got to the campus?"

"Yes, she said Jay came and picked her up; that they met at Wendy's Restaurant near the campus."

"Did you ask her how she got home?"

"She said she didn't remember because she had been drugged."

"Did you get a definite date of when these events occurred?"

"She gave the police officer the date. She told me she wasn't sure."

"Once you knew the date did you ask your housekeeper or your son, Jeff, whether they had noticed that Jennifer was ill or upset around that date, or out late that night?"

"I asked Jeffrey if his sister had been upset around that time."

"What did he say?"

"Do I have to answer that?"

Mercer nodded his head.

De Leon took a deep breath. "Jeffrey said that Jennifer was just her usual nasty self. He and Jenn don't get along too well. You know brother-sister stuff."

"Did you ever take Jennifer to see a psychologist or any other professional for help after this alleged trauma?"

"We talked about it, but Jennifer didn't want to go. She said she just wanted to put it out of her mind."

"Reporting the incident to the police meant bringing all of this up repeatedly. So even though she wanted to put it all out of her mind, she had the charge filed against Jay?"

"She didn't want to do that either, but I insisted. I couldn't see having that boy possibly doing this to some other girl."

"I'm almost through Mr. de Leon, just one last question. Is it fair to say that the only sign that Jennifer had been assaulted was the time when you discovered the nude photo in her phone and that was three months after the alleged assault?"

"I suppose so."

"Okay, that's all my questions. Thanks for your patience, sir. Fred, do you want to ask any questions?"

"Just a couple." Fred looked through his notes while we waited. "No, thanks, no questions."

We all stood up to stretch and Annie headed out the door. It was time for a break before confronting Jennifer.

Chapter Seventy-Eight

Frank and I went down to the cafeteria and got coffee while everyone geared up for the deposition of Jennifer.

"You did a good job on the father, Mary, but this next deposition is going to be tough. It appears that Jennifer is an accomplished liar," Frank said.

"It looks like you're getting into the case after all," I said.

"You know I like to win. I'd like to hire a psychologist that I use in some cases to examine Jennifer and have a professional be able to say that she's a troubled girl who consistently lies."

"My client can't afford to pay an expert even though it's a good idea."

"Never mind that. My office can do this as a pro bono project."

"That's really generous of you, Frank. I'll think about it."

We walked back to the elevator and to the conference room without speaking. I was gathering my momentum for the next hours. I looked at Frank and realized that he was staring at me like Sam does when he's waiting for his dinner.

Annie, Fred, Frank and I settled back into our usual seating pattern. Fred cleared his throat and motioned to Annie that we were back on the record.

"Before we begin the questioning of the victim in this case, I want to let you know that her father has insisted that he be present with his daughter during her deposition. He has the right to be with her since she is a minor."

"She looks pretty grownup in her photo," Frank said.

"Don't you want to get to the truth, Fred? With her father present, she's going to continue to perpetuate what she has told him. It's my belief that she is a pathological liar. I want the opportunity to challenge her assertions. Her father can't object to the questions. They could have hired an attorney to represent her and sit with her here today," I said.

"I explained that to Tim, but he said he didn't want a lawyer messing with her, so I think you have to let her father be in here."

"You know, Fred, I could have insisted that Jay be present. It's his right to confront the witnesses against him. Maybe I should postpone this until Jay can be present too," I said.

"I would fight that before the judge," Fred said.

I told Fred that Frank and I needed a minute to confer. I motioned Frank to follow me into the hallway.

"Mary, I think the father gets to stay, but I will caution him that he can't interrupt or object and that we could have a judge present to make any decisions about the questions, and that will take more time while we find the judge in the case," Frank said.

I nodded in agreement and we returned to the conference room. I asked Annie to bring in Tim and Jennifer de Leon. They came into the room behind Annie. Tim had his hand on Jennifer's shoulder. We were all seated with Jennifer at the table next to Fred and Tim relegated to a chair next to the door.

Annie swore in the witness who answered 'I do' in a shaky voice. Then Frank explained to both de Leons that Jennifer was to answer truthfully, Tim was not to interrupt, and if there were too many objections, we would move the deposition to a courtroom with the judge present to make decisions, causing a delay in the completion of the deposition.

Then I explained that I would not be leaving here today until the deposition was completed even if we had to wait hours for the judge to be present.

De Leon sighed. "Jennifer intends to answer your questions but I don't want her to be beaten up."

I ignored his remark and began the deposition that I hoped would save the future of Jay Lincoln.

"State your full name for the record, please."

"Jennifer Susan de Leon."

"How old are you, Jennifer and what is your date of birth?"

"I'm sixteen. My birthday is June fifteenth."

"Do you attend school?"

"Of course. I'm a junior at Coral Gables High School."

"Who else lives in your home?"

"My dad and my little brother."

"What about your housekeeper? Does she live in your house?"

"Sometimes when my dad is away."

"What is her name?"

"Jonelle Geiger."

"Do you get along well with Jonelle?"

"Sure. She's okay."

"Where does your mother live?"

"In Orlando."

"Your best friend at school is Candy Gomez, correct?"

"She's one of my friends."

"Now you were on the University of Miami campus on the night that you accused Jay Lincoln of some misconduct, is that correct?"

"Yes, I was there."

"How many other times in the last nine months did you visit the campus?"

"I went there once to use the library."

"What about the other five times you went there with Candy?"

"I don't know what you're talking about."

"Candy Gomez has given a sworn statement that she accompanied you there on five occasion. You have sworn to tell the truth here today. Do you want to rethink your last answer?"

"I might have forgotten some other times I went to work on a school project."

"Do you recall the night that you and Candy went to the campus and crashed a fraternity party?"

"I don't know anything about a fraternity party."

"Let me try to help you remember. Don't you recall that you got a ride to the campus and you and Candy pretended to be students at the university when you went to the fraternity party?"

"No, that didn't happen."

"Don't you remember that you and Jay Lincoln were making out when Candy asked you to get her home, that she was drunk and sick?"

"That's just not true."

"Don't you recall calling Jonelle, your housekeeper to come and get you?"

"You're just making this up."

"Don't you remember telling Candy that you gave Jonelle money to keep her quiet about your activities?"

"Daddy, make her stop saying these lies."

"Your father is here as a courtesy. Jennifer, I will be subpoenaing Jonelle to give a statement in this case. Now you stated to the police officer that Jay Lincoln tricked you into going to his dorm room. When did you first meet Jay?"

"I'm not sure when."

"Well, was it before the fraternity party you attended with Candy or after that?"

"It was a long time ago, so I can't remember. Maybe he hung around my high school"

"It was when you waited for him outside the football locker room last spring, wasn't it?"

"I didn't do that."

"Isn't that where you took pictures of him that are in your phone?"

"Do I have to keep answering her?" Jennifer looked at Fred Mercer.

Before Fred could answer her, Mr. de Leon stood up. "You will have to answer every question, Jennifer. I want to hear some answers too.

"I guess I took some pictures of him and some other players."

"And at some point you took a picture of yourself and sent it to Jay, correct, and you saved that picture in your phone?"

"Jay took that picture of me and sent it to my phone."

"Let me show you exhibits one and two, Jennifer." I passed the screen-shot and phone to Jennifer. Isn't this the picture that you sent Jay?"

"No, he did this to me when he raped me." Jennifer had begun to cry.

"You look pretty happy in this photo, wouldn't you agree?"

"I don't have to agree with you."

Jennifer, please look at the addresses above the picture. You can see that it says from you to Jay's e-mail address and it says in the subject line, Do you think I'm hot? You can read that can't you?"

"You're trying to trick me."

"Now how did you get to the campus on the night you ended up in Jay's dorm room?"

"He picked me up at a restaurant."

"What kind of car did he drive?"

"I can't remember. I think it was a black SUV."

"You texted Jay and made a date with him, didn't you?"

"No, he called me."

"Well, I have Jay's phone right here and I have also subpoenaed all his phone records from last May, and it shows more than one call from you to Jay. Shall I go through the phone and see when you called him?"

"I don't want to answer any more questions."

"You have to complete the deposition, Jennifer," Fred Mercer said.

"How did you get home after this alleged assault by Jay?"

"I can't remember. Jay gave me stuff to drink and I think I was drugged."

"When did you wake up again?'

"I think I was in Jay's car again."

"Well, where did you go in that car?"

"I guess he drove me home."

"So first he assaulted you and then you got in a car with him and let him drive you home?"

"I guess so."

"How did he know where you lived?"

"I must have told him."

"But he thought you lived in a dorm on the campus. Didn't he offer to walk you back to your dorm?"

"I'm not going to answer any more of this."

"Mr. Mercer, please instruct the state's witness to answer the question."

"Ms. de Leon, you must answer the questions put to you," Fred said.

"Jay believed you lived in a dorm and were a student at the university didn't he?" I asked again.

"I don't know what he thought. You are one awful bitch." Jennifer pounded the table with her fist.

"Please just answer my questions. This deposition will take longer if you don't answer. Now you told your father and the police that this alleged assault took place in May, correct?"

"You already know that."

"But the first time you reported this to anyone was in August when your father found your nude picture in your phone, isn't that right?"

"Yes, I told him in August."

"Is the reason you didn't make a report sooner because you were the aggressor, you set up the date with Jay with the intention of having sex with him?"

"No, that's not right. He raped me." Jennifer was staring at her father who looked away from her.

"Okay, Jennifer, I think we've all heard enough. Let me just ask you one last question. Isn't it true that you made Jay believe that you were a student at Miami, and isn't it also true that you pursued him, that you told Candy you were going to have sex with him, and that your plan worked?"

Jennifer stared straight ahead tears running down her cheeks. She remained silent.

"Can the witness be excused?" Fred asked.

"Yes, I don't believe I need to ask this witness anything else," I said.

Jennifer, please wait outside for me for a minute." Tim de Leon pulled Jennifer from her seat and escorted her to the door. He looked close to tears himself.

The door closed behind Jennifer. I stood too and moved over next to Tim.

"I didn't want to do what I just did to your daughter, but I have a client who will lose his whole life because of Jennifer's accusation. I was hoping that she'd tell me the truth during this deposition."

"I will have to talk at length with my daughter. Needless to say, I am dumbfounded by the idea that she has been going behind my back to the campus, and acting out, if this is true. She has had a bad example due to the actions of her mother, my ex-wife."

"One thing remains clear," Fred interjected. "The fact is Jennifer was a minor and Jay Lincoln had sex with a minor. He doesn't deny it. It's still a felony."

Frank stood and walked around the table. He loomed over Fred. "Are you telling me that you still want to go forward with this case? That you're going to subject this young girl to questioning on the witness stand in front of a jury and a courtroom full of voyeurs? If you think this was a rough day, you've never really seen Mary Katz on a cross-examination."

"I'll speak to you about this in private," Tim said staring at Fred.

"There's nothing to talk about. The charge has been filed. The State has filed this case and I'm the only one who can drop it."

"Hey, was all this on the record too? I took it all down," Annie said.

Chapter Seventy-Nine

By the time I arrived home, I was bleary eyed and felt as if I'd been running a marathon. I hadn't even been to the gym since returning from Vermont. Maybe Carlos and I could go this evening if the doctor had cleared him for exercise.

Carlos and Sam met me at the door. Carlos was dressed in khakis and a white button down shirt.

"Are you dressed for a Great Gatsby costume party?" I asked after a quick kiss.

"You don't remember do you? We're supposed to have dinner with your parents tonight."

"Oh, no, not tonight. I'm wrung out from depositions."

"Sorry, Mary, they're your parents and you've been neglecting them. Go get into comfortable clothes and let's go."

I dumped my suit, and panty hose, and found my favorite jeans. When I pulled them over my hips, they didn't glide. It was more like a tug-of-war with a too short rope. They didn't button at all. Not even close. "Oh, my God," I screamed.

Sam and Carlos ran into the bedroom. "What's wrong? Are you okay?" Carlos grabbed me.

"I haven't been to the gym or even walked Sam, and I'm going to lose Jay's case, and I'm fat!"

"You are not fat. You are as sexy as always. I thought there was a rat in here when you screamed." Carlos was laughing. He pulled the jeans off of me and pushed me on to the bed. Sam decided to pop onto the bed as well, and soon in a tangle of arms and legs and paws we were all laughing, except for Sam who was licking my face.

"Maybe later I said," as I got up, washed my face, pulled on a maxi-dress generally used for a beach cover-up and now used to cover up lack of exercise. I remembered to brush my hair in hopes that Mother wouldn't do her usual number about how nice I'd look if I'd just take the time to blow dry.

We got into Carlos's Escalade and as we roared across the causeway to Miami Beach, I fell into a comforting sleep.

Chapter Eighty

The condo that Mother and Dad were renting was on the fifteenth floor. I smelled Mother's pot roast as we arrived at their door.

I hugged both of them and remarked about how well they both looked. Dad was as slim as he had been when I was a teenager. He was suntanned and looked totally rested. Mother was beaming as she showed me the view from the balcony. The beach and the ocean were visible in the fading daylight. A yacht swished by, its lights reflecting on the water.

"This is peaceful. No wonder you and Dad look so rested," I said.

"It's just what your dad needed and me too, I guess. We love being here. Last night we went to the performing arts center and saw a play and this weekend we're going to the antique show. But how do you like the décor in the apartment? Everything is white. I was afraid to serve meals at first."

We moved to the table in an alcove off of the living room. Pot roast, mashed potatoes, fresh veggies and hot rolls awaited us. Mother's comfort food was making the stress of the day recede.

"What have you decided about staying in Miami?" I asked

"We're going to take the plunge," Dad said. "Mother is going up to Boynton Beach next week to meet with the realtor and get the house on the market."

"That's right, and William has been house hunting down here himself. The Fort Lauderdale commute is too far. He likes the real estate agent that he's using, so we may use her too. Carlos, didn't you recommend her?"

"I did. She's worked with me on selling some houses and condos that I built. She's been in the business a long time. Her name is Tanya Toronto. Catchy isn't it?"

We took our dessert of fresh fruit into the living room. I assumed we weren't having one of Mother's chocolate cheesecakes in deference to Dad's cholesterol.

"Now let's talk about Thanksgiving. Carlos, your mother suggested that we could have it at your house. You have that huge dining room," Mother said.

"Everything in that house is huge," I said.

"I think it's a good idea to use it before I sell the place," Carlos said

"Why would you do that?" Dad asked. I thought you liked it. You built it."

"Mary doesn't feel comfortable in it. It's not her house, and I only moved in because I couldn't get it sold during the recession."

"Are you going to move into Mary's house?" Mother asked.

I could see the wheels turning in Mother's brain, but I didn't want any announcement made about our tentative plan to sell both places and move in together in some imagined dream house. I shook my head at Carlos.

"I don't know. If it sells quickly maybe I'll just get a bachelor pad in one of my buildings," Carlos answered.

I saw Mother and Dad look at each other, so I changed the subject. "What have you and Angie come up with for Thanksgiving dinner?"

"Oh, it's going to be such fun. I'm going to make a roast turkey and cornbread stuffing and a sweet potato casserole from my mother's recipes, and Angie and J.C. are going to deep fry a turkey, Cuban style. Maybe your grandmother or Aunt Myrna will want to do desserts."

"That sounds so multi-ethnic and interesting. What can I bring?" I asked

"You and Carlos don't have to do a thing, just show up. Maybe you can bring us some good news," Mother said.

"Let me help you clear the dishes, Mother, and then we must be going."

"Mary's had a long day," Carlos said, catching my escape signal.

Chapter Eighty-One

Carlos was still sleeping a few mornings later when I tiptoed out before seven. The quiet of the office in the early morning was what I needed to start writing Motions to Dismiss in Marco's case and Jay's case. A pile of transcripts of sworn statements were on my desk. Catherine and I had worked almost around the clock to tie down Mr. Habib, Mrs. Morehouse, and Manny. I had the letter from Sheila Bird, and the investigative report that Marco wrote. Reuben Porter took a sworn statement from Marty Lantz and his wife. Both of them told Reuben they would testify in court if necessary.

In Jay's case, Catherine and I visited with Candy Gomez and her family and took her statement under oath. Annie Miller accompanied us and prepared all the transcripts. She was ecstatic over so much work, and told us she had already picked out her holiday wardrobe at Nordstrom. I had the depositions of Jennifer and her father and the arresting officer. The only way that Jay's case would disappear was if the judge granted the motion. Fred Mercer was not about to drop the case even though Mr. de Leon didn't seem to want to proceed.

I worked at my computer writing and re-writing for the bulk of the day. At six o'clock, Catherine appeared in my office, backpack slung over her shoulder.

"Mary, is there anything else you need tonight? If not, I need to get the boys. Marco's mom picked them up after school and I need to get them home. I haven't spent any time with them this week."

"I'm so sorry, Catherine. I just want these motions to be perfect."

"I know how hard you're working for Marco and me. I don't know how we can repay you, but Marco's parents asked me to give you this." She held out an envelope.

I opened it and found a certified check for fifty thousand dollars. I gasped and dropped the envelope and check.

"Can they afford this? I never asked them to pay me. Marco is almost like a brother to Carlos, not just another of the clan's cousins."

"They worked it out. They are so grateful to you and so am I. This is all my fault anyway. Marco would never have been in this position if I hadn't been associated with Brady. What a stupid mistake I made."

"Catherine, stop beating yourself up. The good that came out of your bad marriage was your super sons. Just keep thinking about them."

I heard the door close as Catherine left. Then I returned to the computer and began correcting the motions. I checked my e-mails before shutting down for the night. I found an e-mail setting the times for the motion hearings. They were both set the week of Thanksgiving, one on Monday and one on Tuesday. I glanced at the time on the computer and was surprised to see that it was eight-thirty. I hadn't realized it was so late. I closed down the computer and printer and began closing up the office. As I checked the locks on the windows, I saw a car pull into the parking lot. The lights in the car went out and two men began walking toward the building.

With the office lights out, I clearly saw the two figures illuminated by the parking lot lights. They approached the outer door of the building. My heart started thumping, loud enough for them to hear me, I thought. Maybe they're going to the upstairs office that belonged to a group of CPA's, and I'm being paranoid. Then I heard noises on the vestibule door to my offices.

Last June when someone threw a rock through my window, Carlos had insisted that I take one of his guns. I didn't want it, but he insisted, reminding me that everyone in Miami has a gun from pizza delivery men to society mavens. The gun was in my desk drawer hidden under my extra pairs of pantyhose.

"Hey man, this door is unlocked," one of them said.

I shook my head in disbelief when I realized I hadn't gotten around to locking doors yet.

I pointed the gun at the door and put my hand on the light switch. As the door swung open, I pushed the light switch. Two scruffy looking guys stood stunned just feet from me.

"Don't move. Keep your hands where I can see them. I am an accurate shot. Who are you and what do you want?" I hoped they didn't notice that my hand was shaking.

"Wait a minute. We're not here to hurt you."

"Better tell me who you are fast," I said.

"We're DEA agents," the one with the straggly beard said. "I'll show you my badge."

"I said keep your hands in sight." I took a step closer and leveled the gun. The truth was I didn't even know if it had any bullets. "What are you doing in my office at this hour? Didn't you ever hear of making an appointment?"

A noise from the outer doors startled all three of us. Carlos and Reuben Porter came bounding through the door behind the two men. Both Carlos and Reuben had guns pointed at the heads of the two. Both whirled around and then looked back at me. They each raised their hands in the air.

"Get down on the floor," Reuben yelled.

Both guys hit the deck. I could see fear on their faces.

"Carlos, how did you and Reuben get here?" I was half-laughing and half-crying.

"We drove, I mean I was trying to get you but your cell didn't answer. The office phone must have been forwarded to Catherine. She told me she left you at least two hours earlier and she thought you were getting ready to leave. Marco called Reuben and told him to meet me here. Thank God we got here," Carlos moved around the agents who were in a heap on the floor. He took the gun from me and pointed two guns at the floor occupants.

"Enough of this game. What are two DEA agents doing breaking into my law office?" Anger began to replace fear as I looked at these men who looked more like drug dealers than drug cops.

"Mary, I recognize these guys. They actually are agents." Reuben pointed to one of them. "This is the guy who gave me the pictures of Mr. Polar Bear and his pals."

"Listen, Ms. Katz. We had orders to check you out. We weren't sure why you were trying to find *Oso Blanco*. We thought you might be mixed up with a rival drug cartel. It wouldn't be the first time a lawyer was part of an organization," the bearded agent said.

"What?" You were breaking into my office to do what? Go through my files? Find out who my clients are?" That is despicable. I will call the Justice Department and see how they feel about your tactics. I'll call a press conference. In case you didn't get it, I am pissed." I leaned over and tried to take the gun back from Carlos.

"Do you want me to call the Miami Police to haul their asses to the Dade County Jail?" Reuben asked.

I thought for a long minute. "No, I want these poor excuses for law enforcers to give me some help," I said. "I hope you realize that without a search warrant, you have violated my right to be free from unwarranted searches. Something tells me that this isn't the first time you've ignored the Constitution.

"I am defending Marco Perez who is accused of murdering Brady Aynsworth. The reason Reuben obtained the photos for me is that I have reason to believe the kingpin drug dealer you want to nail is the person who actually killed Brady or at least had his people do it for him. Brady owed him considerable dollars." I stopped talking as one of the agents held up his hand.

"Can I speak, please, and can we get up off this floor? Reuben told me some of this, but my boss wanted to be sure this wasn't some bull shit. I apologize for our unannounced visit, but you need to understand that we have a job to do and that's to rid South Florida of enormous drug dealing."

"The ends don't justify the means. Do it right; you could have come to see me and questioned me about my need for your information. Now in lieu of calling the cops to arrest the cops, I need your help in arresting

Oso Blanco and charging him with the murder of Brady Aynsworth. You want him shut down so here's a way to do it. I think I have enough facts to allow you to get an arrest warrant for him and I will share what I have, but I need this to happen ASAP. Once you get him, a confession would be nice too. Carlos, let's put all the guns away before one of us gets shot. Wasn't your last visit to the trauma unit enough?"

Chapter Eighty-Two

The show and tell with the agents was productive. They were impressed with the witness statements, picture identifications and Sheila Bird's letter. They left with copies and were intent on getting the go-ahead from their superior to try for an arrest warrant. They went away happy and we went away to end a long and complicated day.

I felt like I'd only been asleep a few minutes when my cell phone rang and almost immediately I heard Carlos's distinctive phone ring mimicking the chimes of a loud church. I fumbled for the phone and saw the time printout as six a.m.

J.C.'s voice boomed out of my phone, but it didn't sound exactly like him.

"Mary, I'm sorry to wake you, but I need your help right now."

"J. C. what's wrong?"

"I'm at the airport. When I checked in for my flight to Argentina, two NSA officers appeared and sort of arrested me. I'm sure this is some stupid mistake, but I need you to come to the airport if you possibly can."

"Of course, I'll be there in thirty minutes. J.C., listen to me this time. Don't talk to them. Don't answer any questions. The only thing I want you to say is that your lawyer is on the way. Where are they holding you?"

"It's some Miami-Dade airport police station."

"I know where that is. Try to stay calm and just sit there."

"Oh, I can't go anywhere. I'm handcuffed in a holding cell."

I jumped up and started throwing on clothes. Then I heard Carlos on his phone.

"Yes, Mama, Mary is right here getting ready to leave. Yes, I'm sure she is. Please don't worry. We'll sort it all out."

"Your dad called Angie? I've just spoken to him and I'm on my way to the airport."

"I'm coming with you. I can 't believe this. What is this country doing arresting an honest businessman and letting murderers run around loose?"

"Come on, I'll drive. I know how to find the police station in that maze of an airport." I put Sam in the backyard, grabbed my briefcase and keys and wondered how J.C. Martin, a successful entrepreneur could be so naïve.

A scant half hour later we were rushing into the block building that served as a police office and holding area for the airport. Traffic at this early hour was beginning to build but we were a bit ahead of it.

"Well, if it isn't Mary Magruder Katz," Sergeant Masconi called out from the front desk.

We lucked out that he remembered me from Luis Corona's case last June when I was at that airport office trying to find Luis.

"Sergeant, you have a great memory. I'm here representing J.C. Martin. I understand you have him here."

"Yes, ma'am, he's the newest guest of the place. It's been a busy night. We're out of room; two smuggling suspects and an illegal entrant."

"I can help you clear out one cell. Just release Mr. Martin to me."

"You sure have a great sense of humor. The U.S. Attorney's office is on the way over here as we speak to take Mr. Martin. Who's this guy with you?"

"This is Carlos Martin, Mr. Martin's son. Why are they holding my client?"

"There's a material witness hold on him so he's now on the 'no fly' list."

"I need to interview him right now. Can I see him?"

"Yeah, I'll take you back there, but the son can't go. He stays here."

"Now, just a minute," Carlos said. His face turned that fire-engine red that meant he was about to throw a temper tantrum.

"Carlos, it's okay." I squeezed his arm. "You can't be there anyway or attorney-client confidentiality is destroyed."

"Have a seat over there, Sir. Mary, as soon as I search your briefcase and you fill out this form, I'll take you back to him." The sergeant winked at me and smiled.

Chapter Eighty-Three

J.C. was seated on a bench in the stifling holding cell. His face was covered with perspiration.

His always impeccably fresh white button down shirt was wilted. The expression on his face looked like an overripe wrinkled orange.

"Mary, thank you for coming so quickly. This is so embarrassing."

"You needn't be embarrassed. You could have saved yourself this unpleasantness if you had listened to me and not run off to meetings with prosecutors without my knowledge or presence."

"Don't scold me, please. Is that meeting what this is related to?"

"The feds have placed you on material witness status. They have the ability to hold you indefinitely pending a trial against the bank officers if they feel you are fleeing from testifying. That is what they believe you are doing, running away to Argentina. Who is the assistant U.S. attorney who you met with?"

"His name is, let me think. I'm so upset I can't think clearly."

"This is important, J.C. Just take a deep breath and concentrate for a moment."

"Oh, I've got it; Patrick McDonald. Yes, that's it."

"According to the desk sergeant, he's on his way here. I need to call a friend at the U.S. attorneys' and see what I can do to straighten this out. Did you make any deals with McDonald, or did he promise you immunity? Did you tell him you were represented by counsel?"

"We didn't make any agreements. I was stupid not to nail down something."

"I'm going out to the lobby again to make some phone calls. I'll head McDonald off as soon as he arrives. Do not talk to anyone about anything without me present."

"Okay, Mary. Listen, maybe you can get Senator Gilberto's office. Maybe he can help. He's an old friend of Angie's family."

I sat down next to Carlos and asked him for his cell phone.

"Can you fix this, Mary? How bad is it?"

"I hope so. I don't know how bad it is yet."

Chapter Eighty-Four

My first call was to Lucy Stern, my best friend for life, as my nephews would label her. Lucy's husband is an assistant U.S. attorney. The time on the wall clock above the front desk said seven-thirty. If I was lucky, Steve would still be at home.

"Hello, Carlos?" Lucy must have read the caller ID.

"No, Lucy, it's Mary. Is Steve still at home? I have a problem and I need his help."

"He's here. Are you and Carlos okay?"

"Yes, it's Carlos's dad who isn't okay."

After explaining to Steve where I was and what had happened to J.C., I told him the case belonged to Patrick McDonald.

"Oh, shit," Steve said. "He's a real hard ass. Let me call my division chief and tell him the facts you've just given me. I'll try to help."

My next call was to Senator Gilberto's office in Miami. I didn't expect to get anything but voicemail this early in the morning. Instead a pleasant baritone voice answered.

"Good morning, my name is Mary Katz. I'm an attorney representing J.C. Martin. Is the assistant to the senator who heads his Miami office available?"

"No, she doesn't come in until nine but maybe I can help you. This is Glenn Gilberto."

"Senator Gilberto? You're answering your own phone? And you're in Miami?"

"Yes to both questions. I spend three day weekends here in Miami whenever I can and I like to hear what's going on in my office. Now what's this about J.C.?"

I filled the senator in on J.C.'s predicament. He was startled to hear that he was being held at the airport and promised to begin making calls at once.

I handed the phone back to Carlos just as the door opened and two men in dark suits and power red ties walked in. One carried a briefcase and the other a large file.

"Is one of you gentlemen Patrick McDonald?" I asked.

"Yes, that's me," the briefcase carrier said. "Who are you?"

"I am Mary Katz, J.C. Martin's attorney. This is Carlos Martin, Mr. Martin's son. I am angry right now about the treatment of my client who is a well- known businessman and civic donor in Miami-Dade County. I am also puzzled as to why you took a statement from Mr. Martin who voluntarily came to see you, and who told you he had an attorney, without first contacting me. How could you put him on a 'no fly' list after he assisted you in your investigation? You should appreciate that he acted as a concerned citizen."

"Now just a minute Ms. Katz," McDonald said as he glanced at the card I thrust into his hand. Mr. Martin came to see me of his own free will. If he wanted you there with him, he could have invited you to join him. We know of his ties to Argentina and suspected that he might return there."

"Mr. Martin has been a U.S. citizen for thirty-five years. If anyone had bothered to look, they would have seen that his ticket to Argentina is a round trip ticket, returning here in less than a week."

"That doesn't mean that he was actually going to come back," the other dark suited man said.

"Excuse me a minute," McDonald said. "I need to take this call from my office."

He stepped to the side of the lobby and we could hear him saying 'yes, I understand' several times. He turned the phone off and started toward us when his phone rang again. This time he went outside the front door and was gone for several minutes. When he returned, he was the color of his power tie.

"Ms. Katz, please step outside. You and I need to have a conversation. McDonald's invitation came out like a threat as he hurled his words at me.

"I'll come with you," Carlos said.

"No, Carlos this is an attorney conference," I said as I gave him a slight shove back into his chair.

I followed McDonald out into the now sunny fresh air.

"I guess you think you're pretty smart, bringing the influence of a senator who just happens to be on the judiciary committee that funds my office's budget. You may prevail today, but this isn't the end of J.C. Martin's problems. I've been instructed to lift the hold on him for now, but I really mean for now."

"Look Mr. McDonald, Mr. Martin is not your enemy. I'm not your enemy either. But I'm not going to let my client cooperate further with you until I've worked out an immunity package with your office. Once that occurs, I will allow my client to answer your questions and provide you with any information that he has regarding Seaside Bank. Mr. Martin's family lives here. They have been a part of Miami for more than fifty years. They own businesses, homes, and raised families here."

"Right now I'm not in the mood to discuss anything with you. I will do the paper work to release your client as I've been instructed to only because I have a family to feed and I need my job, not because I'm impressed with your little speech."

McDonald slammed through the door of the police station. I followed him in. Carlos and I waited for the subdued J.C. to appear in the company of Sergeant Masconi who handed him his watch, wallet, wedding band, cell phone, carry-on case, and St. Christopher's medal. As we walked him to my car, J.C. was on his phone booking another flight to Argentina.

Chapter Eighty-Five

It was only nine-thirty when I pulled into the office parking lot after driving Carlos and J.C. to J.C.'s condo in the Grove. It seemed like late afternoon.

Catherine met me at the door. "Mary, thank goodness you're here. Humberto Mesa, the DEA agent has been trying to reach you. They have the arrest warrant for *Oso Blanco* and they want to go over some things with you and ask you a few questions about locations where they can look for him."

"That's great. I'll call him back as soon as I take a restroom break. You don't know the morning I've had."

I told Catherine J.C's airport arrest and my rescue mission. She stopped me before I could finish the story.

"Don't call the DEA guy. He wants you to come over to their office right away."

"Oh, no. Isn't that back by the airport?

"It's in the Doral office complex. Yes, it's near the airport. You should have answered your phone. I left you a message. You could have gone directly there."

In a few minutes I was back in the car headed through traffic. I turned onto the 836 toward the airport and Doral. Traffic was stop and go. I kept hitting the brakes but they didn't seem to be responding, so I pulled into the far right lane and then on to the shoulder. A funny burning smell was filling the car. The heat indicator was all the way to hot. The motor trembled and stopped. When I tried to engage it again, it was as silent as a graveyard. The trembling might be my poor Ford SUV's death rattle, I thought.

I reached for my cell and speed-dialed Franco. One of the mechanics picked up and went into a long Spanish explanation of the shop's hours and location.

"Hi, it's Mary Katz. Let me speak to Franco."

"You can't."

"Why not?"

"Because he went to Bimini for the weekend. Not here 'til Monday."

"Well, my car has died. Can anyone come over from the shop? I'm stuck on the 836."

"Oh my God, that's bad."

"I know that's bad. Can you come or send one of the guys?"

"No, not today. Maybe tomorrow. Only two of us here and the other guy don't know nothing about how to fix anything."

"Then why is he working there?"

"Who knows. Ask Franco. He felt sorry for the guy. He just got here from Domican. He needed a job. Sorry, got to go now. We're real busy."

My next plea for help went to Catherine. "Hi, it's me. My car just died. Do you still have Marco's car? Can you come and get me?"

"Sure, I'll lock the office and forward the phone. Give me your exact location, and should I call the DEA agent?"

"Better yet, call Reuben and send him over there. He knows everything that I do about Brady's killer. Just come and get me off of this frigging freeway."

Chapter Eighty-Six

Catherine pulled up behind the dead Explorer. She gave me the news that she had called Carlos who was arranging for a tow truck.

"Why did you call him?" He'll just start worrying and he'll go into his rant about buying me a new car."

"Oh, poor you," Catherine said. "Excuse me for a lack of sympathy. Just about every single woman in all fifty states would love to have a handsome guy offering her a new car. Stop being such a jerk. I promised Carlos you'd call as soon as I got here. We have to sit here and wait for the tow truck anyway."

We got out of the car and stood in the weeds, far from the noisy traffic. The car was too hot to stay in it for long without the air conditioning. The windows wouldn't open without the motor running. We could only open one door. The driver side door would be ripped off by the on-coming traffic. There was nothing to do except call Carlos.

"Mary, listen, I have a whole surprise weekend planned for us. Just listen, and don't interrupt. We need some relaxation, so tonight we're going to the hockey game and finally use the tickets you wanted. Tonight it's beer and hot dogs and hockey.

"Who are they playing?"

"It's the Montreal Canadiens."

"Great, the place will be jumping with the crazed Montreal fans."

"First thing tomorrow morning we will take off for my parents condo on Marco Island. Two days on the beach, just you and me and Sam."

"Carlos, it sounds like heaven, but I can't do it. I have the motion hearings next week in Jay's case and Marco's case. It's probably my last chance to free both of them without being forced into risky jury trials."

"Mary, you are super prepared for those hearings. We can be back by five o'clock on Sunday and you can do your review for the fiftieth time Sunday evening. Just stop and think. I could have been shot to death. You could have been shot to death at that football game. Instead of a relaxing weekend, one of us could have been attending a funeral. And there's another good reason for this getaway."

"What reason?"

"It's your birthday tomorrow."

"Oh, my God, you're right. I've been so busy I never remembered."

"Now there's one additional event just added today," Carlos said. "As soon as that tow truck leaves, Catherine is dropping you off at my office and we are going to pay a visit to my cousin Miguel."

"Who is Miguel? I don't remember your mentioning him."

"We all call him Mikey. He's Marielena's younger son, so that makes him my second cousin, or third. I know you don't like Marielena. No one does. I'm not even sure that Mikey likes her, but he's a great guy."

"Please tell me he's not in trouble and needs a lawyer."

"No, at least he's not in trouble right now. He's a car broker. He gets cars for people at good prices, and you need a new reliable car, unless you're enjoying standing on the shoulder of a freeway in the hot sun. He's bringing in several SUV's for you to look at. You have no car at this point and you're too busy to drag in and out of different car dealers and bargain with them. Go and look and if you don't want any of them, you can rent a car temporarily. How will you get to court on Monday? Hitchhike?"

"Well, I'll look at the cars, and the weekend sounds wonderful, but I really don't want you to pay for a car. Maybe we can work out a repayment plan where I pay you each month like a bank loan."

"Or I could think of a lot of things you could do for me instead."

I realized I was blushing as I thought about Carlos's last remark and the birthday weekend at the beach.

Mikey's place of business was an office on the upper floor of a strip mall in West Kendall. The store fronts were a conglomeration of fast food joints, electronic shops, and cheap linen outlets. The office consisted of two desks, several computer screens, and a gum chewing secretary named Madeline.

Mikey explained that he had pulled together a few cars delivered by dealers who were his clients in the immediate area. I wasn't sure why the dealers would be dealing with Mikey instead of keeping their profits in total, but I decided to keep my lawyer questions unasked for the time being.

"I've got the SUV's in the back parking lot. Let's go take some test drives, Mary," Mikey said. "I'm finally getting to meet you, but I can see why Carlos kept you all to himself. Didn't want to risk introducing her to me, Carlos?"

Mikey put his arm around my shoulders and shoved me toward the parking lot. I was sure that he would be one of my clients someday soon. He had all the indicia of a defendant.

The back lot contained a row of shiny SUVs in a variety of sizes and colors. I walked around peering through heavily tinted windows. Carlos and Mikey trailed behind me.

"Here we got a Lexus hybrid, a fuel efficient model, and over here, this blue one is a BMW Xfive. I can get it in another color if you like the ride. This black model is a Cadillac SRX. It's built super strong, in case you have a lot of accidents," Mikey explained.

"These are going to be way too expensive," I said. "I need transportation, not a trophy."

"Yeah, but you got to impress your clients when you drive up," Mikey said.

"When I arrive at the jail to interview new clients, they're not seated next to picture windows. In fact, there are no windows."

I walked among the row of cars that nearly blinded me as the sun glanced off their new car gloss. I stopped next to a red model, looked at the back and realized it was a new model of my old Ford Explorer. It looked nothing like my old car but the familiar Ford insignia on the back looked comfortable.

"How about this one, Mikey?" I opened the door and viewed tan leather seats and the leather trimmed interior.

"I'm not sure you want that one. It's a demonstrator. Has about 700 miles on it, but I can get you a brand new one."

We all piled into the car. Mikey handed me a fob and explained the new cars don't have a key. I pulled out on to Kendall Drive teeming with trucks. Within minutes I discovered bunches of buttons that operated just like my smart phone with a fingertip. There was a sunroof and a moon roof. I could picture Sam in the back seat with his head protruding from the open roof. There was a satellite radio and a navigation system with a woman's voice giving directions. When I backed into a parking place in the lot there was a camera to guide me.

"I can't believe how cars have changed," I said.

"That's what happens when you drive the same car for seven or eight years," Carlos said.

"I'd like to work out a good deal on this car," I said.

"I can get you a good price but there will be another new model out in December," Mikey said.

"This car better not have ever been in an accident or a flood, Mikey, or Angie will come after you," Carlos said.

So that's how I drove out of West Kendall in my new Explorer feeling guilty that I hadn't even said a proper goodbye to my old car.

Chapter Eighty-Seven

We arrived at my house Sunday evening at six, sun-tanned and sleepy, having gorged on fresh seafood. The beach and J.C.'s boat, and being together were all the entertainment necessary to promote the feeling that all was well in our world.

Sam was slimy with sand and needed a bath, so Carlos took him in the backyard and hosed him down while I unpacked Carlos's car. My new Explorer was resting comfortably in the garage where it barely fit.

Now it was time to work. Marco's hearing was set for one o'clock Monday. Catherine had subpoenaed the witnesses for eleven at the courthouse so I could go over their testimony again. I had enough time to reassure myself that everything that could be done would be done. What would Carlos's family think of me if I didn't get Marco free from this disaster?

Carlos found me in the dining room spreading papers on the table from my now thick file. "I'm going to leave you to work. I don't want to distract you, so I'm going to stay in Pinecrest tonight, and I'll be in court tomorrow with Marco. I hope this was a good birthday."

I ran over to Carlos and hugged him. "It was my absolute best birthday ever. Thank you for all of it."

Carlos smiled. Then he kissed me for a long minute and went quickly out the front door. I sat staring at my paper-laden table and wished that our weekend could have gone on forever.

At nine o'clock, I heard Sam scratching on the back door and remembered I hadn't fed him. I put his food dish on the back step and sat down beside him. Then I heard a rattle at my back gate. Sam heard it too and the hair on his back stood up.

"Mary, are you back here? I rang your doorbell but I guess you didn't hear it."

I recognized the voice of Frank Fieldstone. "Frank, what are you doing here?"

"I tried to get you over the weekend, but your cell didn't answer. I left you three messages."

"Is anything wrong?" I asked. Sam growled and jumped on the gate. "Come around to the front door while I get Sam quieted down.

"That dog never liked me." Frank said.

Frank glanced at the suitcase and picnic basket in the living room and the papers spread out in the dining room, all visible from the front door as he entered.

"I guess you were away over the weekend. Did you have your phone with you?"

"We were at Carlos's parents condo on Marco Island. I had my phone turned off. Why are you here?"

"I had a call from Tim de Leon. He couldn't reach you and he actually said he felt better talking with a male."

"What? You talked to the father of the so-called victim in Jay's case. You can't do that without the state present. What were you thinking?"

"He called me. I didn't contact him. He's very upset about his daughter. He's hired a psychologist to work with her and he doesn't want her subjected to questioning in open court."

"Then he should tell Fred Mercer that she doesn't want to go forward in the case. Without a victim, Fred will have to do what's right."

"He told Mercer, but the guy is stubborn and said he intends to continue even if he has to haul Jennifer into court with a police escort."

"The only thing we can do if he won't drop the case is to go forward with the motion to dismiss. Tim's statement can be added to our reasons for dismissal."

"I just thought you should know this before the hearing on Tuesday."

Sam suddenly rushed to the front door tail wagging furiously. The door opened and Carlos stepped inside.

"Mary, I got home and realized I left my shaving kit in your suitcase." He stopped when he saw Frank. "What are you doing here?" he shouted. The minute my back is turned you invite this *ladron*, this thief over to god knows do what. Thanks a lot."

"Carlos, stop it. Frank invited himself here with news about Jay's case. I was unavailable over the weekend and there's been a new development."

"I'm sorry, Mary, I'll leave," Frank said. "Well, Carlos, now you know how it feels to trust your girlfriend and find her with someone else, but at least I have my pants on." Frank made a quick exit before Carlos decided to punch him. This looked imminent as Carlos was advancing toward Frank.

"You jumped to a nasty conclusion just like I did when I saw you with Margarita. Can we both just stop this jealousy business? Can you realize how much I love you?" I threw myself against Carlos's tense body and felt him relax.

Chapter Eighty-Eight

Monday arrived with a bang. I worked on Marco's file until midnight. Once in bed with Sam in his usual place near my feet, I couldn't keep my eyes closed. Nervous energy was building to a crescendo. At three, I turned on the TV and found a movie on the sci-fi channel filled with beings from outer space invading New York City. I fell asleep on the sofa until a loud bang woke me.

The time was seven-fifteen and the bang was thunder. Rain cascaded down the roof making rivers on the windows. "It can't be raining. This is almost the end of November. Isn't this the dry season?" I asked Sam who had nothing to add to the conversation, except to look mournfully at the rain.

I was too nervous to eat anything. I made a pot of strong coffee, fed Sam, dressed in a black suit that matched the weather, packed my briefcase and loaded my new red SUV. The new car wouldn't look new for long driving through the deluge.

At ten o'clock, Catherine and I left the office for the courthouse. The rain hadn't abated and the satellite radio's weather-traffic report for Miami was more of the same for the whole day. Catherine loved the new car. She kept up a barrage of nervous chatter for the whole ride. I didn't even try to answer because I knew she wasn't really expecting me to chime in. I listened with one ear and re-thought every part of the hearing to come.

"When you get Marco released, we're going to get married. I mean immediately. You'll be my maid of honor, of course." Catherine was saying.

That got my attention. "Are you sure, Catherine? That's a big step. And we don't even know if he'll get out any time soon."

"I'm sure. If he goes to prison, we'll get married anyway. This situation has shown me that life is too short to be undecided about everything.

Just because Brady was a disaster, I shouldn't have to be alone forever. Marco and my boys have a solid relationship. He's the only father figure in their lives. I know this is right."

"Will you go on working? I don't mean to be selfish."

"Of course, I'll still be working for you. I love my job and you're the best friend I've ever had."

I pulled the car into the expensive lot and we huddled under umbrellas. We climbed the courthouse steps, a part of the multitude of lawyers, witnesses and defendants ahead of us and behind us. The odor of adrenaline mixed with the antiseptic smell of cleaning products used to cleanse the courthouse was overwhelming.

The witnesses were to meet us in the attorneys' lounge on the fourth floor near Judge Sylvia Cohen-Cueto's courtroom. Seated in the few chairs available were Marty and Drucilla Lantz. Mr. Habib was smiling broadly, excited to be in the same room with Marty, the star of the Miami Heat team and an NBA legend. When I saw Marty Lantz I realized why there was an extra- large crowd outside the door.

There was a knock on the door and Reuben Porter entered. "I hope this isn't a conflict of interest or anything, Mary. I'm here to make sure no one bothers the Lantz's as well as acting as a witness for Marco."

Before I could answer, there was another knock on the door and Manny, the regular from Mr. Habib's store entered. He was carrying a basketball which he thrust at Marty. "Can you sign this for my nephew? His name is Grayson but everyone calls him Buddy. I'm so glad to be a witness here and get to meet the great Marty Lantz."

I pulled Reuben aside. "Did you tell everyone that the Lantz's would be here?"

"Sure. It was the way to make sure everyone showed up."

"Everyone except Mrs. Morehouse. Where is she?'

"Oh, she'll be here. Turns out she watches all the Heat games on TV."

Another knock sounded on the door. Catherine opened the door a crack and then stepped outside. She returned a minute later. "Mary, remember Harlan McFarland from the Herald? You kind of got him his start last June when he covered your press conference. He asked if you could possibly come out in the hall and answer a few questions."

"Well, maybe a little press won't hurt," I said and stepped out of the Marty Lantz fan club.

Harlan looked as young as ever, but he had proved himself to be a good reporter despite his lack of polish. As I closed the door behind me, Harlan dropped his notepad. He bent to retrieve it and dropped his cell phone. I scooped it up before he did any more damage.

"Harlan, good to see you again. Hold on to your phone," I said as I placed it firmly in his hand.

"Thanks for remembering me, Mary. What's going on in there? Everyone out here says you've got Marty Lantz in there with you. Is he in trouble?"

"Not at all. He's a witness in Marco Perez's case set for a Motion to Dismiss hearing today."

"That's the murder case, isn't it? The new boyfriend alleged to have blown away the ex-husband?" What's Lantz a witness to?"

"Why don't you stick around for the hearing? Then, if you have questions afterwards, I'll make time to talk to you."

"Okay. Sounds interesting," Harlan said. He backed away into the crowd and nearly knocked over an elderly woman.

I looked at the woman who was snarling at Harlan. Then I looked again and realized it was Mrs. Morehouse. She was wearing a print dress over which she wore a Heat tee shirt. Her hair was pinned up in a braid topped off by a bright red hairband. She was also sporting makeup of some sort that seemed to lodge in her wrinkles. Blue eye shadow and bright red lipstick topped off the outfit. I took her by the arm and marched her into the witness room where she reached out and hugged Marty Lantz.

Chapter Eighty-Nine

When I finally got the group's attention away from Marty, I went over the ground rules for the hearing. No one was to discuss their testimony with any other witness. I handed out each witnesses' sworn statement for them to review, and explained that they might not all have to testify.

"The best result would be the judge dismissing the case based on the written motion and their sworn statements, but she may want to hear live testimony. Please make yourselves comfortable in here in the meantime. Reuben Porter is bringing sandwiches and drinks from the cafeteria for your lunch. If you are called to testify, you may remain in the courtroom after that, but you can't be present before you are called. Finally, thank you for giving up your time to help Marco Perez. I know he will thank each of you himself when he is able."

There were murmurs of 'no problem' and 'you're welcome' from the assembled group.

"Reuben, what about the DEA agent? Wasn't he supposed to be on call if we needed him?"

"Agent Roberto Padron is on call if needed. I met with him Friday when your car bit the dust. He's trying to find *Oso Blanco* and his numero uno helper. They've got the arrest warrant but the guys keep eluding them."

"Okay, if we need him, you'll be in charge of getting him here."

At twelve-thirty, I entered the courtroom. Catherine accompanied me and helped me arrange my notes and the contents of my file on the defense table. I kept an eye on the door for Marco's arrival. Carlos was bringing him. This was the one time, Marco was allowed to leave the confines of his home. House arrest makes your home into a jail and even the most pleasant living space soon becomes confining.

For Marco, who was accustomed to being out on the street most of the time investigating, it was his private hell to be unable to investigate his own case.

Ten minutes passed before Carlos and Marco entered the courtroom followed by Marco's parents.

I settled Marco at the defense table. He was pale and looked as if he had shrunk over these weeks. Catherine rushed over to him and kissed him. Then she went to sit with the Perez's and Carlos. The smell of nervous tension filled the courtroom.

A minute later Louise Margolis entered. A young man carried her files and placed them on the State's table. I guessed he was an intern. I crossed the aisle and shook hands with Louise.

"Mary, thank you for getting your motion and the statements to me ahead of this hearing."

"All of the witnesses are here and prepared to give testimony, if the judge wants to hear from them," I said.

"I hear you even have Marty Lantz and his wife here. It's the talk of the courthouse. The bottom line is that this might be fine before a jury, but this is just a motion hearing, and this is still a murder charge."

Louise wasn't going to go away quietly. That was obvious, but before I could respond, the bailiff entered through the door behind the bench with the judge right behind him.

"All rise, the Honorable Sylvia Cohen-Cueto presiding. Please turn off all cell phones."

Sylvia looked much as she had when we were in law school, the only difference being at least twenty extra pounds. "Ladies and gentlemen, please be seated. We are here in State vs. Marco Perez. Everyone please announce for the record."

"Louise Margolis for the State, your honor."

"Mary Magruder Katz representing Marco Perez."

"I want to put on the record that Ms. Katz, Ms. Margolis, and I were in the same law school class and at the time all of us were friends. However, I have had little or no contact with either of them since then. I don't believe this will prejudice either side, but I need to know if anyone has any objection to my hearing this case."

We both mumbled 'no objection', although I couldn't remember Louise or me being friends with Sylvia.

"Ms. Katz, I have had the opportunity to read your motion and to review the witness statements. Thank you for having everything here well ahead of the hearing. It's your motion so please let me hear from you.

I stood and moved to the lectern. "Judge Cueto, Marco Perez has been charged with the murder of Brady Aynsworth. It is true that Mr. Perez is the fiancé of Catherine Aynsworth, the ex-wife of the deceased. Catherine and Brady Aynsworth have been divorced for seven years. He walked out on her leaving her with no money and two babies. He never provided child support and was totally out of their lives.

"Objection, Judge, this isn't family court. All this is beside the point," Louise said.

"Your honor, I am just setting the scene with important background information," I countered.

"Listen, Mary, I mean Ms. Katz, this has nothing to do with the murder charge. Let's get on with this," the judge said.

"Very well, Judge. I will show the court that the police zeroed in on only one suspect, Mr. Perez. They didn't do the background work that I have done to show that Mr. Aynsworth had numerous enemies who would have loved to see him dead.

"Brady Aynsworth was thrown out on the street by a woman in Ft. Lauderdale with whom he had been living or I guess you could say sponging off of. He was a known drug user in the Broward area. He next lived with a young Native American woman, Shirley Bird, who he got addicted to drugs. Ms. Bird is now in rehab but I have submitted her letter in which she describes having been accosted by a drug lord trying to extract money owed to him by Aynsworth. This drug lord, nicknamed *Oso Blanco*, the Polar Bear for his huge frame and shock of white hair and beard, was looking for Aynsworth.

"Brady Aynsworth was desperate. He had no money and no place to live and also had a big drug addiction. That's when he began showing up at his former wife's apartment. She obtained a stay-away order a few days before he was gunned down. You will see a copy of the order from the domestic violence court as one of the exhibits with this motion.

"Numerous witnesses are able to identify the Polar Bear from pictures along with photos of his lieutenants. They were spotted by Mrs. Morehouse who owns the apartment building where Catherine Aynsworth lives. He was spotted again a few doors from the apartment building at a convenience store. The store owner and one of the customers can also attest to these drug dealers hanging around the area and asking where to find Brady.

"The DEA is actively seeking *Oso Blanco* and plan to arrest him if they can locate him. Now to Marco Perez. Mr. Perez has lived in Miami all his life and has never been arrested for anything before, other than one speeding ticket. He is the owner of a well- known private investigation firm. On the day of the murder, Mr. Perez can account for every hour of his time. The medical examiner's report places the time of Aynsworth's death between the hours of two and six p.m. The state furnished copies of the report with her discovery. Mr. Perez was engaged in a surveillance as part of his work. Drucilla and Marty Lantz were involved in this investigation, and have been kind enough to offer to be witnesses in this case. They have even allowed me to make available with this motion a copy of the report filed by Marco Perez that concluded this investigation.

"Now before the media pounce on this, let me make clear that Mr. Lantz was trying to plan a surprise for his wife for their anniversary and was visiting a jeweler at a hotel in Coconut Grove. Mr. Perez followed him to his own home where he presented his wife with some beautiful custom made jewelry commemorating their twentieth anniversary. This took up Mr. Perez's hours from one-thirty to three-thirty p.m. A few minutes later he was at the Coral Gables Middle School picking up Ms. Aynsworth's sons. They were together continuously. At five p.m., he picked up Ms. Aynsworth and they proceeded to a restaurant for dinner. At seven-thirty, they returned to Ms. Aynsworth's apartment. That is where they found the police and the body of Brady Aynsworth. It was impossible for Marco Perez to have committed a murder. Every hour of his day is accounted for.

"If the court wishes to hear from any of these witnesses, they are all in the courthouse except the DEA agent who is on call."

"Thank you, Ms. Katz." The judge smiled at Louise. "Let me hear from the state."

"Your Honor, Ms. Katz is very persuasive. However, the State is not prepared to drop a murder charge. I would like to call the police officer who made the arrest of Mr. Perez. I want his live testimony in this record. As to the defense witnesses, the only one I would like to hear from would be the DEA agent."

"Not even Marty Lantz?" Judge Cohen-Cueto asked. "The whole courthouse was hoping to get a glimpse of him. Just kidding, Ms. Margolis."

Several people sitting in the back of courtroom got up and left, making quite a stir as the door swung open and shut. I guessed that they actually had been hanging out waiting to see the star player live and in living color.

"Judge, can we take a short break while I summon Sergeant Jaime Ruiz from the homicide bureau to the courtroom?" Louise had sent her intern out before she began speaking. "We are locating the detective now."

"Good idea. Ten minute break everyone," Sylvia said as she quickly exited through the hidden door behind the bench.

Chapter Ninety

Marco turned to me. "The State isn't going to dismiss this case. I can see that."

"You don't know that, Marco. Wait 'til I get through with that detective on the stand. Haven't you ever heard, it isn't over 'til the fat lady sings?"

"Yeah, I've heard that, but the fat lady here is the judge and she won't do anything if the state won't budge."

I walked Marco back to where Carlos and the rest of the family were seated. Marco greeted everyone and then said he needed a restroom break.

"Carlos, go with him and stay with him, please. He's a little depressed," I said.

Carlos sprinted out behind Marco.

"You can't believe Marco would run away," Catherine said.

"People do strange things when they're lives are disrupted. Let's not take any chances." I said.

"Reuben, what about Agent Padron. Have you called him?"

"As soon as Margolis said she wanted to hear from him, I left a message on his cell phone. He hasn't answered yet."

I decided to take a break to the ladies' room. I had just walked in and glanced at my slightly frizzed hair when Louise came in.

"Mary, off the record. I'm between a rock and a hard place. I'd love to drop this case. It's beginning to look like a big loser, but I can't. The State Attorney is the only one who can authorize dropping a case. Maybe if he reads the transcripts of the witnesses and of this hearing, he might be persuaded, but it can't happen today."

"I understand, Louise. Let's see what the judge is thinking after we finish the witnesses. Thanks for being honest with me."

We returned to the courtroom where Jaime Ruiz was seated in the witness chair. He was dressed professionally in a suit and tie, but the jacket barely covered his paunch. He looked uncomfortable.

Carlos walked Marco back to the well of the court and we all settled in for part two of a long afternoon.

The judge asked the clerk to swear in the witness, as Louise laid her yellow pad on the lectern.

"Please state your name and position for the record." Louise said.

"Sergeant Jaime Ruiz, detective in the Miami-Dade Police Homicide Bureau."

"How long have you been assigned to homicide?"

"Five months. Before that I worked gang related crimes."

"The scene of the murder was in the jurisdiction of the Miami Police Department. Why was Miami-Dade County answering the call?"

"The Miami P.D. was swamped with crime scenes. Our department handles homicides all over the county so we helped out."

"Were you the first officer on the scene?"

"No, Miami uniform patrol was called regarding a man lying in the street in front of a row of apartment buildings. When he found the body cold, he called for homicide. Miami Homicide called us and I was assigned to go there."

"Who was there when you arrived?'

"Well, the patrol officer was trying to hold back a crowd of people who were curious."

"How many people?"

"Maybe a dozen. People on bikes and walking dogs after dinner, I guess."

"Anyone else there?"

"Yeah, there was a couple with two kids who drove up. They got out of the car and the woman started screaming."

"What did you do?"

"I was helping get the crime scene tape up and calling for the medical examiner to come. I told the couple to stand aside and not to leave. The woman said she lived in the apartment upstairs and asked if she could send her kids up there to get them away from the scene. I told her okay, but she had to stay right here. I said it looks like you know this guy. She told me it was her ex-husband. She was pretty shook up."

"Now do you see anyone in the courtroom who was on the scene that night?"

"Sure. The defendant seated at the table over there. He was with the woman who later became known to me as Catherine Aynsworth. She's sitting back there." He pointed to Catherine.

"What happened next?"

"I put on my gloves and went to examine the body. It was cold and rigor mortis had set in. I saw two bullet holes, one on his side and one in his chest. I also picked up one shell casing and bagged it. Crime scene still hadn't arrived."

I separated the defendant, Mr. Perez, and Ms. Aynsworth. I sat her down in the Miami patrol car. I sat him down in my car."

"Did other officers arrive?"

"Yes, a detective from Miami P.D, Jim Avery, tried to assist me. He was from the robbery unit. Crime scene and the medical examiner arrived, so then I went to talk to the two people. I was speaking to Ms. Aynsworth who identified the body as her ex-husband, Brady Aynsworth. I was trying to interview her but she was crying very hard and then the defense lawyer arrived, Ms. Katz over there."

"What did you learn?"

"Not too much. Ms. Aynsworth said her ex had been hanging around harassing her and her kids. She told me the identity of Mr. Perez and said he was her boyfriend. Ms. Katz asked if I could finish the interview at a later time. The witness's kids were alone upstairs and she wanted to get them away from this area. I decided to let her go ahead and leave with her kids. Then I went to talk to Perez. Ms. Katz insisted on sitting in on that interview also."

"Did you read the defendant his rights?"

"Of course."

"Tell us about that interview."

"Perez tried to answer my question about his whereabouts that afternoon and evening, but he had a hard time relating where he'd been. He said something about being out on a surveillance all afternoon, but he wouldn't give me the facts about what client he was working for or what the case was about."

"Did you ask him if he'd had any contact with the deceased?"

"Yes, he told me that he'd seen the guy in his girlfriend's apartment where they quarreled, and then he said that he had no use for the guy and the best thing for his girlfriend and her kids was that Aynsworth was dead. I took that as a possible admission."

"Now who else did you interview?"

"We spoke to a Mrs. Morehouse who lived in the apartment downstairs of Ms. Aynsworth and was her landlady."

"What, if anything, did you learn from her?"

"She said the deceased had broken into Ms. Aynsworth's apartment on more than one occasion and the defendant had come bursting in one evening when the deceased was having a squabble with his ex-wife and dragged Brady out of there and that the defendant had had a gun with him."

"What else did you do to investigate this case?"

"I tried to get some background on the deceased. It appears that he was homeless. I obtained the name of a woman he had been living with and her address, but she was no longer there, so I hit a dead end. I tried to find any of his relatives. His parents had lived in Deland, Florida, but they were no longer there. Based on my investigation, everything pointed to Marco Perez. I got an arrest warrant and I arrested him."

"Okay, Detective, thank you." Louise sat down.

"Cross examination Ms. Katz?" Judge Cueto asked.

"Yes, Judge, thank you," I said as I shuffled through my notes, stalling for time to get my head around the testimony I had just heard. I approached the lectern, laid out my notes, and turned the lectern sideways so I could look directly at the judge and the witness without the barrier of the lectern between us.

"Detective Ruiz, you learned that Catherine Aynsworth had obtained a restraining order against her ex-husband, didn't you?"

"Yes, she told me that."

"You never mentioned that when Ms. Margolis questioned you, correct?"

"I didn't think it was important."

"There were several occasions where Brady Aynsworth threatened Catherine, correct?"

"I never looked into that."

"You spoke about an interview with Mrs. Morehouse, the landlady, correct?"

"Yeah, that's right. She told me about the defendant having a gun at the apartment."

"Now did Mrs. Morehouse claim that she observed Marco Perez with a gun?"

"Well, no, she said another neighbor told her about it."

"Did you obtain the name of the neighbor and interview her?"

"I got her name, but when I went to see her, she said she was late for work and wouldn't talk with me then."

"So when did you return to talk to her?"

"I didn't. I was called away on another case."

"Judge, I ask that all mention of Mr. Perez appearing with a gun be stricken from this record as hearsay," I said.

Louise was on her feet. "But Judge, it's not being offered for the truth of the matter, just to show a pattern of violence of the defendant."

"I'm afraid not, Ms. Margolis. That portion of the record is stricken. Continue, Ms. Katz. Let's move this hearing along." It appeared that Judge Cueto was losing patience.

"You asked Mr. Perez if you could examine a weapon in his car that he uses in his work as a private investigator, didn't you?"

"Yes, he allowed me to examine it."

"Did you compare the caliber of his weapon to the shell casing you picked up on the scene?"

"They were different."

"Mr. Perez invited you to come to his office to examine all the firearms owned by his firm, didn't he?"

"I think so."

"Well, did you ever go there and look over those firearms?"

"No, like I said, I was called away on another case."

"You testified that Mr. Perez was unclear about his whereabouts for the afternoon of Brady Aynsworth's death. Was that your testimony?"

"That's correct."

"Well, didn't he tell you that he had been working on a case and was on a surveillance at the Ritz Carlton Hotel in Coconut Grove? And that he couldn't give you the name of his client as the matter was confidential?"

"I guess that's what he said. But I wasn't buying it."

"Well, you didn't have to buy it. He gave you all the other hours leading up to the finding of the body, didn't he?"

"I think so. I really can't remember. I've worked several homicides since then."

"But I have furnished Ms. Margolis and the court with the full report of Mr. Perez's hours once Marty and Drucilla Lantz allowed the report to be used, and you could have viewed the report before coming here today, isn't that correct?"

"Just because a report has been produced doesn't mean it's accurate."

I drew a breath and asked, "Judge, would you like me to call Mr. and Mrs. Lantz to testify as to the accuracy of the report with Mr. Perez's hours on the day of the murder?"

"I don't think it's necessary," Judge Cueto responded, "in spite of the fact that everyone in the courtroom would love to see Marty Lantz."

"Now you stated that you couldn't find the woman Brady Aynsworth had been living with. What was her name and where was she supposed to be living?"

"Can I look at my report?"

"If it will refresh your memory."

The detective pulled out several sheets of paper from his file and began reading through them. We waited while he shuffled through the pages. People shifted in their seats and the judge called the bailiff over. She whispered something to him and he left the courtroom. I had a momentary picture of the bailiff canceling the judge's hairdresser appointment or visit to the nail salon. I stifled a giggle.

The judge finally spoke. "Detective do you have the name in your report?"

"I can't seem to find it, Judge. I thought it was here somewhere."

"The name of the woman is Renee Francis and at the time Brady Aynsworth lived with her she lived on 39th Court. You should have read that in my investigator, Reuben Porter's, report furnished to Ms. Margolis in discovery and attached to my motion. Does this jog your memory?"

"Not really."

"If you had read the private investigator's report you would have learned that Renee Francis moved to Hollywood and was readily available. Did you follow up on that information?"

"No, I had already closed this case."

"You never learned that the deceased, as you have referred to him, next moved in with Shirley Bird, did you? And that Ms. Bird led us to a drug ring run by someone called *Oso Blanco?*"

"No, I didn't learn that."

"And that this drug dealer threatened Ms. Bird and Brady Aynsworth if Brady didn't pay up for the drugs he received from *Oso Blanco?*"

"No, I wasn't provided that information."

"Well, wasn't it your job to find this information, or do you always wait for others to provide you with key information in your cases?"

"Objection, Judge, Ms. Katz is arguing with the witness," Louise said.

"Sustained, are you nearly finished with the witness, Ms. Katz," the judge ruled.

"I withdraw the question and I have nothing more for this witness," I said, registering my disdain for him.

"Your Honor, would you like me to call Mr. Porter, or Mrs. Morehouse to corroborate the information in my cross examination?" I asked.

"That won't be necessary, counsel. I see the statements and reports attached to your motion. Ms. Margolis, do you have any other witnesses you wish to call?"

"I was hoping that Ms. Katz would be calling the DEA agent she mentioned. We don't have any report from him or her," Louise said.

"I will be glad to call him. I believe we have him on standby," I said.

"Let's take a few minutes break while you locate him. I'm sure the court reporter would be grateful for a break." Judge Cueto was out of her chair and through the door behind her bench before anyone could answer.

Chapter Ninety-One

I returned to the room where all the witnesses had gathered. I excused the Lantz's and asked the others to stay a little longer until we were sure that the DEA agent would appear.

Reuben walked the Lantz's to the freight elevator that would lead them to a private garage away from the hoard of gawkers who were hanging around the hallways.

I explained to the remaining witnesses how appreciative Marco was for their help and begged them to be patient a bit longer.

Reuben returned with Agent Padron, who was out of breath and wet from the rain that persisted.

"I hope this doesn't take long, Mary. We've got a solid lead on our drug kingpin. Last night we arrested the guy in the photo that your witness ID'd, and after we talked murder charge, he talked up a storm. I need to get back up to Broward County. My crew is trying to move in to make an arrest before this asshole gets tipped off."

"I'm really sorry to pull you away at a time like this, but the state is insisting on my calling you. It is crucial that we conclude this motion on a positive note. If not, my client will be standing trial on a murder charge that he is innocent of. You know what a crap shoot a jury verdict can be."

"You better believe it. So let's go."

I returned to the courtroom with Agent Padron and the remaining witnesses who were now able to listen to the testimony since they would not be called. I told the bailiff that I was ready to proceed with the DEA agent. He left to escort the judge back to the bench and to phone the state to return. The court reporter was in her seat as was the clerk. The two women were engrossed in conversation as we entered, and I suspected that it was the usual game court personnel played, deciding whether the defendant was really innocent or faking it.

"All parties present and ready to proceed, Your Honor," the bailiff called us to order.

"Judge Cueto, I have before the court Special Agent Padron."

"Your Honor, I apologize for my appearance," Padron said. I've been on a stake-out since early this morning after making an arrest late last night."

"Not to worry. I understand, but may I ask you a question before the clerk swears you in?" the judge asked.

"Of course, Judge."

"Your official title is Special Agent of the DEA. Why are all of you called Special Agents?"

"That's just the titles adopted by the Drug Enforcement Agency. Maybe it's to separate us from the personnel that are not sworn officers, like lab technicians, and psychologists and the like, but honestly, no one ever asked me that before."

"Okay, just curious. Proceed Ms. Katz."

Padron stood and was sworn in. He looked expectantly at me, impatient to return to his real work. He stated his name and title and duties speaking rapidly.

"Agent, you have been working of late on apprehending a drug ring working mainly out of Broward county, correct?

"Yes, ma'am."

"During this work you and I had occasion to meet recently."

"Yes, it turned out that we were both attempting to find the members of this ring, particularly the head of the organization."

"Did I turn over to you the product of my investigation in the case of State vs. Marco Perez?"

"Yes you did. But I am reluctant to divulge names and places in open court at this time."

"If we were to adjourn to the judge's chambers, would you be able to answer questions about your investigation?"

"Yes, that would be better."

"Come sidebar, counsel," Judge Cueto ordered.

We gathered in front of the judge's bench with the court reporter huddled between Louise and me.

"Your Honor, the DEA is about to make an arrest that impacts the case before the court. Until that arrest is procured, this information must be kept sealed. Otherwise, weeks or months of undercover work will be blown," I explained.

"Dear God," Louise murmured. "Now Ms. Katz wants to turn this into a cloak and dagger mystery."

"You wanted to hear from this witness, Louise," I said.

"Ladies, please, talk to me, not each other." Judge Cueto couldn't stifle her annoyance.

"Judge, I have every reason to believe that the head of this drug ring ordered the murder of Brady Aynsworth in retaliation for his owing a great deal of money for unpaid drugs. He was a user and a foot soldier seller."

"Let's adjourn to chambers so I can hear all of this," the judge said as she picked herself up, robe flapping behind her. The bailiff called out "Fifteen minute recess," as he hustled to accompany her .

Louise and the court reporter, followed by Agent Padron, went through the outside hallway and into the formal entrance to the judge's chambers. I brought up the rear accompanied by Marco. There had been brief argument about Marco being allowed into the judge's chambers. However, my argument that an accused is entitled to hear all argument and witnesses in his case won the day. We were met by the judge's judicial assistant, a motherly looking woman, who asked us to wait in the outer office while she checked with the judge.

"Send them all back, Linda. I need to get this matter concluded before Thanksgiving, but at the rate we're going it looks like it'll be here 'til Christmas," Judge Cueto called.

We seated ourselves around the long table that took up most of the room. Judge Cueto sat at the head of the table at a mahogany desk. Agent Padron sat next to me and across from Louise. Marco sat on my other side nervously drumming his fingers on the table. The court reporter positioned herself next to Padron, her fingers poised over the keys of her steno machine.

"Judge, may we temporarily ask that this part of the record be sealed?"

"Yes, temporarily only," Cueto answered. "Go ahead, Ms. Katz".

"Agent Padron, please explain to the court who you hope to arrest and why."

"Your Honor, the DEA has been trying to put an end to a pervasive drug operation headed by a man known as *Oso Blanco.* We have been cooperating with agents from New York who have an outstanding arrest warrant for this man. He has eluded us on several occasions. The New York warrant charges him with attempted murder.

"In the midst of this investigation, we were contacted by Reuben Porter, a private investigator working for Ms. Katz in Marco Perez's case. She had a lead that this same ring leader had either ordered the killing of Brady Aynsworth or did the killing himself. We furnished Ms. Katz with surveillance photos. She obtained sworn testimony from three witnesses who identified *Oso Blanco* and one of his workers, as having been in the area where Aynsworth was shot and having asked questions about him in the surrounding neighborhood. Ms. Katz also had evidence that these same men were seeking Aynsworth in Broward County where he was liv-ing with a young woman named Sheila Bird. They threatened Sheila and tried to extract a payment from her. She was aware of Brady Aynsworth's drug dependence and money owed to this drug dealer.

"We arrested one of the regulars in the drug organization late last night. In questioning him, we have an excellent lead on the location of *Oso Blanco.* We also learned that *Oso Blanco* had stated on more than one occasion that he would take care of Brady Aynsworth if he wasn't paid the money he was owed."

"How do we know that this drug guy did the killing, or maybe it was one of his assistants?" Louise asked.

"Judge, what difference would it make which of these did the killing. The point here is that Marco Perez was not the killer, the point of my entire motion to dismiss the case against an innocent man." I felt anger rising in my chest.

"Ms. Margolis, what I have heard is compelling information, but I think the state has to evaluate the testimony elicited here today. I know you can't dismiss this case on your own. I am asking you to speak to the state attorney today. I will set this on my calendar for Wednesday morning at nine. My preference is for the state to act in the interest of justice." Judge Cueto stood illustrating the end of the hearing.

"Let's go back into court on the record, ladies, so I can adjourn this hearing formally," the judge said.

We trooped back into the courtroom as the bailiff quieted the spectators.

As soon as we were all back in place, I stood to address the court again, pushing my luck just a little. "Judge, I believe you have the ability to end this case today, yourself, but I understand you are asking the state to do this. However, based on what you have heard today, I am asking for Mr. Perez to be released on his own recognizance, his bail money returned to his family and that he no longer be confined under house arrest."

"The state objects," Louise said without much conviction.

"So noted. I hereby grant a change of status for Mr. Perez as requested. Bailiff, please notify the house arrest supervisors of this immediate change of status. Get someone over to the courtroom to take off the defendant's electronic bracelet. Mr. Perez, do not leave Dade County and be sure to appear here on Wednesday with your lawyer. Until then, if I were you I wouldn't even throw a gum wrapper on the sidewalk. The police might haul you right back in here. Bailiff, show these folks out." Cueto bolted for her door before being accosted by the news media.

Chapter Ninety-Two

A semi triumphal march paraded down the courthouse steps and into the parking lot. We hadn't received a dismissal of the case, but it seemed imminent. Meanwhile, Marco was free to move around Dade County once again.

My remaining witnesses left together after Marco's profuse thanks. Carlos took Marco, his parents, and Catherine in his car to drop them at Marco's own house for the first time in weeks. I told Catherine to forget about the office for today and to enjoy Marco's freedom.

I climbed into my shiny new Explorer, turned on the satellite radio to a music station and made my way back to the office. I was tired but still had Jay's hearing set for tomorrow morning. I needed a wake-up coffee so a quick stop at Starbucks was imperative. The drive-through on Dixie Highway had a backed up line of cars, so I parked and went inside. No sooner had I placed my order for a double espresso when I felt a tap on my shoulder.

I whirled around and found Harlan McFarland staring at me.

"Harlan, did you follow me here?"

"Yes, sorry, you left pretty fast and you promised to talk to me after the hearing, so here I am."

"Let me buy you a coffee to make up for running out on you." I upped the order to two espressos.

We settled in the lounge chairs by the window. I stirred my coffee to cool it. Harlan promptly spilled half of his cup on the little table between us.

"I'm not supposed to let anyone buy me even a coffee; journalism ethics, you know, so let me pay you back."

Harlan reached into his pocket, pulled out some dollar bills and dropped them in the puddle of coffee.

"Harlan, never mind that. What questions do you have?"

"Well, do you really believe that Mr. Perez is innocent? Didn't he have a real motive to get rid of his girlfriend's ex-husband?"

"You didn't get to hear the testimony of the DEA agent in chambers. This must be off the record. Okay?"

"Sure, but I gathered that the agent was arresting some drug guy who was going to be charged with the murder."

"That's true, and hopefully, he's making the arrest as we speak. As soon as that happens, there's your story. Drug ring busted, Marco Perez freed."

"It's all too convenient. I guess I've turned into a cynic covering the courts the last few months."

"Again, off the record, one of the ring has been arrested already and he told the agents that the main guy had threatened to kill Brady. I'm sure you'll see all of this clearly once Agent Padron makes the arrest."

"I'll be waiting to see what develops. I'll be covering Jay Lincoln's hearing tomorrow. You're keeping busy."

"That's for sure, Harlan. That's why I've got to get back to the office now. See you tomorrow."

I thought about Harlan's skepticism as I drove and wondered how many people in this town would always believe that Marco Perez was a murderer.

I turned into the parking lot of my office and found Jay Lincoln and his mother getting out of a car.

"Mary, thank goodness, we've been trying to call you since noon. I kept getting a voicemail. We were getting worried what with Jay's hearing tomorrow, so Jay said maybe your phone was out of order with the heavy rain this morning," Lorena said.

"I've been tied up in court all day, but everything is ready for the hearing. Come into the office so we can talk."

I led them inside just as the rain began again. The message light was blinking and the computer screen showed forty-seven e-mail messages. We gathered around my desk. Jay's long legs squirmed in the small guest chair.

"Sit up straight, Jay. For heaven's sake, I hope you don't slouch like that in court tomorrow," Lorena said.

Jay gave his mother a look of exasperation. "I'm not six years old anymore, Mom. Mary, what are our chances on the motion tomorrow? Do we have any chance of winning?"

"Of course, we do, or I wouldn't be arguing the motion. I am hopeful especially because Jennifer's father doesn't want her to testify. I'm sure he realizes the truth after hearing her answer my deposition questions."

"Well, if she doesn't testify, the state has no case, right?"

"Fred Mercer, the prosecutor, doesn't want to take no for an answer. He's made noise about dragging her into court anyway. I can't believe he would do that."

"Is he a racist?" Lorena sat forward in her chair.

"No, I think it's about his hatred of me," I said. "I have some ideas about how everyone can save face. Let's not jump to any wrong conclusions. Jay, I want you to sit quietly in court tomorrow and look like you aren't worried, but keep a serious face."

"I want to tell my side of the story, Mary. You have to let me do that," Jay said.

"No, Jay. That's why I'm here, to speak for you. Don't you understand if you testify, Fred will cross examine you and make you look like a conceited jerk who thinks he can have sex with whomever he wants whenever he wants. You must trust me on this."

"We do trust you, Mary," Lorena said. "I've been meaning to ask, how's that Carlos friend of yours? Has he recovered from the shooting?"

"He's almost one hundred percent again. Jay, thanks to your team member, Brett Fieldstone, the shooter, Roy Carter was arrested."

"I always thought Carter was a weirdo, but he's not a bad quarterback. It's just that I'm a better one," Jay said.

I gave Lorena and Jay copies of the depositions and my motion to go over again. While they studied the pages, I cleared up the phone messages and read a few of the e-mails.

I could hear Lorena comment aloud as she read Jennifer's deposition. "That lying hussy," she said.

Jay answered, "No, Mom, what that girl is, is a beautiful bitch."

Chapter Ninety-Three

Carlos called to tell me that Marco and his family were preparing to have dinner at the new Argentine steak house in Dadeland Mall. Catherine was insisting that I join them.

"Please tell everyone that I need to review everything for tomorrow's hearing and I need a good night's sleep," I said.

"I think I'll stay in Pinecrest again tonight," Carlos said. "I need to be sure everything is set up for Thanksgiving at the house. Our mothers have been unloading food and china and God knows what else out there. They're turning Thanksgiving into a cook-off between the Old South and Havana, Cuba."

"At nine o'clock that evening, I fell into a sound sleep and never stirred until Sam woke me barking at seven. The morning of Jay's hearing had finally arrived. I dressed in my white suit, pulled my straggly hair into a pony-tail and hoped that this judge knew that the good guys always wear white.

When I stepped off the elevator, I was met by a stream of people lining the hallway. Some were dressed in orange and green University of Miami shirts. Others were wearing matching blue shirts with the CRUM letters marching across their chests. I hadn't realized that this hearing would be a repeat of the demonstrators for and against Jay.

A man pushed to the front of the crowd and stood in my path. "Mary Katz? I'm Toby Crenshaw, sports reporter for Channel Seven. I need to ask you some questions about your defense strategy for Jay Lincoln."

"I don't need a strategy. My client didn't commit any crime," I said pushing past him.

I managed to get through the courtroom door where I encountered Harlan wearing his press credentials.

"Mary, our sports editor is right over there. I'd appreciate your giving any Herald interviews to me. This is a court matter, not a football game. I'm shocked that the sports department is trying to grab my story."

"It's okay, Harlan. I'm not giving any interviews right now. Jay is a sports figure, but you've got the inside track with me."

I finally got to the defense table and deposited my files. Fred Mercer was already at the state's table with a young woman assistant. A minute later Frank Fieldstone appeared, but he wasn't coming from the main door. He came through a side door followed by the bailiff.

"Mary, I was just about to look for you to see if you needed someone to run interference through the mob scene. I was doing a little warm-up with the judge; a little schmoozing and a few hints about what a great guy Jay is. It can't hurt," Frank said.

I looked up and saw Jay and his parents in a back row. I motioned for them to come forward.

"Jay, you need to sit right next to me at this table. If you have any questions or notes for me during the hearing, write them on this pad. I need to have your parents seated in the first row right behind us. I motioned for the bailiff to come over to us. Judge Luongo's bailiff was a tall blond woman. Her white official bailiff's shirt struggled to keep its buttons from popping. In other words, she was a babe.

"Bailiff, I need your assistance. I need my client's parents seated in the first row. Can you please explain to the two gentlemen seated there that they need to move and make room for the Lincolns?" I asked.

"You want me to do that?" the babe asked. "I'm not sure that's my job."

"Trust me, it's your job. How long have you been with Judge Luongo?"

"I started last year when we were in civil c ourt, but mostly what I did there was sign people in and open the mail."

"Well, criminal court is different. You're here to keep order and protect the judge."

"You're kidding, right? He needs to protect me from these sort of people."

"Never mind," I said. Frank, would you go tell those people in the front row to move and get the Lincolns seated there?"

"Sure, but I have to leave the courtroom for a couple of minutes. I have a new lawyer from the firm handling a hearing here and I need to look in on her," he said.

"One of your lawyers is in criminal court?"

"She's of counsel to the firm, but she's handling some of the motions and court appearances on the civil side for us. We've been short-handed since you left in case you've forgotten. She's got an arraignment and a case conference on some football player named Roy Carter."

"Roy Carter? That's the guy who shot Carlos and almost got me. What is this, payback for my breaking up with you?"

"What? I didn't know who that was, or I would have asked her not to take the case. It's too late for that now. I'm truly sorry and I'll talk to her. I won't leave right now. Let me get the Lincolns seated."

I tried to stop thinking about Roy Carter. Jay's case was the important issue now. A big part of my brain was saying that Frank was a big liar. I just hoped that he wasn't going to try to screw Jay's case. Maybe his schmoozing with the judge was not in Jay's best interest.

I turned to look around the courtroom and saw Tim de Leon slip into a seat in the back row. He was alone. Jennifer was nowhere in sight.

Chapter Ninety-Four

"Y'all come to order now. Judge James Luongo presiding, and no cell phone use, you hear?" the bailiff, aka the babe, spoke in a honey-dripping accent.

Court was in session and I felt my legs shake as I got to my feet.

"We're here on State vs. Jay Lincoln this morning. Counsel please announce for the record," Judge Luongo stated as he gave a long look at his bailiff.

"Your honor, Mary Magruder Katz on behalf of Jay Lincoln. We are here on my motion for dismissal of all charges against Mr. Lincoln."

"Judge, Fred Mercer on behalf of the State of Florida."

I saw Jay write on his pad, the whole state of Florida is against me? I ignored him for the moment as the judge began speaking.

"Ms. Katz, I've read your motion with great interest. You have made some points about which I have questions. I have also read the sworn statements of the witnesses and the depositions that were furnished to the court. First of all, you have brought to my attention the so-called Romeo and Juliet laws. I understand that Florida has adopted a law that allows the court to find that a defendant, who is five years or less older than the minor victim, need not be put on the sexual offender list.

"But you appear to be asking the court to go further and utilize laws in other states such as California that allow a finding that no crime occurred in the instance where a minor has willingly entered into sexual relations with someone who is not a minor but is close in age to the victim."

"Judge, this is an opportunity to make new law by such a finding. I can envision this becoming a precedent called Luongo's Law in future law textbooks."

Mercer moved to the lectern in front of the judge, scowling as he interrupted me. "Your honor, this is an insult to the integrity of this court. The State knows that you are not an activist judge that presumes to usurp the province of the legislature."

"Just a minute, Mr. Mercer, courts in this state and every state have a duty to protect the rights of those who appear before them. They also have a duty to oversee the laws that may be unconstitutional. Those are duties of the court. Remember checks and balances of the three branches of the government?"

The judge spoke passionately, and I must have hit a nerve when I mentioned a law being labeled for all times as the Luongo Law, I thought.

"Judge, you don't have the right to fashion new laws from the bench. You can overturn a law but that doesn't give you the right to write a new law to replace it." Mercer was lecturing the judge.

"Mr. Mercer, are you saying I don't understand my duties as a judge?"

I stood watching Mercer angering the judge while I stood idly by. The state was winning my case for me.

Judge Luongo pushed himself forward in his chair. I thought he might stand up and accost Mercer. "Having read the depositions of the alleged victim and her father, I'm thinking this might be the perfect case to alter the consent laws in Florida. I would like to hear live testimony from the victim in this case."

Now I had my opening to jump into the fray. "That's just it, Judge. It is my understanding that the victim is not willing to appear in court. In fact she is not here today, and doesn't want to testify in this case."

The judge looked at Mercer. "Is that correct, Mr. Mercer? Are you trying to proceed without a victim?"

"Well, she isn't here today, that's correct, but I haven't had a chance to counsel her as to her witness testimony."

"What is that supposed to mean?" the judge asked. "Does she want to proceed or not?"

I glanced around and saw Tim de Leon approaching the front of the courtroom.

"Judge, could I speak, please?" de Leon asked. I am the father of the victim.

"Your honor, I believe we should discuss anything about the victim in chambers due to her young age. As a rape victim, her identity must be kept confidential," Mercer said.

"I am willing to continue in chambers, Judge, but I insist that my client be allowed to be present. He has a right to hear all important aspects of his case," I said.

I was thinking that I had just been through the same circumstances in Marco's case. We always seem to end up in chambers. What happened to the public's right to know?

"Of course, he is to accompany you to my chambers along with the court reporter," Judge Luongo said. "We will reconvene in chambers in five minutes where I will hear from the gentleman who asked to be heard. Mr. Fieldstone, do you have anything to add? You've been very quiet."

"No thank you, Judge, I think the hearing is moving along without my muddying the waters," Frank said. He and the judge exchanged smiles.

Chapter Ninety-Five

Judge Luongo's chambers differed from the others I had visited. The room was extensively decorated with eighteenth century furnishings; a large mahogany desk, wing chairs and a sofa covered in deep blue velvet. There were dark oak bookcases and a teacart with glasses and a crystal carafe. I guessed his wife had decided to go all out to create a royal bearing for her husband.

We were seated comfortably, Jay between Frank and me on the sofa, the court reporter on a straight chair, Mercer and Tim de Leon in the wing chairs and the judge behind the ornate desk. It looked like a book club meeting instead of a motion hearing.

"All right, Sir, please state your name and tell me what you wanted me to know," Judge Luongo said staring at Tim.

"Judge, I am Tim de Leon. My daughter, Jennifer, is the victim in this case, but that's just the point. After Ms. Katz's depositions and my own talks with my daughter and others, I don't believe that this young man, Jay Lincoln, coerced her into having sex. I think it was the other way around. Let me say that I am deeply worried about my daughter. She has begun working with a psychologist."

"Mr. de Leon, when you say you talked to others about this, with whom did you speak?" the judge asked.

"That's not really important, Judge," Mercer interrupted.

"I believe it is, Mr. Mercer. We need to find justice here," Judge Luongo said.

"I spoke to the mother of Candy Gomez, Jennifer's friend. She filled me in on the girls' sneaking over to the university campus on several occasions. I also spoke with my ex-wife. Jennifer spent a month with her this summer. Let me say that I avoid speaking to her most of the time. She is a poor influence on Jennifer. It turns out that Jennifer told her that she had had sexual relations with Jay. Of course, she failed to tell me this."

"Where is your daughter now?" the judge asked.

"I don't want her to go through the trauma of testifying in court. I have sent her to stay with my sister in another state for the remainder of the school year. She will be out of the temptations of Miami and she will continue working with a psychologist."

"Well, if you're saying that she doesn't want to proceed in this case, then there really is no case." The Judge started to close his file on the desk in front of him."

"Judge, you can't just let this go. It's as if we are condoning the conduct of the defendant and saying every young girl who is a groupie is fair game for him," Mercer said.

"You have a point there," Judge Luongo said. "Ms. Katz and Mr. Fieldstone, do you have any solution to this situation?"

"Your honor, may I have a moment to speak to my client and to my co-counsel?" I asked.

"Certainly. Why don't you step into the corridor for a few minutes?" Judge Luongo stood and motioned to a side door.

We stood in a little circle in the narrow hallway. Jay looked like he'd like to bolt out of this confining place.

"Mary, I thought we'd won. Now what's going to happen to me?" Jay looked like a scared little boy even though he towered over Frank and me.

"I know it seems like we are snatching defeat from the jaws of victory, but I do think there's a way to resolve this to everyone's advantage. There is a misdemeanor charge called Contributing To The Delinquency of a Minor. If you entered a plea to that charge and the felonies are dropped, the judge could withhold adjudication and sentence you to some community service hours," I said.

"What does that mean? I didn't do anything to that girl that she didn't ask for."

"Yes, but that did contribute to her delinquency. She was only fifteen at the time, even though you didn't know it. If the judge doesn't adjudicate you guilty, once you finish the community service hours, I can move to expunge your record. That's like erasing this case. It won't follow you."

"Mary, that's brilliant," Frank said.

"Can I talk to my parents?"

"Of course. Frank could you bring the Lincolns back here so I can explain everything to them?"

A few minutes later we were back in Judge Luongo's chambers. Jay's parents looked around the room at the over-decorated décor. Everyone agreed to the plea agreement, even Fred Mercer. Judge Luongo looked pleased as he went through the plea colloquy with Jay, explaining every aspect of the charge and the penalty.

"I'm very glad this case has concluded to everyone's satisfaction," the judge said. "Glad I thought of this lesser charge."

I decided not to correct him. Always let the judge take the credit, and the next case before this court will be a slam-dunk. We left the chambers and headed to the elevator.

"Jay and Mr. and Mrs. Lincoln, let me warn you. The media will be waiting for us when we leave the courthouse. I think the less said the better. Just that the case has ended with all parties satisfied with the outcome," I said.

Frank chimed in. "The university will probably issue its own statement. We shouldn't do anything to make the judge rescind this good agreement."

As we came down the courthouse steps, we were bombarded. The Herald sports reporter grabbed Jay's sleeve making it impossible for him to leave. "Jay, are you a free man? Tell us what happened in there?"

Jay looked at the reporter and smiled. "I am happy to say my case has been concluded. Now I can concentrate on football and my classes. Our next two games are very important. That's all I have to say."

Mrs. Lincoln removed the reporter's hand from Jay. "My son never raped anyone, just as I said. Now let us leave here and go by our church to thank Jesus who looked out for us," she said as she swept by him as regal as a queen.

Harlan McFarland was standing to one side. I owed him some comments. "Harlan, the alleged victim in Jay's case decided not to pursue this matter. Jay will be doing some community service hours and that will conclude this matter. You should look at the court file for the full findings of the court. I'm very pleased with the outcome of this case. Jay is a fine young man, one whom I am proud to have represented."

Jay and his parents shook my hand and Jay gave me a hug and a kiss. There were still two more football games left in the season and I had a feeling Miami would be victorious. Maybe even go to a bowl game.

Frank and I walked to the parking lot. I unlocked my car with the fob as we approached.

"I guess things are going well in your practice. Nice new car," Frank said.

"Speaking of practices, your new hire will have to depose Carlos and me when she defends Roy Carter. If you involve yourself in the case, I personally will move to have you excluded from the case. You have a definite conflict of interest," I said.

"Mary, why must you always be at odds with me? I just want to be your friend. You did a great job on Jay's case and I'll be the first to admit that I thought it was a complete loser."

"Thanks for the compliment, but as to being friends, it's hard to forget your breaking into my home and trashing it, among other things. Friends don't do that to friends."

"It was stupid of me. You just don't understand how you hurt me. I've always liked working with you on cases and I hope we can do that again someday."

Before I could escape to my car, Frank pulled me close and kissed me. I stood staring after him in stunned silence as he got into his Mercedes.

Chapter Ninety-Six

Wednesday morning was a perfect November day. The sky was clear, the wind tousled the deep purple bougainvillea blossoms and red hibiscus. The humidity had receded and Thanksgiving was upon us in twenty-four hours. I relished the look of early winter in Miami as I drove to the courthouse to hear the state's decision in Marco's case. If the state didn't dismiss the case, I still hoped that the judge would have enough sense of justice to dismiss it herself.

As I climbed the steps of the courthouse yet again, I spotted Catherine and Marco waiting at the top. They were holding hands and looked like two happy teenagers. We went through the metal detectors together and proceeded to Judge Cueto's courtroom.

Standing outside the courtroom door was Agent Padron. He spotted us and motioned for us to follow him to the end of the hallway.

"Agent Padron, this is a surprise. Is everything okay?" I asked.

"It sure is. We arrested *Oso Blanco* last night and charged him with a continuing criminal enterprise. One of the crimes charged in the enterprise, besides the importation and sale of illegal drugs, is the murder of Brady Aynsworth. He'll be arraigned in federal court later today."

"They can't continue to charge me with the murder, can they?" Marco asked.

"That's why I came over here this morning to report this to the court. I'm not sure we would have nabbed this group so quickly without the work you turned over to me, Mary. Oh, and guess what the polar bear's real name is? Marvin *Misterioso*; that means weird. No wonder he liked using his nickname."

We were a jovial group as we entered the courtroom. The judge was on the bench and the calendar showed numerous items ahead of Marco's case, so we settled into a back row to wait our turn.

Catherine leaned over and whispered to me. "I know you have plans for Thanksgiving but please save time for us on Friday. Marco and I are getting married Friday afternoon at four. My parents are on their way down here as we speak. I called Liz Montgomery and she agreed to perform the ceremony. We want you and Carlos to stand up for us."

"I know you said you would be planning a wedding but this is so fast," I said.

"We've been through enough. Now it's our time to be completely happy. The boys are thrilled."

"Where will the wedding take place?"

"Marco pulled some strings and got the private party room booked at Nino's restaurant in the Grove. After the ceremony we'll have a small dinner for everyone."

"You've planned this so fast. What about a dress for you?"

"Oh, my God, that's the one thing I forgot."

"Not to worry. I'll call Chicky, Carlos's sister at Luis's boutique. It'll be my gift. Catherine, I'm going to be the only single girl left."

"You don't have to be, you know, but that's your choice."

The bailiff approached us. "Don't you girls ever shut up? I just called your case."

I hurried to the defense table pulling Marco along with me. Louise was already seated at the state's table and, to my surprise, was accompanied by Jason Jimenez- Jones, the elected State Attorney and Louise's boss. If it was important enough for Jason to appear in court it was either because he was going to announce that there was no way in hell he was dropping the murder charge, or he was going to dismiss the case himself.

We all announced our appearances. I immediately asked to be heard.

"Yes, Ms. Katz?" Judge Cueto asked.

"Your Honor, DEA Special Agent Padron is in the courtroom. He informed me this morning that he has arrested *Oso Blanco* who has been charged with a Continuing Criminal Enterprise and the murder of Brady Aynsworth. With this new charge, I don't think there is any way that the case against Marco Perez can survive."

"Judge, let me stop Ms. Katz," Jason said. "I have come here this morning to announce the dismissal of the murder charge against Mr. Perez. I felt it was important for me to do this rather than having one of my assistants do this in case there was to be any criticism of the state. It's my job as the State Attorney to handle any such matters myself. May I point out that this dismissal was based on all the material that Ms. Margolis furnished to me after Monday's hearing and before hearing the news just now that another person has been charged with Aynsworth's murder."

"Thank you very much, Mr. Jimenez-Jones. The court is very appreciative that you have taken responsibility for the outcome of this case." Judge Cueto smiled and had a look of relief that she hadn't had to act on her own to dismiss a serious case.

"You are welcome, Judge. I just want to state in open court that the office of the State Attorney is always on the side of justice. We aren't just here to prosecute; we are here to stand on the side of justice."

Jason was warming to a full speech, but was interrupted by the judge.

"The case against Marco Perez is closed. Mr. Perez, you are free to go. I'm sure your lawyer will be moving to expunge the arrest in your case. Fifteen minute recess." Judge Cueto left the courtroom.

Marco hugged me and then hurried back to Catherine. I moved across the aisle to shake hands with Jason and Louise. Jason left quickly before being accosted by the press, but Louise stayed behind.

"Mary, do you have a minute?" Louise said.

"Of course, let's walk out of the courtroom together. That should make a good picture in The Herald tomorrow."

"Let's go to our favorite hangout," Louise said, "the ladies' room."

We walked away as the cameras flashed and whirred. Safely alone in the restroom, Louise looked at me frowning.

"You seem to be the queen of case dismissals this week."

"I guess I'm just lucky to have represented clients that were truly innocent of the charges against them. It isn't always this easy, as you well know."

"Mary, the reason I wanted to talk to you is that I consider you a friend over the years. I always think of you as someone who stands up for women's rights."

"I think I always have, and always will," I answered.

"There's a lot of nasty talk circulating about you and I thought you should know. I am puzzled too about how you could have destroyed a teenage girl who was the victim of a rape. I hear that you brutalized the victim in her deposition in Jay Lincoln's case to the point that she refused to testify. Was it that important for you to win?"

"Louise, I'm stunned. Jay never raped that girl. She was a groupie who stalked him for months. This is confidential, since she's a juvenile but I want you to know. She sent nude photos of herself to Jay's cell phone and invited herself to his dorm where consensual sex took place. She also passed herself off as a coed at the university. Jay had no idea she was a high school kid. Then when her father found the photos months later she made up the story that she had been raped. I'm glad you told me about the gossip. I can't help what people say, but I'm glad I could let you know the truth."

"I'm glad too. Maybe I can put a stop to some of the gossip. Please, don't be angry with me for telling you what people thought; maybe even what I thought. And I am glad Marco's case ended well. He seemed like a nice guy."

"He is a nice guy. And you're a good friend. Happy Thanksgiving."

Chapter Ninety-Seven

Catherine and I went directly to my car. I told her instead of going to the office we would go directly to see Chicky at the boutique and get her outfitted for her wedding. I made a quick call to Carlos and left him a message on both his cells about Marco and the wedding. My next call to Chicky alerted her to our shopping quest.

By the time we reached the Corona Boutique, Chicky had pulled out a stack of gorgeous dresses.

"Welcome, Catherine, we are very excited about helping you select a dress for your wedding. This is Christina," Chicky said as a tall brunette came out of a back room carrying several more dresses.

"I didn't know you had hired another person here," I said.

"Oh, Christina is an old friend from school. She wasn't working so I told her to hang out here and give me some help. Catherine, start looking through these dresses and see what appeals to you. We can alter anything overnight if it's necessary. Christina is a whiz at making things fit."

Christina smiled at Chicky and they looked at each other for a long second.

"Chicky, are you coming to Carlos's for Thanksgiving dinner? I asked.

"No, Luis's parents are here and I promised to eat dinner with them. Mr. and Mrs. Corona send their best to you. I know they'd love to see you and so would Luis. They'll never forget how you saved his life last June."

Christina took Catherine into a fitting room with an armful of outfits. I looked through the ones still on hangers scattered around the room.

"What will you be wearing to the wedding? You said you will be Catherine's only attendant," Chicky held up a hot pink mini dress.

I hadn't even thought about it. I guess my only dressy clothes are all black. I don't guess black is appropriate for a wedding."

"Of course not. Let's look around here for something that looks like Mary Magruder Katz." Chicky held up several different dresses and pants suits. I was about to seize a turquoise silk pants and top when Catherine came out of the fitting room dressed in a soft yellow silk skirt and jacket. She took off the jacket revealing a yellow lace camisole. It fit perfectly and she was glowing. I snapped a picture with my cell phone. Then I put on the pants outfit and we paraded around the boutique like French models on the runway.

"Bring on the wedding. We're ready," Catherine shouted.

I delivered Catherine and her gown to her apartment and headed for my neglected office. In my line of work, I seldom confronted so much happiness as the last three days brought. I wasn't sure whether to laugh or to look over my shoulder to be sure another disaster wasn't approaching.

Chapter Ninety-Eight

There were few messages waiting at the office. With Marco's case and Jay's case resolved, I needed to find some new clients. I listened to my voice mail messages. There were only three. The first one was from J.C. "I am back from Argentina and all set to do my famous deep fried turkey. Let's talk before dinner tomorrow."

The second message was from my gym telling me my membership was expiring and for only five hundred dollars, I would be good to go for another three months. I made a note and put it on my pile of unpaid bills.

The third message was a familiar voice. "Mary, it's Dash, your Vermont friend. Remember me? You promised to get back to me about my client and his Uncle's estate. I am coming to Miami on December third with my client. We need to get this matter sorted out. Please let me know that you will have time to help me with this."

I could picture Carlos's displeasure at having Dash in town. Dash helped me a lot when I spent October in High Pines, so I knew I had to help him and I did need a new client. I left a message at his office after hearing Daisy's answering machine voice explaining that the office was closed for Thanksgiving and the end of hunting season. What a different life in Northern New England. The only hunting taking place here was at the South Beach clubs where mini-skirted females hunted for rich boyfriends.

I watered the plants now neglected after Catherine's mother left, turned out the lights, locked the doors and headed for Thanksgiving with a gaggle of relatives all asking when Carlos and I would follow Catherine and Marco's lead and surprise them with a wedding.

Chapter Ninety-Nine

Thanksgiving morning dawned clear and breezy. A north wind rattled the bedroom window panes and sent my wind chimes clattering. Sam and I were awakened by the noise.

I was told not to bring anything to the feast, that there was already too much food; probably Mother's way of discouraging my questionable cooking attempts. I felt funny coming empty handed. J.C. was a wine connoisseur so I knew he had that category covered, and my five dollar Trader Joe's bottle wouldn't be appreciated. Then I remembered the twelve year old bottle of Scotch that an appreciative client had included with his fee payment. I packed the Scotch in a tote bag.

I fed Sam and brushed him so he wouldn't shed too noticeably on everyone's clothes. I showered, tried to dry my hair and packed clean slacks and a blouse for the dinner. For now, I grabbed jeans and a tee shirt and we were off to Starbucks for a quick coffee and roll and the morning Herald.

I was surprised to see that Marco's case did not make the front page or the local section. I searched again. On an inside page, I found an article about the DEA breaking up a drug ring. One paragraph toward the end of the article stated that Marco Perez's case was dismissed after the head of the drug ring was charged with the murder of Brady Aynsworth. Marco's name had been dragged through the mud when he was charged with the murder. Now the paper buried the fact that he was innocent. Most of Miami would never know that he had been completely cleared. Maybe what my father always says about the media is true. They love bad news. Good news just doesn't sell.

We pulled into the brick parking area in front of Carlos's monster mansion at ten o'clock. Mother and Dad's car was already there. J.C. and

Angie's Bentley was also there. I opened the front door and was met by the hunger-inducing odor of Mother's roasting turkey.

In the kitchen, Mother was swathed in a white apron. She was rolling out a pie crust. Angie was by her side dressed in designer jeans and a striped shirt that looked like a painter's smock. She was cutting up sweet potatoes. They were gabbing away like the wild parrots in the backyard.

"Mary, darling, you're here already," Angie stopped her work for air kisses on each cheek.

"Is that what you're wearing for dinner?" Mother asked.

"Hello, to you too. No, I have my 'good clothes' in the front hall. I won't embarrass you in front of the Katz relatives. Where are they?"

"They'll be along in a while. Max and Myrna are bringing Grandma Katz and her new husband. They're all staying at that new beach resort on South Beach, but your aunt and uncle will be moving to a rental condo for the month of December, as soon as they find one they like. You know Myrna. Picky, picky, picky."

"They just got here yesterday. Cut her some slack, and Grandma's husband isn't new anymore. They've had their second anniversary," I said.

I could see Carlos and J.C. in the backyard. They were carrying a huge carton. Sam and I walked through the screened patio, passed by the kidney shaped pool and entered the yard. Sam settled himself under an oak tree.

"What's in there? It's big enough to hold a casket," I said.

"It's my turkey fryer," J.C. said.

"Are you going to cook out here? Why not on the patio where it's cooler?" I asked.

"There's always the possibility of a fire, so we can't chance it," Carlos said. "I forgot to get a fire extinguisher."

"You're kidding, right?"

"No, he's serious. Carlos, remember the fire we had at the old house, and the horses got freaked and one of them jumped the fence and you chased him around for an hour?" J.C. was laughing.

"Do you think I could forget that fiasco? Finally, Chicky coaxed him back with some sugar lumps." Carlos laughed too and the two men looked as happy as I'd ever seen them. I guessed it wouldn't be a good time to try to talk with J.C. about his bank situation.

At noon time, we were all starved smelling the turkey, cornbread stuffing, and apple pies baking. Carlos and I were slicing cheese and putting out crackers, even though our mothers were warning us that dinner would be ready by three.

Jonathan and Randy and their boys were piling out of the family van. Kyle, the eleven year old, was carrying a soccer ball. Thirteen year old Aaron had grown several inches and had noticeable hair growing on his upper lip. Time stood still for me when I was engrossed in my clients' cases. Looking at Aaron made me realize that time was hurtling past like the runaway horse Carlos had described.

Everybody hugged and kissed everybody. Then Jonathan brought up Dash's client.

"Hey, Mary, did you get things straightened out with that client of your friend from Vermont? Dash sounds very nice on the phone. Sorry I couldn't help him."

"I'm going to work on it next week Dash is bringing the client down here and I'll have to see if there is some way to get the feds to release the estate." I said.

Carlos took on his thunder cloud look. "That Dash guy is coming here? You never mentioned that."

"Because I just found that out yesterday. I've been a little busy as you know," I said.

"Carlos, if Mary wanted to be involved with someone from Vermont, she wouldn't be back here spending every spare minute with you, so stop acting like someone took your favorite toy," Angie said. "I've seen that look for more than thirty years when Jose took your baseball or your bat. Enough already."

"Thank you, Angie. Maybe you should have given him a good spanking." I said. That lightened the mood and soon we were all munching cheese and crackers and pouring shots of the twelve year old S cotch.

At two o'clock, a Cadillac rental car pulled into the driveway. The brick courtyard was too full of cars to accommodate another one. As soon as I saw the Cadillac, I knew it was Uncle Max who never drove another brand. I ran out to meet the new arrivals. Uncle Max jumped out and grabbed me in a bear hug. Aunt Myrna stepped out gingerly. She had gained a lot of weight since they had moved to New York. When Dad and Max sold Katz's Kosher Markets, Max and Myrna retired to the upper west side of New York City, a lifelong dream to see plays, concerts, galleries and live a totally sedentary life.

Grandma Katz and her distinguished husband, Ronald Morgan, slid out of the back seat. Both sported California suntans. Grandma looked years younger. She had colored her hair and was dressed in a red pants outfit. Ron looked straight out of GQ in white pants and a navy shirt, loafers worn without socks, and his grey hair smooth. He was a total contrast to my grandfather who had been almost bald when he died and usually looked rumpled.

"Grandma, I don't know what to call you now. You're not Grandma Katz anymore, and Grandma Morgan doesn't sound right," I said.

"Just call me Bertha. That will do and we'll be like a couple of girlfriends," she said.

I introduced Carlos to the new Katz family arrivals. The two women looked charmed when he bent to kiss each of them.

"He's such a good looking boy," Aunt Myrna said. "the best looking one of the bunch you've gone out with."

We all gathered in the kitchen tasting the dishes as they came out of the oven and generally getting in the way of Mother and Angie. Angie and Aunt Myrna were discussing Broadway plays and concerts. J.C. and Carlos were preparing their turkey for the deep fryer. They were adding all kinds of spices and garlic to the bird. Ron followed them into the yard where they were pouring what looked like gallons of oil into the fryer and submerging the bird. Smoke filled the air causing Sam to run inside the house where he was chased out of the kitchen and finally lighted in the living room where Dad, Jonathan, and Uncle Max settled in to watch the Dolphins play the Jets.

Forty-five minutes later, the fried turkey was hoisted out of its oil bath. The roasted turkey was ready for carving and the long dining room table was groaning with side dishes and salads. Folding chairs were added to the eight dining room regulars. Somehow fourteen people managed to fit in sitting thigh to thigh. J.C. poured the first of several bottles of Argentine wine and Thanksgiving began in earnest.

An hour later, we all sat half asleep in a food fog. Angie and J.C. seemed like they had always been a part of this extended family. I admired the way they always seemed at home with every kind of group. I complimented them on their ability.

"We're used to being new to many experiences. We both emigrated to this country as teens. The immigrant experience gave us curiosity to learn about new people." Angie smiled looking around the table.

"I know what you mean," Bertha said. "My parents came here from Germany as teenagers, so I am a first generation American. It's different than how my sons and grandchildren were raised."

"Maybe you and Carlos will understand this better when you have children," Mother said. "Their childhood will be different than yours."

"Who said anything about us having children," Carlos and I said together.

"Can we go out and kick the soccer ball around?" Kyle broke the silence in the room after our reaction.

"Go, and take Sam with you," Randy said.

Then I spoke, startling everyone including Carlos. "Actually Carlos and I do have a sort of announcement. We're thinking about selling both our houses and finding a house we both love so that we can move in together. We're going to talk to Tanya Toronto who is making her career on our family's real estate transactions."

"Well, that's a start," J.C. said and reached over and slapped Carlos on the back.

"Why not get married instead of just moving in together?" Mother asked.

Before we could answer, Bertha intervened. "I think that moving in together is a good idea. It never hurts to test the water before plunging. Times change. I got married at eighteen before I ever got to grow as a person. You two do it your way and it will turn out just fine."

Mother stared at Bertha as if she had grown a second head. I got up and moved around the table and gave my young-old grandmother a kiss.

Then we all got up and started shuttling dirty dishes into Carlos's already overwhelmed kitchen.

"You surprised me," Carlos said. I didn't know you were going to announce our plan. I wasn't even sure you were going to go through with the move."

"You still want to, don't you?" I asked.

"Ah, *mi amor*, you know I do."

Chapter One Hundred

Carlos and I decided to spend the night at my house. We left with a bag of leftovers as did Jonathan's family. The rest of the crowd was sitting by the pool enjoying each other's company and telling stories of past Thanksgivings. J.C. promised to lock up and be sure the fire was out in his turkey fryer. Sam waddled to the car. He had begged turkey tastes from everyone. He settled into the back of the new car and was asleep before I backed out of the electric gate.

Turkey is noted for containing sleep inducing endorphins, so we followed Sam's example. Carlos and I were sound asleep almost as soon as we arrived home.

"It really was a perfect day," I said to Carlos as we snuggled together.

Friday, the big day for Catherine and Marco, began looking as lovely as the Thanksgiving weather, but by noon dark clouds filled the western sky. November is a fickle month in South Florida. It can't make up its mind. Is it the beginning of the dry season or the end of the rainy season?

The waitress at Coral Bagels, where we went for a very late breakfast. said we should be glad to have a bit more rain, knowing the dry season would soon bring the threat of grass fires.

By two o'clock, big rain squalls shook the trees as we dressed for the wedding. We used our biggest umbrellas as we dashed from the car into Nino's Restaurant. I went directly to the ladies' room to grab some paper towels to dry off my shoes. Catherine was there with her mother. Patty was braiding Catherine's long hair and tying a satin bow to hold it.

"Mary, I'm so glad to see you and thank you for all you've done for Catherine and Marco," Patty said pumping my hand up and down.

"Catherine you look beautiful. Are you nervous?" I asked.

"Not a bit. I feel like I'm starting a whole new life. Wait 'til you see Cory and Phillip. They're wearing suits and ties and they're going to be carrying our rings. I've never seen them so excited. Phillip said this was a way lot better than Christmas."

"What about Ricky, Marco's son. Is he here?"

"No, don't say anything to Marco. He so wanted him here but his ex is being her usual bitchy self. She took him to her parents in Sarasota for Thanksgiving. It was her turn for the holiday, but she could have gotten him back here today."

"Never mind, you'll all come to visit us at Christmas time and we'll all go to Disney World," Patty said.

"Catherine, where are you going to be living?"

"We're going to live in Marco's house in Westchester for a while at least. I've already given notice to Mrs. Morehouse. Then we'll look for something closer to the boys' schools."

"So here's where you're hiding." Judge Liz Montgomery said as she came through the door. "I just need to put on my robe and we'll be ready to start. I hope you don't mind that I brought my husband, Joe, with me."

"That's great," Catherine said.

A few minutes later we assembled in the party room with its Italian lanterns and fresh flowers in huge baskets placed at the front of the room. Catherine held a cymbidium orchid and Marco and the boys wore carnations in their lapels. Carlos and I took our positions on either side of the bride and groom.

Patty and Doug sat on the front row of seats. Just behind them sat Marco's parents and then I saw who they brought with them. It was Marielena, the dreaded Perez cousin and friend of Carlos's ex-wife. Just entering the room were J.C. and Angelina, late as usual. Angelina sat next to Marielena and they did their air kissing. The door opened again and Franco and Lucinda arrived. It was clear to see that they were arguing as they came in. I hoped the argument didn't turn physical. They sat on the other side of J.C. who shushed them. Joe Fineberg, Liz's husband took a seat in the back row watching Liz and smiling at her as she prepared to begin the ceremony.

I leaned over and whispered to Catherine. "Why is Marielena here?"

"She sort of invited herself and Marco's mom couldn't tell her no."

Liz cleared her throat and began the ceremony.

"Friends and family of Marco and Catherine, we've come together today to join in the joy of the melding of two people who have weathered many storms to arrive at this special day. To find a rainbow, you must endure the rain. Catherine and Marco, you have endured the rain in your lives and now arrive at the promise that the rainbow of love brings to you.

"Marriage is the image of the interlocking fingers of two hands. They can move away from each other while still touching with fingertips. They can create space between themselves. They can create a tent, a home that is a safe place to be. That will be the picture of your marriage. You will not be asked to do great things; only small things with love and that will bring about the great things you will accomplish in your newly united families. And now each of you will commit to the vows that you have written for each other."

Catherine looked angelic as she gazed at Marco and began to speak in a steady voice. "Marco, you and I have found each other through our friends, Mary and Carlos, and we knew we were right for each other from the first moments together. You are the person I always dreamed of finding to spend my life with. You have already shown yourself to be the father that Cory and Phillip have longed for. I trust you and love you now and forever."

I could hear sniffling from the audience and I felt tears forming myself as Marco took Catherine's hand and began to speak.

"Catherine, you are the most selfless person I have ever known, always trying to make everyone around you happy and seldom thinking of your own needs. From now on, I will be there to be sure that you are happy and never in need of anything. You deserve the best. I will devote myself to making sure that you have the best of everything but especially my best love. Always know that there is nothing I wouldn't do to keep you safe wherever you go."

Liz removed a handkerchief from the sleeve of her robe and wiped her eyes before continuing.

"Do you each promise to love and care for each other for all of your lives?"

Catherine and Marco spoke together, "I do".

"Cory and Phillip, please hand the rings to your mother and Marco, and as you place these rings on each other's fingers remember each time you look at your rings that they symbolize the circle of love that you are entering today. "And now by the power vested in me by the State of Florida, I pronounce you husband and wife."

Marco beamed at Catherine as he gathered her in his arms and kissed her. Then they both turned to Phillip and Cory and kissed them. Phillip clung to Marco as if he were afraid he would disappear. Then they all hugged and kissed Carlos and me and the families rushed forward to hug and kiss the beautiful bride and grinning groom.

We gathered around the long table Nino had prepared. Platters of steaming Italian dishes began appearing as waiters poured Champaign in the waiting goblets. How fitting, I thought. A Cuban marries a middle American Army brat and their wedding supper is Italian. That is so Miami.

Marielena stopped on her way around the table and patted Carlos on the shoulder, basically ignoring me. I was not about to let her ruin this occasion.

"Marielena, how good to see you again," I said. "I'm glad we're having the opportunity to see you. Carlos and I are going to be so busy for the next few months."

"Really, why is that?" Marielena asked.

"We're going to be selling our two houses and looking for a perfect house for the two of us. We're moving in together." I watched her expression as I spoke.

"Well, isn't that nice. I suppose you want something grander than Carlos's lovely home."

"Not at all. We want a house we can furnish together, and I am very thrifty. It doesn't take a lot of money to make me happy," I said. I knew

Marielena understood this was a dig at Margarita, Carlos's ex-wife who was all about spending.

"Well, good luck with that," Marielena said as she moved away quickly.

Carlos laughed so loudly that everyone turned to look at what could have been so funny.

Then we began a series of toasts and emptied several bottles of bubbly.

Chapter One Hundred-One

Catherine's Story Revisited

Patty and Doug herded the two boys into their car. They would be taking care of the boys for the weekend in Catherine's apartment while the newly-weds had a brief honeymoon. Marco remembered a resort in Marathon Key. It was not high season so it should be quiet and they were looking forward to the beach and just being together with nothing to worry about.

The rain stopped as they passed over the line between Miami-Dade and Monroe Counties. The last town before Monroe County and the Keys was Homestead where Catherine had once lived in a trailer with Brady and the boys when they were infants. It was a terrible time in her life and she dreaded even seeing the town again.

Homestead looked completely different. When she lived there, it was still recovering from Hurricane Andrew. In the midst of the many farms was the Nascar Race Track and not much else. Now the farms had become housing developments and stores dotted the main street. She was glad that there was little to remind her of the life she left behind when she drove out of there in a broken-down car with her few possessions and her sleeping babies. She never wanted to think about that time again. Her life was finally complete. She had a great husband and a good job and friends. She had a father for her kids.

"What are you thinking about?" Marco asked.

"Oh, just how lucky I am today, and how everything has changed since the time I left Homestead."

"I don't want you to think about Brady ever again. We'll make life seem like he never existed."

"Is that what you meant when you said in your vow that you would always keep me safe?"

"Of course, Catherine. There's nothing that I wouldn't do for you, no matter what."

Catherine stared at him. A disturbing thought crossed her mind. "You would do anything for me? What are you saying?"

"I'm just saying I love you, and I can't wait to get to the hotel." He took his eyes off the road and placed his hand on her breast.

"Hey, watch the road. We've got all the time in the world to play." Catherine vowed to herself to put away any silly thoughts and concentrate on her honeymoon weekend.

Epilogue

We were still filled with good food and drink and the happy glow from the wedding when Carlos and I settled in for the evening. Sam was content lying on the foot of the bed after eating the turkey leftovers from the fridge.

"You sure gave it to Marielena. She looked like she'd been hit over the head. I think she actually cringed."

"She deserved it. It was a beautiful wedding. I'm so glad it's worked out for the two of them."

"I'm glad it's working out for the two of us. You really are enthused about selling the houses and finding our new place?"

"Yes, it's hard to part with this little house of mine, but I know this is the right move. We'll never find out whether everything is right for us until we have our own place. Tanya Toronto is due to become a wealthy woman just from our family. She gets to find us a house, sell both our houses, find William a house, and find my parents their permanent condo."

"Not to worry you, but speaking of your parents, I thought your dad didn't look like himself at Thanksgiving. His usual feistiness was missing."

"Maybe he's just getting used to you, or maybe having so much family around was a bit much.

Speaking of dads, I promise that I will get your dad's situation with the bank investigation resolved starting this Monday."

We were quiet for a while. I thought Carlos had fallen asleep. Then I saw that his eyes were open and he was staring at the ceiling.

"Are you worrying about something?" I asked.

"I was just wondering why your friend Dash had to come all the way to Miami with his client. His client ought to be able to board a plane and come to Miami to consult you by himself. I think it's just an excuse to see you again."

"I made it clear to Dash that I was committed to you. I think it's more about being sure the client remains his client and that he gets his fee out of this. You need to understand that there aren't many big cases in the villages in Vermont. Please, don't do one of your jealousy macho routines."

We were both quiet again. Then Carlos asked me what I was thinking about.

"I'm mulling over something that Marco said in his vow to Catherine. He said he would always keep her safe and that he'd do anything for her. I read something a bit sinister into that."

"What is your lawyer brain concocting from that earnest statement?"

"Maybe, Marco would kill someone who wanted to hurt Catherine."

"Are you saying that Marco was really the one who killed Brady?"

"I'm saying we'll never really know for sure. I'll feel better when that drug dealer gets convicted of the murder."

"Okay, Ms. Lawyer, close your eyes and get some sleep before you think of some other crazy theories." Carlos turned out the lamp and kissed me goodnight making my heart flutter and my thoughts focus only on our future. November, with its neurotic pace, was almost over. December couldn't be any more hectic, or could it?

Acknowledgements

The characters and events in this fourth Mary Magruder Katz mystery novel are all fictional. However, most of the places, streets, freeways, and traffic are real. The University of Miami is a very real institution of which I am an alumna of its law school.

The situation involving the fictional football player Jay Lincoln is not a real incident. The sports programs at the "U", as the university is nick-named, bring student athletes from all over the United States as well as internationally and the various sports programs add to the enjoyment of the South Florida community.

The wedding ceremony of Catherine and Marco comes from my file of ceremonies I presided over during my tenure as a judge. The first time I was invited to participate in a wedding, I was at a loss as to how to pro-ceed especially since the couple said they were leaving the ceremony completely in my hands. I turned to another judge who graciously shared her file of ceremonies. Over the years I added poems and suggestions from books and the internet and included thoughts of my own, so the ceremony in this book is a conglomerate of multiple weddings that I conducted

The Romeo and Juliet Law is an actual law, Florida Statutes, Section 943.04354 (2008) as is Contributing To The Delinquency of a Minor, the misdemeanor that Jay Lincoln enters a plea to in the book.

The description of the courtroom utilized for bond hearings is an accu-rate description of the process utilizing closed circuit television between the jail and the courtroom. In the book, a retired judge presides over the bond hearing. Retired judges are often used for bond hearings as well as many other hearings wherever there is a backlog of cases.

On the next pages you will find recipes for two of the dishes described at the Thanksgiving dinner of the combined Katz – Martin families. Enjoy!

Thanksgiving Recipes

Traditional Southern Cornbread Stuffing

Four leaves of fresh sage, finely chopped
Two sprigs of fresh thyme, leaves only
1 ½ cups celery chopped
1 cup onion finely minced
¼ stick of butter (for sautéing)
½ stick of butter (reserved)
One cast iron skillet of fresh baked cornbread, crumbled (approx. 5 cups)
2 cups fresh French bread crumbs
¼ teaspoon salt
¾ teaspoon black pepper
¼ teaspoon granulated garlic
1 apple peeled and finely chopped
2 large eggs, beaten
2 tablespoons fresh whipping cream
2 ½ cups chicken broth

In a skillet, sauté celery and onions with sage and thyme in the ¼ stick of melted butter

Combine cornbread crumbs, salt pepper, garlic, and apple in a mixing bowl. Add the celery, onions, and herbs from skillet.

Beat eggs with whipping cream and stir into mixture. Slowly add **1 ½** cups of the chicken broth as you stir. **If using to stuff the bird, mixture should be a little dry as it will absorb juices from the bird. If using for dressing to be cooked separately, use two full cups of the chicken broth.**

If stuffing the bird, cut remaining butter into chunks and add to cavity as you put in the stuffing. Roast the bird according to your recipe. Be sure both the bird and stuffing are at room temperature before setting in oven for more even cooking.

If using for dressing, slice remaining butter into thin slices, using some to grease two pie plates. Spoon dressing mixture into pie plates and pat flat with the back of a spoon. Lay remaining slices of butter around surface of dressing and bake for 45 minutes in a 375 degree oven until browned and an inserted knife comes out clean.
RECIPE COURTESY OF TONY SEARS (from an old South Carolina recipe)

Deep Fried Turkey

Use a large stockpot or a turkey fryer and a drain basket. Fill with 3 gallons of peanut oil.

Open the neck of the bird at least two inches. Insert one white onion and ¼ cup of seasonings. Creole seasonings work well, or mix one clove pressed garlic, 1 tablespoon dried oregano, ½ teaspoon ground cumin, one tablespoon thyme or lemon thyme, salt and pepper. Rub some of the seasonings on the skin of the bird as well. For a tangy taste add a small amount of orange or lemon juice.

Fry for 3 ½ minutes per lb.; around forty-five minutes for a 12 lb. bird. Internal temperature should be 180 degrees.

Remove carefully using the drain basket. Hot oil should be cooled completely before handling.

(Recipe from numerous sources in Miami)

Hope you enjoy trying these recipes at your next family dinner. And watch for another Mary Magruder Katz adventure, DARING DECEMBER, when Mary and her diverse family and friends celebrate Chanukah and Christmas. There's sure to be more than your normal holiday headaches.
Barbara Levenson

About the Author

Barbara Levenson is a retired judge who has resided in Miami, Florida for 38 years. She is a cum laude graduate of the University of Miami law school and has worked as a prosecutor and run her own law practice specializing in criminal defense.

Barbara and her husband raised and showed German shepherd dogs and finished eleven champions in the show ring. Mac is the current shepherd residing in the Levenson household. She has two sons who are both attorneys.

Barbara was born and grew up in Central Ohio and was the first woman elected to the Columbus, Ohio board of education, its first woman president, and the first woman to receive the Ohio newspaper "man of the year" award.